Never too LATE

a novel

a novel

NANCY L. CRATTY

Covenant Communications, Inc.

Cover image by © Photodisc Blue Images

Cover design copyrighted 2004 by Covenant Communications, Inc.

Published by Covenant Communications, Inc.
American Fork, Utah

This is a work of fiction. The characters, names, incidents, places, and dialogue are products of the
author's imagination, and are not to be construed as real.

Printed in Canada
First Printing: January 2004

11 10 09 08 07 06 05 04   10 9 8 7 6 5 4 3 2 1

ISBN 1-59156-268-6

Library of Congress Cataloging-in-publication Data

Cratty, Nancy L., 1969-
    Never Too Late : a novel / Nancy L. Cratty.
        p. cm.
    ISBN 1-59156-268-6 (alk. paper)
    1. Mormon women--Fiction. 2. Young women--Fiction. 3. Friendship--Fiction. I. Title.

    PS3603.R39N485 2004
    813'.6--dc22   2003062709
                                                                          CIP

Dedication

I would like to dedicate this book to my husband,
Joseph J. Cratty Jr.

Acknowledgments

I would like to thank my husband Joe and our children, Logan, Trevor, and Kayla for their unconditional love, support, and sacrifices in helping me achieve my goals. I would also like to thank my parents, Roger and Gloria Patchin, my grandmother, Carol Bertolino, my sister and brother-in-law, Susan and John Toomer, Ron and J. P. Piotter, and the Cratty family for all their love, encouragement, and help over the years. A special thank you to Evelyn Tankersley for believing in me more than I believed in myself. You told me I could do it, and even when I doubted myself, your words always gave me hope. And a thank you to Angela Colvin and the staff at Covenant for this opportunity, your help, and hard work.

Prologue

I'm not prepared for this day, he thought, as he glanced up through his windshield at the clear blue sky. He felt that dark, dismal clouds should have formed to match his grim mood. It seemed cruel to him that this new day had actually dawned when he felt as though his life were over.

His hands firmly gripped the steering wheel as he drove to his destination and he tried to keep his gaze locked as firmly on the road, but he felt compelled to glance behind him as he looked at his newborn son. His heart ached for their loss.

Watching his son contentedly sleeping, he thought of his wife and how she would have loved and adored their first child. She had known in her heart that their baby was going to be a boy from the day she'd discovered she was pregnant, and she had been anxious to be a mother. She was a woman that would have given their child all the care and love possible. Truly grateful that his son was too young to witness this loss, yet sorrowful that the infant would never feel his mother's embrace, the young father forced his thoughts to the task ahead of him.

Knowing that a crowd of people was awaiting his arrival, he took a deep breath and hoped that he had enough strength to face the realities of the day. He pulled his truck into Bridger Cemetery, parked next to his parents' car, and quickly switched off the engine. He sat for a few moments, admiring his son and wishing that fate had treated them differently. It was difficult to leave the cab of his truck, and he sat longer than he could afford, willing himself to move. Finally, he glanced at his watch. The last feeding and changing before leaving had taken longer than expected, and he realized that he was now twenty minutes late.

Although he had only been a father for four days, he felt deep parental pride. He reached behind to the back seat and carefully pulled his son out of his car seat, cradling him in his arms. Despite how tiny the boy was, there was already a resemblance between father and son. He sighed. There was so much to learn about babies that he felt overwhelmed. Fortunately, his mother had been eager to teach him how to care for the new baby, and perhaps in time the burden would be lighter.

Careful not to wake the sleeping baby, he climbed out of the truck and swung the diaper bag over his shoulder. He pulled a blanket off the front seat and arranged it so that it would shade the infant's eyes from the glare of the sun without making him too hot and uncomfortable. The June heat was nearly unbearable, but luckily a slight breeze was blowing. Birds chirped in the nearby trees, oblivious to the events that were about to unfold. He felt that the day was far too bright and cheery to be on record as the day he buried his wife.

As quickly as possible, without disturbing his son, he headed toward the congregation at the rear of the cemetery. He approached the front of the group, ignoring the stares and sympathetic looks.

"Kolton." His mother noticed him immediately and softly called his name as she rose from her seat. Then she gathered the baby in her arms as their bishop reached out to shake Kolton's hand. As he'd handed the baby over to his mother, Kolton could tell she'd seen the obvious anguish on his face, and he knew her heart ached for him and her new grandson.

The bishop gave him a silent nod of acknowledgment, indicating it was Kolton's right to authorize the beginning of the dedication, and Kolton nodded back his permission. Then his mother quickly led him toward an empty seat in the front row between her and his father.

He sat down, dropped the diaper bag between his feet, and folded his arms. Stoically he listened to the words of his bishop, but their meaning barely registered. The shiny white coffin sat only a few feet in front of him, and he refused to comprehend that her body was about to be laid to rest. He couldn't accept that her earthly life was over.

Bishop Wynn spoke of their temple marriage and the blessings that they would be given. The bishop's words made Kolton think of the day he was sealed to his wife. He pushed the memory out of his mind and glanced again at his mother. She had begun to rock the baby, and tears streamed down her face. He looked at his father and noticed that his father's eyes were filled with tears, and he quickly looked away for fear of losing control of his own emotions.

Kolton sighed and swallowed hard before he looked back at the bishop and tried to concentrate on the words he spoke. His own tears were spent. Dark circles surrounded his eyes, and the lines in his face were drawn. There wasn't a fresh tear left to cry. There were so many emotions flooding his mind that his sorrow had no room to express itself. Disbelief and anger were beginning to rule his thoughts. He knew that there were different stages of grief, but he had never lost a close loved one before. The emotional pain was excruciating, and he was completely unprepared for it or the anger.

He heard a cry of emotion to his left and noticed his wife's family huddled together. He instantly looked away. He was confused and angry over an incident that had taken place with them earlier that day. Terrible accusations and harsh words had been exchanged with his in-laws before the funeral services. In his heart he wanted to forgive their angry accusations, knowing their pain, but he was hurting too much to worry about anyone else at the moment. Besides, their intolerance for him had always been obvious, and without his wife to love and defend him, they had wasted no time revealing the depth of their feelings.

In his anger, he fully recalled the morning's incident. As usual he had lost control of his temper. The funeral services were to start in minutes, and he had stepped outside the chapel with his son to have a breath of fresh air and clear his head. His mind had been overrun with emotions, and he hadn't slept for days.

As Kolton turned the corner outside the church building, his in-laws and their extended family members were hugging and comforting each other. They were also clearly discussing their private opinions about him, as they momentarily quieted at the sight of him. He'd wanted to walk by peacefully, but there was too much tension. Then the accusations began to fly. Initially he knew that their words were the direct result of their suffering, but when they began to blame him for his wife's death, he became enraged.

Kolton's only response was a direct order. "Stay away from me and my son. I don't want any of you near him for the rest of his life!" His mother had walked onto the scene behind him, turning pale upon hearing the accusations directed toward her son and his angry reply. Yet, unlike her son, she had a deep regard for the feelings of Kolton's in-laws. She tried to discuss the situation calmly and offer condolences, but it was too late. Too many ugly words had been spoken. His mother-in-law had begun to weep uncontrollably as he and his mother departed.

Pulling himself from his thoughts and reaching over to his mother, Kolton gently took his son back in his own arms. The baby squirmed momentarily, then curled into his father's chest and resumed sleeping. Closing his eyes, Kolton silently vowed to always protect his son from the hate and anger of his wife's family. Kolton would raise him with all the love and guidance a child could be given, and keep him from ever knowing the hatred his father had faced. This promise to his son gave him a reason to continue with life. He then opened his eyes and tried to focus on the graveside service and the heartfelt words of his bishop.

Chapter One

Eight Years Later

"You don't need to do this, Carly." Adam tried to control his emotions, but Carly heard his voice crack.

"Yes, I do. This is very difficult for me too, Adam. You know how much I care about you, but our differences are a problem whether you want to acknowledge it or not."

Adam shook his head. "You're making a big deal out of nothing."

Carly's eyes filled with tears as she softly spoke, "I don't want to hurt you, Adam. I never intended to string you along." She paused for a moment, studying his expression. "I just wanted to stop by and say good-bye before I left town."

Silently he glanced back and forth between her and her car, then focused on the small car packed high with her belongings. It was as if he was realizing for the first time that she was actually leaving town and leaving him. He shook his head in disbelief.

Carly had to look away from him. Even early in the morning he was as handsome as ever. She'd miss his stylish brown hair, only a shade darker than the eyes she'd miss even more. She glanced back at his face. His eyebrows were taut with emotion, and she resisted the urge to reach out and comfort him. "I just wanted to say good-bye, Adam. And to let you know that I'm sorry it has to end this way, but I wish you the best."

"But it doesn't have to end," he insisted. He reached out to touch her cheek, but she turned her face. His hand fell to his side. He was hurting, but he looked at her hopefully. "Come on, Carly. Let's talk this over. Come in and talk with me," he offered, and waved to motion her into his apartment.

She shook her head. "No, Adam." In the past she had been charmed by his personality, and had allowed her emotions to be led wherever he wanted to take them. He possessed many good qualities, and she still found him very attractive, but she had made a decision to leave him, and she was going to follow through.

He glanced at his watch. "Carly," he spoke softly. "Let me take you out to breakfast. We'll go to that little country inn off the highway. You love that place, and they have a great buffet on Saturdays. We can relax and talk more openly."

She did love that restaurant. And she loved the way that he always remembered what she liked. He had been a very thoughtful boyfriend. She remembered the last time they had eaten there. He had taken her to dinner for her birthday, and surprised her with a dozen yellow roses—her favorite. She hadn't recalled ever mentioning that they were her favorite, but somehow he had found out.

She found his offer to go out to breakfast tempting, but she had to be strong-willed. Adam had recently made it very clear to her that he was not interested in her religion. And no matter how thoughtful or charming he could be, she needed to make wise choices, and her choice had always been to prepare herself for a temple wedding.

"I'm sorry, Adam. But I need to get going. I have a job waiting for me in Bridger, and I have to be out of my apartment this weekend."

"I figured that you had a job somewhere—putting in your resignation at the office like that."

"I feel like this is what I need to do. As much as I care about you, I just don't think we could work out our differences."

His voice turned cool. "You mean to say that you don't think I could change to fit your beliefs."

"It's not just a matter of changing, Adam. It's a respect and understanding for my beliefs." In the past few weeks she had repeatedly become defensive over her religion, and she disliked seeing this close-minded side of Adam. He was usually kind and considerate, but when the topic of her religion would arise, he would become impatient and argumentative.

Unable to break her resolve, he changed directions, "Remember the first day that I started working at the law firm with you?"

She smiled and nodded. He gave her a wide grin and cocked his head as he reached out to hold her hand. He continued, "I walked up to your desk and asked you for a pen, remember?"

Again, she nodded. She had been hoping that he would notice her that day. She admitted, laughing, "For some reason I was so nervous, I was trembling. I dropped the pen twice before I handed it to you."

"Did I ever tell you that I really didn't need a pen? I was just looking for an opportunity to talk to you then." He smiled at the memory, then his face became serious. "Look how far we've come since then. Carly, we have had some really good times together. You have to admit we both felt something between us from the start, and it led into a good relationship once we discovered how much we have in common." He gave her hand a squeeze, but she pulled away.

It was true. She couldn't deny she had felt an instant connection, and they had never argued over anything besides religion. But there was more to life for her, and she wanted to prepare for her future. "Adam, physical attraction is what we felt. And we have personalities that complement each other. But now we know that it's not enough."

"I want us to try again, Carly. We can figure out a way to overcome our religious differences."

In her heart she had hoped that he would make an effort to learn about her religion and why she believed so strongly in her values. In fact, she almost expected him to do so now, once he realized that she was leaving town. But none of her hopeful wishing could change him into the person she wanted him to be.

"Adam, the argument we had a couple of weeks ago made me realize that we aren't compatible. And it's not just our religious differences."

Adam nodded that he understood, but his eyes showed his agitation.

Carly glanced at her watch. "I need to get going. I want to get there early and unpack, so I can spend some time with my family before I start work next week."

He sighed and folded his arms against his chest. "I think you're making a mistake, Carly. I really think that we're a good match."

She quickly blinked her eyes to prevent tears from falling. She had prayed about her decision to leave, and felt that she had made the best choice, but there was a small part of her that wanted to stay with

Adam. There was so much about him that she adored, and she had always felt special and cared for when she was with him. She forced back the desire to give in to the temptation, then said, "Good-bye, Adam."

He swallowed hard and shook his head. "Don't go, Carly."

She turned to leave without a word. As she pulled out of the parking lot she noticed him standing still, watching her go. His expression was grim, and it made her heart ache to know that he was hurting as much as she was.

She drove to Bridger unable to rid herself of thoughts of Adam. By their first date she had known that she was interested in him. He had offered to pick her up one Saturday night, and she had accepted, not knowing what he'd planned. When he arrived at her apartment, he'd surprised her by asking to borrow an old blanket. She'd been grateful he'd asked, when later that evening the wind picked up. He'd planned a picnic in the park and an outdoor musical by a community theater.

He prepared the meal himself, and she had been flattered by the amount of time he'd spent preparing fried chicken, salads, and a dessert. They had both agreed on how much they enjoyed theater productions, and as they chatted they found other common interests to discuss. At that point she'd felt as though she had good reasons to consider dating him. She felt fate had somehow interceded in her life. Over time, they both discovered that their essential values and interests were the same, except the one thing that meant the most to Carly—the gospel.

As she recalled their time together, she felt frustrated and sad, and nothing seemed to distract her from the melancholy that had overcome her. Carly's thoughts were solely concentrated on her relationship with Adam by the time she entered her childhood town, and when she arrived at her parents' home, she was emotionally exhausted. Luckily, her parents had come to her apartment a few days earlier and picked up most of her furniture and belongings. Her mother had already organized her things, which would make the transition much easier for her. Carly spent the first few days in her parents' home, organizing her remaining possessions and visiting with her family. She needed a few days to rest and reflect on the changes in her life.

Her parents had never pried into her affairs, and she was grateful they were interested in other aspects of her life besides her breakup. They talked about her new job and recent events in their small country town. She wanted to talk to her mother about Adam, but she decided to wait until her emotions had settled down.

A few days after her return home, she decided to venture out and visit an old friend. The March winds were cooler than Carly remembered from her youth. She pulled her coat tight around her chest, pushed her long blond hair out of her face, and lengthened her stride. It was only a half mile to the farmhouse in the distance. She would have to walk through undeveloped desert, full of weeds and rocks, in hopes that there would be a slight remnant of the old, well-trodden path. Gazing upward, she noticed the gray clouds billowing above her, and the faint smell of rain in the air. She walked swiftly, hoping she would make it to her destination before the rain fell.

It had been fifteen years since she had followed this familiar path to Jennifer Wright Parker's house. Besides a few cards and telephone calls immediately after graduation, there hadn't been much communication between the two friends through the years. Carly regretted neglecting their friendship, but she hoped that they could renew it now that she had returned to their hometown of Bridger, Nevada. As she stepped cautiously, trying to stay on the faint path that had begun at the back of her parents' property, she noticed that not much had changed since she had left home. She smiled at the familiarity of having to cross a few acres of raw desert and walk through a large field of alfalfa before ending at the Wrights' big, green barn near the edge of their yard. Carly smiled even wider, remembering how Mrs. Wright had always disliked red barns, and she had often changed the color of the old barn during Carly's childhood.

Once Carly arrived at the barn, it took her only a few seconds to reach the front porch of the house. Before she could knock on the door, it quickly opened, and Jennifer came flying out to throw her arms around her old friend.

"It's been so long," Jennifer cried as she squeezed Carly tightly before pulling away. Jennifer held her friend at arm's length and exclaimed, "Look at you. You look fantastic! I've never seen your hair so long, and you are so thin! You look fabulous!"

"Thank you. And look at yourself," Carly countered with a big grin. " I didn't know you were pregnant again. Congratulations!"

Jennifer put both hands on her belly and her eyes softened. "I had an ultrasound last week, and it's finally a girl. After three boys, I just can't believe I'm finally having a girl. But Rich isn't getting his hopes up—he won't believe it until he sees her!"

The two women shared a laugh, and Jennifer exclaimed, "Well, come in. I didn't mean to attack you at the door. This weather is so nasty—come in and warm up."

Carly entered the house and felt as though she had traveled back in time. The carpet, kitchen tile, and wallpaper were the same as they had been when they were children. Most of the furniture was the same too. The only differences were the pictures of Rich and Jennifer's children covering all the walls and end tables. A few stray toys and a rocking horse in the center of the room made Carly smile. *Jennifer is so lucky to have a family of her own,* she thought.

Jennifer motioned for Carly to sit on the couch in the living room and said, "This is the perfect time for a visit. My baby, Timmy, is taking a nap, and the other boys are at a friend's for another hour."

As Carly shed her coat and sat down, she mused, "I feel like I'm sixteen again! Everything feels so familiar. It's as though I've traveled back in time."

Jennifer sat down close beside her and explained, "As soon as my father retired, my parents bought a fifth-wheel trailer and decided to travel. So, four years ago we moved into the house to take care of the place in return for not paying any rent. We had assumed it would be a temporary arrangement, but as soon as my folks were done traveling, they decided to serve a mission. They were gone for eighteen months in West Virginia, came home for three months, and they just left for another mission in Australia for another eighteen months!"

"That is so great. Doesn't your mom miss your kids, though?"

Laughing, Jennifer responded, "Rich and I are convinced that the grandkids are the reason they keep leaving!"

At the comment, Carly gazed at the pictures of Jennifer's children. "They are so cute, Jennifer. They're all a combination of you and Rich."

"Thank you. They're a handful, but I love being a mom." Carly and Jennifer exchanged glances, both in awe of how strange it was to be together again, and how different their lives were now.

Carly couldn't believe how wonderful it felt to be with her old friend again. Although Jennifer's auburn hair was shorter, the years hadn't changed her face much, and Carly felt as comfortable with her as when they had been kids.

As friends, they had always seemed an awkward pair since Carly was tall and lean and Jennifer was small and voluptuous. In high school Jennifer had been a popular cheerleader while Carly chose to spend her time more on the sidelines; she had participated in school choir, taken piano lessons, and joined the local 4-H to show rabbits and sheep, though. Those days were long over, but she still enjoyed quiet activities and being involved in small groups. They did have things in common that drew them together, though. Both had been good students and well respected by their peers and teachers. They also shared the same value system and love for the gospel.

Jennifer tucked her legs beneath her. "I heard you were moving back to town. I talked to your mom at church on Sunday, and she said you had moved back and that you have a job at the elementary school."

Carly nodded. "Yeah, I've been home for a week, and I start work on Monday. I was here last Sunday, but I wasn't feeling well so I didn't come to church." She didn't want to admit to Jennifer that she wasn't feeling well *emotionally* due to her breakup with Adam.

"Are you excited about your job?" Jennifer asked.

"Yes, I am. I applied as a secretary in the office, and they called me up for an interview. I came home last week for it, and by the time I'd arrived back in Langdon, they had left a message on my answering machine asking if I could start this next week. It will be a little difficult to start work in the spring, but at least I'll have this last quarter of school left to learn how things are done in the office."

"That is so great. The elementary hasn't changed much since we were kids—it'll be déjà vu. Actually, the entire town hasn't changed much," Jennifer said with a laugh. "I think the population here in Bridger is still less than two thousand." Jennifer suddenly caught Carly's thoughtful expression. Jennifer stopped talking and absent-mindedly rested both hands on her swollen belly.

"Why did you come back, Carly?"

Carly explained, "I felt I needed to come home. It's going to be a change for me after living away for so long, but I'm excited for the change." She briefly thought of Adam, hoping she wouldn't regret the changes she had made in her life. She continued, "I also want to spend some time with my family. I think I'll stay at home for a few months before I look for an apartment."

"Are you okay?" Jennifer asked, concerned.

"Yes. Why?"

"You just seemed sad for a moment."

"Oh, you know, I'm just going through some changes right now. Leaving Langdon was difficult for me. I was involved with someone special, and . . . it ended. I guess I just need some time to adjust."

Jennifer nodded that she understood, but didn't press her friend. In the next hour, Jennifer updated Carly on some of their mutual friends from school, her own children, and her current calling in the Relief Society at church. Carly was an avid listener, but tried to steer casual conversation away from herself. She wasn't ready to discuss Adam yet.

Jennifer finally began asking direct questions so Carly would talk, but respectfully stayed away from the topic that Carly clearly wanted to avoid. Besides, she was anxious to learn about her friend's travels. "Now that you know all about me, what have you been doing all these years?" Jennifer asked. "Your mother tells me you're doing great."

Carly took a deep breath. "Well, after graduation I took a receptionist job with a small bookstore in Langdon. Since it's such a long drive from here I hardly ever came home. Then when you got married, I had already planned a trip east to visit my grandmother in Maine. I always felt bad about missing your wedding, but Grandma was so ill. I ended up staying there for a couple of years to take care of her. Although her health gradually got better, she still needed someone to help her around the house.

"Then, she got really sick again, and my folks both retired and came to Maine too. That was . . . nine or ten years ago. Everyone thought it would be a short stay because we weren't expecting her to live very long. My folks were going to sell their house, but then decided to rent it to Chad and Leann. So the rest of us were all living with Grandma, and she lived another five years. Mom and Dad were able to come back to Bridger for visits, but I always stayed with Grandma because she needed the help."

"I loved having your brother and Leann live in your parents' house," Jennifer interjected. "When we were all growing up, Chad was always your bossy older brother, but now we're all good friends. Leann was a great neighbor, and Rich works for the county road department with Chad."

"I knew Chad worked for the road department, but it never occurred to me that he and Rich were good friends." Carly leaned back into the couch and continued. "That's another reason why I chose to come home. I need to spend more time with him and Leann. But anyway, after Grandma died, Mom and Dad moved back into their house. Since Chad and Leann found a house nearby, I decided to come back to Nevada. The job opportunities were better in Langdon, so I moved there. Plus, it's a short drive from Bridger, and I wanted to stay close to family."

"Did you go back to doing secretarial work?" Jennifer asked.

"I did. Actually, I took some classes and I got a job as a legal secretary with a good firm. The work was great—I really enjoyed it. Unfortunately, the senior attorney, Matthew, passed away recently. The other attorneys decided to keep the firm together, but I decided it was a good time for me to leave."

Jennifer listened intently as her friend continued. "Anyway, I feel good about coming home. Mom knew that I was thinking about leaving my job, so she told me about Mrs. Green having to quit her job at the elementary due to some health problems. Luckily they hired me, and I start on Monday."

"Are you a little nervous?" Jennifer asked.

"Yeah, but I'm excited. It'll be hard to come in during the middle of the school year, but I'm sure I'll learn a lot. And I'll have the summer off to prepare for the next school year."

"So, while you've had an independent life of excitement and leisure, I've been changing diapers and doing four loads of laundry a day," Jennifer said with a chagrined smile.

Carly's expression turned serious. "No, Jennifer. You've had a wonderful life. Never compare working to raising a family. I've always wanted a family. I would quit work in a second for marriage and a family."

Jennifer replied, "I am fortunate. I just get tired sometimes and wonder what it would be like to be in your shoes." She paused, sensing it was possible that Carly felt so strongly about family because of what had happened in Langdon. She decided to ask the question they'd been avoiding. "You mentioned that there was someone special in your life. Is there any chance of reconciliation?"

Carly realized she did want to talk about it after all. She admitted, "I really don't know. Everything was great in the beginning. Adam was kind, caring, and respectful. But we don't have the same religious beliefs. I really think that we need to be more compatible in our values. I just can't see us making a marriage work."

Jennifer nodded that she understood, but before she could respond, both women heard a truck pull into the driveway.

Jennifer kept one hand on her belly and turned awkwardly to look out the window. "Oh, it's our feed delivery. I didn't think he was due until tomorrow." She turned back to Carly, an impish grin suddenly lighting her face. "You know who that is, don't you?" she asked.

Carly leaned over the back of the couch to get a better view. Pulling back the curtain, she saw a tall man with a good muscular build get out of the driver's side door of a pickup truck and move toward the back of the truck. He pulled down the tailgate and began pulling a bale of straw out of the bed. Then he carried it over to the side of the barn, where it would be protected from the rain. He took long strides back to his truck, and Carly noticed that his dark hair had a slight wave. The top of his hair appeared to be casually combed back as though he had recently raked his hand through it. Soft curls brushed the back of his shirt collar. His face was shadowed with a close-cut beard, and his skin was well tanned.

"Hmm . . . he's handsome in a cowboy sort of way, but I don't know him," Carly replied, still looking. A drizzle of rain softly pelted him, making his tight red T-shirt appear spotted. He occasionally wiped his face on his sleeve. His nose was straight, and his cheekbones high. He had an angular look that others might think rough, but to Carly it was very attractive.

Jennifer's smile grew sly and her green eyes sparkled as she observed Carly's piqued interest. "You know him. We went to school with him," she said knowingly.

"Really? You look like the cat that ate the canary," Carly laughed, and looked closer while the man unloaded the last bale of straw and a couple sacks of chicken feed. As though he could feel someone watching him, he suddenly glanced up at the window and waved before he reached into the cab of his truck.

Perplexed, Carly admitted, "He doesn't even look familiar. Does he know me?"

Jennifer laughed, "Of course. I bet he remembers you. Once you see him up close you'll recognize him."

He began to walk toward the house, carrying a receipt book, as Jennifer got up to open the front door. Carly watched him from the window, but she still couldn't attach a name to the handsome face.

As he approached the open door, Jennifer welcomed him. "Hello, how are you?"

"Good, thank you. How are you?"

"Great. Come on in. I'd like you to see someone."

The man stepped into the house but stopped near the door. "My boots are a little dirty. I shouldn't come in," he stated. He nodded at Carly and asked, "How are you, Carly? It's been a long time."

Carly didn't recognize the voice or the man, but at close range the combination of dark eyebrows and lashes surrounding those very blue eyes was definitely familiar. Unconsciously, she was biting her bottom lip, but she couldn't remember who he was.

Smiling back, she tried to hide her quizzical expression and answered, "Good. How are you?"

The man looked at Jennifer and laughed. "She has no idea who I am." He handed the clipboard to Jennifer to sign the receipt. "I guess I didn't leave a big impression on you," he teased, giving Carly a wink.

Carly felt at ease with his teasing and noticed that he seemed comfortable with her. She didn't want to be rude, yet she couldn't help but stare. The more she looked at him, the more things about his appearance began to register in her memory, but she still couldn't place who he was.

Jennifer offered, "Well, in her defense, it has been a long time. Carly's been gone from Bridger since high school. She'll figure it out."

The man said to Carly, "Are you back home to stay?"

"Yes," she answered. "I start work at the elementary school on Monday."

"Good." He seemed pleased as he turned to Jennifer and said, "I'm a bit short on your order, so I'll drop by as soon as I can with the rest of it."

She handed back the paperwork. "It's no problem. If you don't drop it off I'll have Rich pick it up when he stops by to pay."

"Sounds good. See you later, Jennifer," he said and turned to leave. He glanced back at Carly and commented, "It was good seeing you again. I'm sure we'll run into each other."

Carly said good-bye but he was already out the door. "Jen! Tell me who that is!" she demanded as she watched him return to his truck and drive away.

Jennifer sat down on the couch and hinted, "We grew up with him."

"I can't imagine who he is."

"I'll give you some more hints. He went to church with us, he was always quiet, his parents owned the feed store—"

Suddenly Carly exclaimed, "Kolton Raywood! That was Kolton Raywood?"

Jennifer smiled smugly. "Doesn't he look great?"

"I can't believe it! He was the skinniest, shyest kid in school." Carly looked out the window again, but his truck had disappeared from view. "He was always so short. He must be almost six feet now. I always thought he was cute, but I towered over him all through school. What's his story—how has he been since high school?"

"He hasn't had an easy life." Jennifer chose her words carefully before she spoke. "He's not shy anymore, but he isn't real outgoing either. Despite what life's handed him, he's still a good person. A few years ago he bought the feed store from his folks, and he lives in their old house next door to the store. He pretty much keeps to himself."

Carly grew inquisitive. At first, she didn't remember much about Kolton except that they had all gone to elementary school together, and he had always been shy and quiet. Carly had a vague recollection of him from her memories of high school. Most of her time had been spent with Jennifer and Rich, and sometimes with her brother, Chad. Small fragments of memory from her youth began to surface. "He had a shaved head in grade school, didn't he? I remember him better now. He used to come regularly to the youth meetings at church, right?"

Jennifer nodded her head, confirming Carly's memories. "Yes, his family is very active in the Church, and both he and his parents are still in our ward. They only moved a few blocks over from the feed store. Kolton moved into their house next to the feed store because it's more convenient to live right there. And, of course, he still attends our ward."

Carly recalled, "Didn't he have a good sense of humor?"

"Yeah. Remember when Mr. Wayne, our government teacher, threw a fit in class because someone had glued his mug to the desk on April Fools' Day?"

"Oh, I'll never forget that. I laughed so hard I almost fell out of my chair. The entire class was hysterical."

"That was Kolton," Jennifer said. "He and Rich thought it up together."

"But the mug wasn't the only thing," Carly remembered. "Didn't they tape pictures to Mr. Wayne's maps? Girls in swimsuits sitting on race cars or something?"

Jennifer began to laugh. "Mr. Wayne pulled a map down from the roll over his chalkboard, and he turned bright red to see some cover girl wearing a bikini plastered on his map." Carly joined her friend's laughter. She felt good reminiscing about high school and old friends. It made her feel as though she belonged at home in Bridger.

Carly mused, "Kolton was the type to do things quietly, but he had personality. You know, I remember a time in high school when some kids were picking on Yolanda Herring, and he defended her."

"Oh, I remember her. The kids were so mean to her because she was a little overweight. She was a really nice girl—and she was funny, too! It makes me so mad that people didn't take the time to get to know her."

Carly began to remember the details. "We were doing a ward service project at her house. The men were working on the roof and the women were helping with some of the yard work because her dad had been sick for a while and out of work. Anyway, a group of guys were taking a break under a tree near the house, and Keith Jackson said something about Yolanda's weight. I don't remember what he said, but they all started laughing. All of a sudden a roof shingle came flying out of nowhere and hit him in the back. I looked up at the roof and there were some guys still working, but not one of them was watching or looking down at us. I thought I caught a glimmer of satisfaction in Kolton's expression, though. I couldn't prove it, but I always figured it was Kolton."

Jennifer smiled. "It probably was. As small as Kolton was then, he'd have been no match for Keith if he'd approached him face-to-face."

Carly continued, "And Keith's mom found out what had happened because he had that huge welt on his back. He ended up apologizing to Yolanda, and she hadn't even heard his mean remark. But I always thought it was so interesting how Kolton reacted. I know it wasn't nice on his part to throw that shingle, but we all knew what a bully Keith was. I was amazed Kolton had any aggression in him; he was always so quiet."

"I guess people aren't always as they seem," Jennifer said.

"Yeah," Carly agreed thoughtfully.

"It seems you might be a bit interested in Kolton. You know, he's single," Jennifer teased. "Perhaps I could have him over to dinner, and you could just happen to drop over the same evening, and . . ."

Carly raised her hand defiantly and announced, "I am *not* interested in men right now. Besides, there will be no matchmaking. Remember the last time you did that to me with your cousin, Ned? He got a bloody nose on the dance floor, tripped over his own feet, stepped on mine a few times, and we agreed to end the date by nine o'clock! He was the clumsiest boy alive."

Jennifer began to laugh. "Would you believe he's a heart surgeon now? He works in Chicago."

"No way!" Carly laughed until her eyes filled with tears. She reached out to touch Jennifer's arm. "It's so great to see you again."

Jennifer smiled warmly, "You'll have to come over for dinner soon to visit with Rich and the kids. We'll bake up some treats like we used to do when we were kids, and we'll talk all night."

"I would love to. My mom is so worried about fat grams and cholesterol that there isn't anything to eat at her house except fruit and vegetables. That reminds me, I better get home. I want to be there in case my mom needs help with dinner."

After exchanging another hug and promising they'd get together soon, Carly left and hurried through the light drizzle of rain toward home. It had felt so good to remember the old times she hadn't thought of in years. Her parents were happy to have her home with them, and she felt more comfortable there than she'd expected. There were so many big changes in her life right now, and she was relieved to feel good about her decision to move back to her hometown.

As she stepped over weeds and brush, she thought again of Kolton. There was something earthy and masculine about him that she hadn't noticed in high school, and she was intrigued by Jennifer's comments about what life had dealt him. It suddenly dawned on her that she hadn't thought of Adam for over an hour. That realization was a welcome one, as lately, Adam had seemed to dominate her thoughts and emotions. The nine months that they had dated had been wonderful, and memory after memory had assaulted her since the day she'd moved home.

She couldn't deny that she'd have strong feelings for him for a while; she'd never been so deeply in love before. She was beginning to understand why her Young Women leaders had encouraged her to date young men who shared her religious beliefs. She had once hoped that their love would be eternal, but deep in her heart she knew Adam would never accept her religion or her choices in life.

Any other thirty-three-year-old single woman would have jumped at the opportunity to date a rich, successful attorney. But there was so much more at stake for Carly—Adam could never fulfill her heart's true desire of a temple marriage and an eternal family. Now she wondered if she would ever have an opportunity for love again. She wondered if she should have been more patient with Adam and tried harder to bring him to the gospel. Maybe in time she could have helped him learn of the truthfulness of the Church, and they would have been sealed in the temple for time and all eternity. But she knew it was too late to wonder. She had made her decision to leave, and she would just have to face the consequences of being single, again.

Chapter Two

Carly arrived at home just before the rain began to fall in heavy sheets. It was common for desert storms to produce flash flooding, and Carly was grateful to be out of the weather. Entering by the back door, she rushed through the kitchen and carried her damp jacket into the adjacent laundry room.

As she threw her wet jacket into the washing machine, she called out, "Mom, I'm home." Her voice echoed through the house, but no one answered.

Her parents' home was a single-story ranch house with a full, wraparound covered porch. Carly's father had built the house himself, and—although it wasn't large—it was handsome and well cared for. The wooden exterior had been recently painted butter cream with a dark brown trim. Inside, the house was decorated with country accents and antique furniture. Carly's mother, Emma, loved to decorate, and every room had its own style. Carly had noticed the remodeling, but hadn't really taken the time to appreciate her mother's work. As no one was home to talk to, she figured it was a good time to explore.

She walked into the western-style living room and saw no one. She paused to glance around the house, letting it sink in that she was really home. Pictures of cowboys, cattle, and horses adorned the stained-wood walls. The brown leather couch and matching chairs were worn and welcoming. Her father's favorite heirloom—a one-hundred-year-old antique saddle—hung on the wall over the couch. Carly made her way down the hall and peeked into her parents' room. The master bedroom had recently been decorated in deep shades of green and rose. Floral drapes complemented her mother's bedspread and throw pillows. The wooden bedroom set had belonged to Carly's paternal grandmother, and it was a beautiful walnut with few scratches or dents.

Glancing across the hall, Carly looked into the two bedrooms that had once been designed for her and Chad, who was fourteen months her senior. His room had been painted a cool blue tone, and now served as an office. Her mother's computer, file cabinets, and genealogy work covered every square inch of floor and desk space. The wooden shelves that had once displayed Chad's athletic trophies were still there, as well as a built-in chest under the window that had held all of his athletic equipment, but no other sign of Chad was left.

Carly's old room had a bay window with a covered bench seat and a small rolltop desk. The same four-poster bed that she had loved in her youth was still in her room. Now it was a guest room adorned with a matching blue plaid comforter and curtains. The walls were painted a soft yellow, and childhood pictures of Chad and Carly were hung around the room. Although much of the decor had changed, Carly still felt comfortable staying in her old room. She enjoyed that the room added to her sense of positive change. The new look made her feel less like she was running away to an old self, and more like she was moving on to new things.

Carly retreated to the kitchen. The kitchen had Spanish floor tiling like the living room, but the walls were a soft peach color. A border of pastel, floral wallpaper matched the fabric of the kitchen window curtains. Antique cream pitchers, butter trays, and serving plates filled the kitchen hutch. The solid oak cabinets were hand-built by her father.

The kitchen was still Carly's favorite place in her parents' home. The appliances were old, the cabinets a bit dented, and some of the tile counter tops chipped, but every flaw held a story from her past. She smiled as she surveyed the room. One chip in the floor tile had been caused by a plate Carly dropped when she was eight. A small indentation in one of the cabinet doors was from a shoe Chad had intended to throw at the cat, but his aim had been off.

She grabbed a soda from the refrigerator and sat down at the table. As she opened the tab, she noticed a note from her parents. She read it quickly and discovered that they had gone out to pick up some groceries and a health-food pizza, and they would be returning soon.

The phone rang, and Carly jumped to answer it in the living room. "Hello."

"Hello, Carly."

She hadn't heard his voice for days. "Hi, Adam."

"How are you?"

"Good." She smiled and sat on the couch. "How have you been?"

"Okay. I've been busy with work. You know how it is—there's always something going on."

Carly had been hoping that he would call. She was anxious to know how he really was. "So, what's going on?"

"Well, I wanted to tell you something. I've been doing a little research about your church, and I've learned some interesting facts."

Curious, Carly asked, "Really? Like what?"

His tone turned more serious as he explained, "Well, the man you call a prophet, Joseph Smith, was a fortune hunter, a liar, and a thief. I'm sure that's why the early Mormon settlers were chased and ridiculed wherever they went."

"Adam, this is nonsense. You haven't been researching my religion at all, you've been—"

Sternly he interrupted, "Listen Carly. You need to know these things. There is a book all about Mormons and all their ridiculous nonsense. You really need to read it."

Carly insisted, "You researched anti-Mormon material. That is different than actually researching my religion."

"How do you expect me to understand your religion when *you* won't be open-minded about it?"

"*Me?*" Annoyed, she threw the accusation back. "You haven't been open-minded since I first brought up religion."

Dismissing her irritation, Adam pressed, "You really need to read these books and pamphlets I have. If this church is such a big part of your life, then you need to do some research on your religion. I think there are a lot of things you're not aware of."

Carly's emotions dulled. She didn't want to argue. "Adam, I'm not going to read anti-Mormon literature when I believe it's trash. I know my religion and the history of my church. I also know that there are people in the world who want to destroy the integrity of the Church, and I won't read any of it." Her tone softened. "I know where you're going with this, Adam—this is all about my beliefs on marriage. And it's not a matter of my faith alone. I've always respected the vows of marriage. Even if I didn't go to church, I would believe in marriage. And you don't have to be a Mormon to be a Christian."

Adam was silent and then questioned, "Christian? I didn't think that Mormons were Christian."

His lack of religious knowledge surprised her. "I know what I am. I'm a Christian. My church is called The Church of Jesus Christ of Latter-day Saints," she said clearly, emphasizing the words "Jesus Christ."

Adam sighed heavily into the receiver. "Fine, Carly. But don't say I never warned you about your church."

"Adam, I'm really not in the mood to discuss this."

"Well, then I'm sorry I upset you." She remained silent until he added, "I'll let you go. Take care, Carly."

"You too."

"Good-bye."

"Good-bye, Adam." Carly heard the line go dead before she turned off the phone. She returned the phone to its base and walked back into the kitchen.

She sipped her drink as she listened to the rain beat down on the roof. For the past few days she had been hoping that Adam would call, yet she hadn't been sure what she was going to say when he did. She hadn't expected him to call and discuss anti-Mormon literature. For her, their conversation had been bittersweet. She missed him, but as he had talked, she felt sure she'd made the right choice to leave.

She thought back to her conversation with Jennifer, and a twinge of envy began to surface. When they had been kids, Jennifer and Carly had both been raised by parents who kept the standards and principles of the Church. Carly knew the gospel was true and her testimony had never wavered. She had made mistakes in her life, but the one thing she had always been determined to have was a temple wedding. For Jennifer it had seemed so easy—her dream in life had been to be a wife and a mother. She had been sealed to her high-school boyfriend, Rich, after he returned home from his mission. She and Rich had their life planned out as soon as they'd graduated from high school. It seemed that Jennifer never had to worry about choosing the right person—Rich had been a perfect match for her.

Carly remembered how she felt when Rich and Jennifer sent an invitation to her for their wedding. She was excited for her friends, but also a bit jealous. At that time she had never had a serious boyfriend, and she felt left out of Jennifer's world. She could have managed a trip home for the wedding, but she hadn't tried very hard to make it a priority. Now she regretted her juvenile actions and wished she had put more effort into being a part of Rich and Jennifer's lives.

Over the years she had dated many men, but she had never felt like pursuing a serious relationship with any of them, until she met Adam. The first time she laid eyes on him she had felt there was something special about him. Looking back, she knew that it had been only physical attraction at first. But over the course of their relationship he had proved himself to be kind, caring, and thoughtful—all the qualities she had hoped for in a husband. She'd also never been approached by such a handsome and successful man, and it had boosted her self-esteem a great deal.

She thought back to the first time she met Adam. As soon as she'd become a legal secretary, she applied at the office of Connelly, Williams and Associates. Matthew Connelly interviewed her himself and hired her on the spot to be his personal secretary. His former secretary stayed on with the firm for three months to train her and help her through any problems. The work was demanding, but she loved every minute of it. Matthew and his wife, Jean, became her good friends in and outside of the office.

After six months, Matthew started looking for another attorney to help with the increasing workload. Business was great, but the current employees were overwhelmed with responsibilities. Adam Masterson was one of many attorneys who applied for the position. The moment Carly saw him, she was intrigued. Although his stature was large, he carried himself with great confidence and grace. His dark hair was cut short and was very stylish. His designer suit was charcoal gray and his shoes were shined to perfection. He was a handsome man with tanned, clear skin, a slender nose, and full lips. Carly remembered her hands trembling slightly when he had inquired at her desk about his appointment.

"Excuse me, I'm Adam Masterson. I have an appointment with Matthew Connelly."

"Yes," Carly said as she checked Matthew's schedule. "He will be with you in a moment."

"Thank you."

Carly had motioned him to a seat, and within moments Matthew had come out to shake his hand and lead him back into his office. After an hour they both walked out of his office and shook hands again.

"Adam," Matthew expressed his thoughts sincerely, "your accomplishments in New York are impressive. It will be a pleasure to have you on board. We'll see you first thing Monday morning."

"Thank you, sir. I do believe it will be a pleasure to work here," he agreed as he looked directly at Carly, his hazel eyes sparkling as he gave her a wink.

Adam Masterson was a definite charmer, and he knew it. For Carly, there was an allure about him that she couldn't resist. He had worked in the office for only a week when tragedy struck—Matthew Connelly suffered a mild stroke.

The office staff pulled together and followed the directions of Mark Williams, the senior attorney, who put Adam on most of Matthew's cases and handed Carly over to him as his personal secretary until Matthew could return. Though Carly was concerned about Matthew, she was thrilled at the chance to work with Adam. Her first day working with him, she took extra time to make her hair and makeup look especially nice. She wore her favorite professional dress suit and crossed her fingers that Adam would notice.

To her surprise, he did notice. By the end of the week he asked her out to dinner, and from there they became close friends. Adam confided in her that he had felt drawn to her from their first encounter, but that he was wary of office relationships. Carly admitted her attraction to him, and secretly felt as though she would like to know him better. But she wanted the relationship to progress slowly. They both agreed to simply start as friends and cross other bridges as they came up.

After work they often stayed late to finish up on paperwork, and on the weekends they planned fun outings. Adam loved to travel, and they took trips to lakes, museums, and small country communities where they purchased homemade jams and relishes. Carly glowed, and she called her mother almost daily to tell her about Adam—something he would say or some sweet gesture. And then there was their first kiss in the moonlight.

Though their mutual attraction and interests were growing and they worked well together professionally, there was one thing continually gnawing at Carly. Adam wasn't interested in her religion. She'd only let herself get as close as she had because she was sure a man of his nature would be interested. But he wasn't.

Carly thought back to when she first told Adam that she was a member of the Church. They were taking a walk in a park near her apartment when she mentioned, as casually as she could, "I wanted to invite you to come to church with me tomorrow. I'm a member of the Mormon church."

He thought for a second and then asked, "Does that mean you have multiple mothers?"

"Of course not," she stated, looking at him quizzically, not sure if he was joking. "I only have one mother—it's not possible to have multiple mothers," she teased.

Adam remained serious "But I thought Mormons were all polygamists."

Carly was slightly offended by how uneducated Adam was on the matter. After all, many national magazines had recently done fairly accurate reports on the Church. "No. There is no polygamy in the Church. Actually, in Church history—"

Adam cut her off. "Actually, I have plans tomorrow."

Now that she was thinking about it more clearly, it seemed to Carly that Adam had always changed the subject when she brought up religion. But her thoughts of Adam were interrupted by the arrival of her parents carrying in bags of groceries and a pizza. "Here, Mom, let me help you with the groceries," she offered as she reached out to take two sacks from her mother's arms.

"Oh, thank you, honey. The one bag goes in the pantry, and the other is milk and cheese. Go ahead and put it in the fridge here in the kitchen. Raymond, give me your wet jacket and I'll hang it with mine in the laundry room." Carly was almost an exact replica of her mother, although Emma Weston was a bit shorter and had gray-streaks in her shoulder-length blond hair. She was a woman who knew how to take control of situations, and she had her household in order at all times. "Honey," she said to her husband, "there is a pair of panty hose in the one bag—just set them on the counter for me, please."

Immediately, Emma began to arrange the table for dinner as she ordered everyone else around. "Raymond, please put the birdseed in the garage, and the bag of frozen goods can go in the outside freezer." Raymond was Emma's biggest fan. He adored her, and although at times she could seem a bit overbearing, he always kept his patience and honored his wife.

Carly knew that her parents' love and support for one another kept their marriage going strong, and together they were a pair that complemented each other fully. Even in appearances they were a well-matched and attractive couple. Raymond was lean like his wife, though slightly taller. His hair was dark, as was his complexion, and his dark gray eyes were striking. Together, the two were hard not to notice.

Being a man of few words, Raymond gathered the bags and nodded. Carly watched her father exit the room and turned to her mother. "It was good seeing Jennifer today."

"How was your visit?"

"Good. Jennifer seems really happy. I saw some pictures of her kids, and they are really cute."

"They are cute," her mother agreed. "I've always liked Rich and Jennifer, and they seem to be a happy family."

Carly had always felt that her parents were a happy couple too. She suddenly wanted to question her mom about it, "When did you know that Dad was the one for you?"

Emma finished placing the napkins on the table and smiled. "I don't believe there's just one person in the whole world for anyone. I believe we're here on earth to make good choices. Your father and I were very happy dating, and I just knew that we could be happy forever. Of course, it takes an effort. Marriage is a lot of work."

Carly nodded in agreement. Her mother's reply was exactly what Carly had expected. She knew her parents well, and their knowledge of the gospel always affected their thoughts and decisions.

Emma turned to her daughter and said, "Carly, your choice in a husband will be yours to make. You can always pray for direction, but ultimately, you will be the one who has to live with the consequences—good or bad."

"I know. It's just that some things are so confusing. I don't know why I would be so attracted to someone so wrong." Carly's voice cracked, and her mother put her arms around her daughter.

"I know what you're going through is hard, Carly. This stage of grief will pass. I have faith that you'll make good decisions in the future. Perhaps this was a lesson you needed to learn. I don't want to sound preachy to you, and I certainly don't want you to think that I discriminate against nonmembers, but maybe now you can teach your own children why we're taught to date members that have the same values and beliefs we do.

"I've known many wonderful couples who have begun as one-member families and the other partner joins the Church. I love to hear those stories, but there are many stories of unhappy members who feel their lives have been somehow shortchanged because their spouse never joins the Church. It's just a lot easier to start a relationship with someone you have those core beliefs in common with."

Carly hugged her mother back. She was so grateful to have her mother's love and understanding. "It was a hard lesson to learn firsthand."

"What's this?" her father interrupted. "Are we eating dinner, or having a hug fest?"

Carly and her mother locked eyes for a moment, and Carly knew that her mother did understand what she was feeling. "Let's eat," Emma announced, "and Carly can tell us about her day."

Over dinner, Carly told her parents about her visit with Jennifer and how she hoped to continue a friendship with her now that she was living at home again. As they finished, Emma remembered something. "Carly, I almost forgot to tell you. We saw Kolton Raywood today."

"Oh, I saw him too," Carly said. "He delivered feed to Jennifer's house today while I was there."

Raymond wiped his mouth and smiled with a twinkle in his eye. "He did, did he?"

Emma smiled to herself and took a drink. Carly felt as though she had just missed the punch line. "What?" she questioned. "What's so funny?"

Emma looked knowingly at her husband. Raymond picked up his plate and cup and announced, "It's girl talk, so I think I'll excuse myself to the garage." He placed his dish and glass in the sink and headed out the back door.

Carly turned to her mother. "So, what is it?"

"Kolton came over this afternoon with our feed delivery, and he asked about you. He'd heard that you were back in town. So I told him you were over at Jennifer's house."

"Oh, I get it," Carly figured. "You think he went over to Jennifer's house to see me. Well he had a delivery to make. He was probably going over there anyway."

Emma raised her eyebrows and smiled wide. "Maybe . . . unless he only delivered two bales of straw and two bags of chicken scratch."

Carly wasn't positive, but that sounded pretty accurate. She had been paying more attention to his appearance than the goods he was unloading. "How would you know what he delivered?" she questioned her mother.

"Because, it was our order! As soon as I told him that you were over at Jennifer's house, he told me he had forgotten Jennifer's order, and he had meant to deliver it today. So he said he would be over this evening to deliver our feed, and then off he went to Rich and Jennifer's house."

Carly thought quickly, amused that his maneuvers were an excuse to see her, and she smiled inwardly. Hoping for confirmation, she asked, "He's coming over tonight?"

"Possibly. I think it would be good if you could befriend Kolton."

"Befriend him? Mom, you make it sound like a service project. Is there something wrong with him?"

"No, it's just that he's had a troubled life. Well, that's not exactly right—I guess it would be better to say that he's had many trials in his life."

"Jennifer said something similar. What happened?"

Emma shook her head slightly. "It wouldn't be fair for me to tell you anything. You need to form your own opinions. I like Kolton.

His mother and I are good friends, and I like his father too. I believe we've known their family since we moved here."

"Mom, you can't leave me hanging like that."

Her mother purposely pressed her lips together, and without a word, she got up to clean the kitchen.

Carly wondered why her mother and Jennifer both seemed hesitant to discuss Kolton. Neither one would probably tell her anything, so she figured that she would have to discover his past herself, in due time. Flattered that he would make a point to see her, she decided to make herself presentable in case he did stop by that evening.

Chapter Three

Kolton stood at the end of his wooden slat porch looking out over the horizon. His hands rested in his denim pockets as he leaned against a post. The sky had partially cleared since that afternoon's rain showers, and the sun was setting behind the mountains, leaving an aftermath of brilliant red and orange hues. Desert sunsets were always beautiful, and the view was spectacular from his front porch. When his folks had offered to sell him their home as well as the feed store, he had been thrilled. It had always been his dream to stay in Bridger and own the family business. His other siblings had all left the small town, but he never shared their desires to leave.

He buttoned up his flannel shirt and ran a hand through his damp hair. Even the view of the sunset couldn't distract him from his thoughts about Carly. For the past couple of hours he had been debating over whether to go over to the Westons' house and deliver their feed. It wasn't pressing, but he wanted to see Carly Weston again. He had never told anyone, but Carly had been the girl he'd secretly admired through his youth.

Turning around, he headed for the old, weathered rocker that rested on the porch. Collapsing in it with a sigh, he thought back to his teenage years. He had been small for his age and an easy target for teasing. There hadn't been anyone particularly mean to him, but he was always thought of as a runt by the girls. It hadn't mattered much that he was a good athlete and an honor student. Most kids his age had matured physically during their teen years, but he hadn't hit his growth spurt until serving his mission.

After serving two years in Oregon, he had grown four inches and gained over thirty pounds. His jaw and shoulders had squared, and his parents had barely recognized him at the airport. But it was too late for all his old friends and the girls from his adolescence to see how he'd changed. A few kids still lived in town, but most of his friends had left to pursue careers outside of Bridger. Though he'd always desired to stay and help his parents run the feed store—this was his home, and he couldn't imagine leaving—he realized with disappointment that there weren't many single women left to share that home with.

He sighed and briefly pulled himself to the present. His truck was loaded and parked in the driveway. It would only take a few minutes to drive over to the Westons' house and drop off their delivery. With his parents looking after his son this evening, he had a couple hours to himself. He imagined what he would say to Carly, but he was taking a gamble that she would even be there. If she was, on the other hand, he worried that she might notice that he'd showered and put on cologne, when he was only supposed to be dropping off feed. He didn't want it to be too obvious that he was interested in her. He hadn't seen her for years, yet, at their brief encounter earlier at Jennifer's house, he'd somehow felt that she was the same sweet girl she'd always been.

He recalled that she always had guy friends in school, but never seemed to be serious with any of them. At their Church activities she had always overlooked his slight attempts to gain her attention. It wasn't that she was unfriendly. It was that she never gave him any indication that she could ever like him *more* than as a friend.

He always admired how caring she had been. Everyone liked Carly, and she seemed to be a good friend to everyone she knew. All during their senior year he wanted to ask her out. Right before their senior prom he finally worked up the courage and approached her in the hallway at her locker. He would never forget that day.

"Hey, Carly," his voice had quivered.

She'd had her head in her locker, looking for something. She peeked around the door and mumbled, "Hey, Kolton, how are you?" before returning to her search.

Kolton stood as tall as he could—which brought him eye level with her chin. "Good. How are you doing?"

"Alright. I lost my chemistry homework," she'd said as she rummaged through books.

He'd looked around nervously and cleared his throat. He'd decided that maybe it would be easier to ask her out without her looking at him. "Prom is coming up, and I was thinking that it would be fun to go."

"Yeah, it will be."

Kolton's heart had soared. "So, do you want to go with me?"

She pulled her head out of her locker, and a wave of realization washed over her face. "Oh, no, Kolton. I meant that I'm going already."

"Oh, I see." He tried to hide his disappointment. "That's good. I think it's going to be a lot of fun."

Carly gave him a weak smile and nodded in agreement. A moment passed and neither one knew what to say. "Well," Kolton stammered, "I have to get going. I'm going to be late for class."

Carly answered, a little too energetically, "Oh, me too. I'll see ya around."

Kolton had walked straight outside to the school parking lot. He'd gotten into his truck and headed home, skipping his last two classes. That entire afternoon he'd pouted and sulked and finally decided that there was more to life than Carly Weston. The prom came and went, and he didn't attend. He'd heard that Carly had gone with Jennifer and Rich without a date, and it surprised him how much that hurt his self-confidence and his respect for her. He had no choice but to assume that she would rather go dateless than with him.

As time passed, his heart had healed. He realized that she hadn't been mean to him at all. She just hadn't wanted to date him, and she had tried not to hurt his feelings by finding another way to say it. He chuckled at the memory. He had been small and shy, while she had been tall, pretty, and popular. No wonder she hadn't been interested.

After his mission he forgot about Carly, especially after he'd met Stacey. But that was another story—a story he didn't want to think about now. His past with Stacey was going to be an issue in his life as long as he lived in Bridger. Her memory haunted him, but he wasn't going to allow it to stop him tonight. This was the first time in eight years that he had felt an attraction to someone else.

The sun slid farther down the horizon until it was dark. He took a deep breath and decided that his fear of loneliness would overcome his pride—at least for tonight. He checked the lock on the front door, pulled on his Stetson hat, and jumped into his truck.

* * *

Carly's parents had left to visit Chad and Leann as the sun set. They'd invited Carly, but she'd claimed to be too tired. She honestly was tired, but she also wanted to be home in case Kolton stopped by. Since talking to her mother, she kept remembering small things about Kolton from her past. The many times that Kolton had shown her deference were suddenly coming to mind. Even the littlest things made her wonder if she'd missed something. For instance, there'd been that time at a combined youth basketball game at the church. Kolton was one of the team captains, and he had picked Carly first to be on his team. At the time she hadn't thought anything of it, but now she wondered if he'd been trying to get her attention.

Well, he had her attention now, she realized. Tonight, she couldn't stop thinking of his piercing blue eyes. In her mind she compared Adam to Kolton. It was like comparing Armani to Levi Strauss, she thought with a smile. They were certainly different, but Kolton had surprisingly sparked her interest.

After a shower and a change of clothes, she glanced at her watch and noticed it was almost eight. Kolton still hadn't arrived. Perhaps it was getting too late or her mother had misunderstood him. She sighed heavily and began looking for the television remote control. Then the phone rang and she rushed into the kitchen to pick it up. "Hello?"

"Hey, Carly. This is Jennifer. What are you doing tonight?"

"Oh, nothing." She wasn't going to confess that she was waiting for Kolton to stop by.

"I told Rich about our visit today, and he wanted to see you if you're up to another visit this evening. We're getting the boys ready for bed, but we'll keep them up for a while if you want to come over and meet them."

"Well," Carly said, "I'm pretty tired. I'd like to see Rich soon, and I can't wait to see your boys, but I was thinking I would just stay around here tonight and watch some TV."

Jennifer persevered. "Come on. We're more entertaining than TV And we have ice cream, soda—"

Carly cut her off with a laugh. "Okay, I don't need to be bribed." She glanced at the kitchen clock. "I'll think about it, but don't count on me."

"Okay. I don't want to force you. We'll have plenty of opportunities now that you live here."

"Thanks, Jennifer. I'll definitely see you at church tomorrow if I don't call back tonight."

"Okay, good night."

"Good night." Carly placed the cordless phone on the kitchen table and looked one last time at the clock. A knock at the door startled her, and she stiffened. *Is that him?* She moved quickly to the living room and saw headlights shining through the front window drapes. Expectantly, she opened the front door.

Kolton stood on the front porch with his thumbs tucked into his front pockets. Nervous, he worked to keep his voice from cracking. "Hello, Carly. How are you?"

She decided she liked his deep voice, then instantly felt silly as her heart sped up at the sound of it. "Good," she replied as she hugged the door. "How are you, Kolton?"

He thought the years had added a polished maturity to her features, and suddenly it was as if they were too different again—almost like in high school. His heart rate increased, and he moistened his dry lips. *Why does she affect me this way?* he thought. *Get a grip.* "I'm good. Looks like you finally figured out who I am." He paused and cocked his head to the side, giving her a sly grin.

"I'm so sorry I didn't recognize you earlier today."

"It's okay. It's been a long time. I guess we've both changed."

Carly smiled, searching for the right compliment. "I do remember your eyes. They're just like your mother's. It just didn't dawn on me who you were until Jennifer told me."

"Everyone tells me I look like my mom."

"Me too," Carly said. This was followed by an awkward pause, the small talk having suddenly run out.

"Well, I have a delivery for your folks," Kolton said to break the silence. "I set it back near the chicken house out of the rain."

Carly offered her thanks, and another silent moment passed. Finally Kolton laughed and confessed, "I also had another reason to stop by."

Distracted by his nearness, she hadn't heard what he'd said. She couldn't seem to take her eyes off of him. She could smell his woodsy cologne, and it stirred her senses. It was a scent that adequately captured his personal country charm. His hair curled out from under his Stetson. It was slightly damp and shone in the light from his truck headlights. His blue, sparkling eyes caught her attention again, and she was fixated suddenly on a small scar above his eye, one she didn't remember from their youth.

She suddenly noticed he was waiting for her to respond. "I'm sorry, what did you say?" *Physical attraction to someone does not mean you need to lose your head,* she silently chastised herself.

He took off his hat and apologized. "Well, I told your mom that I would drop off her feed delivery today. But to tell the truth, I was really hoping to run into you. I heard that you were living back here in Bridger."

Carly nodded and averted her eyes. *Stop staring at him,* she told herself. He had changed so much that it was hard to believe he had once been the boy she remembered. "Yes, I am living here. Like I told you before, I have a job at our old elementary school."

"That's great. I think you'll like working there."

She couldn't think of anything to say. She recognized that the growing attraction she was feeling had taken over her senses, and it worried her. She didn't think she was ready to handle those feelings, knowing that they could be related to her breakup with Adam—just a loneliness and a desire to be with someone again. Her smile faded. "So, you have our delivery?"

"Yeah, I set it up under the side of the house in case it rains again," he repeated awkwardly.

"Thanks. I'll tell my parents," she offered with a polite smile, not knowing where she was headed in the conversation, and trying to buy herself time. Kolton couldn't discern whether she was being aloof or just shy. But he had come over for a reason, and he wasn't going to be a coward now. He looked her squarely in the eyes. "I know it's late, but I was wondering if you had any plans for tonight. I thought we could visit and catch up. Not a date or anything," he explained hastily. "Just old friends reminiscing."

She was so nervous her hands trembled. "Well, I—I kind of have plans—nothing important, but I—I do have . . . an invitation," she stuttered.

His jaw tightened. He put his hat back on and smiled politely. He knew when he was receiving a brush-off. He realized that it had been a mistake to come over, and his voice went flat. "It was good seeing you then, Carly. Take care of yourself." He would have to accept that things hadn't changed as much as he'd thought. She obviously still felt about him the way she had in high school.

Carly's heart was racing. She hoped he wasn't leaving, but she couldn't think of anything to say. Quickly she blurted, "Actually, Rich and Jennifer did invite me over, but I thought it was too late to go over."

His truck was still running in the driveway. All he had to do was say good night and go home, but something nagged at him to say his piece. He slanted his eyes at her, and he knew by the look on her face that she'd instantly felt his contempt. His ego was hurt though, and he couldn't resist leaving without making the cutting remark he was thinking. "I suppose if Rich and Jennifer worked as an excuse in high school, they will work as an excuse now. I'm a big boy, Carly. You don't need to make up things for my sake."

Before she could comprehend his words, he turned, headed for his truck, and climbed in. Without hesitation, she walked after him to the edge of the porch. "Kolton, wait. Don't go."

She stood motionless and confused as she watched his truck pull out of her parents' driveway. "What is he talking about?" she said aloud. She had been so excited to see him, but instead of spending time with him she had somehow driven him off. She didn't know what she had said to make him so upset, but her own temper was beginning to rise. He had no right to be so rude to her.

She quickly grabbed a sweater, jumped into her car, and drove over to Jennifer's house. Rich and Jennifer had just put the kids to bed when she arrived. Rich greeted her with a big bear hug that made her laugh. "It's so good to see you, Carly. Jen's in the kitchen. Come on back."

Rich had always been a bit husky as a kid, and he still had that same little-boy quality. He'd nearly crushed her in his exuberance. Although he didn't have striking features, his warm brown eyes expressed his good nature and made him attractive. Carly was happy that Jennifer had such a good-hearted husband. She felt instantly at ease with him.

"Jen tells me you've moved back to work at our old elementary school."

"Yeah, I think I'm going to like it. If it works out for me I'll probably stay in Bridger."

"Good. It's still a good place to live and raise a family." They talked for a minute or two while catching up with each other and reminiscing about the past.

"It's really good to see you, Carly," Rich said again. "I hope you're home for good."

Carly was touched by the sincerity in his voice. "I think so. It feels good to be home. For now, I'm planning on staying."

"Well, I better go check on the kids and make sure they're sleeping." He turned to his wife. "Jen, after I check the kids I'll be in the family room if you two get tired of talking and want to watch some TV."

"Okay, honey."

As Rich left the room, Jennifer motioned for Carly to come in and sit at the table for something to drink. "What would you like? Hot chocolate? Soda?"

"Oh, definitely hot chocolate. Thank you." Carly laid her sweater over the back of the kitchen chair and collapsed into it with a sigh. Jennifer served her a steaming mug of hot chocolate, and Carly stirred it rhythmically. The kitchen was warm and cozy. At first, neither one said a word, and from the other room they could faintly hear the television.

"So what happened in the twenty minutes since I called you?" Jennifer finally asked. She had poured herself a cup of hot chocolate and was sitting across the table from her friend.

"What do you mean?" Carly purposely tried to keep her voice free of emotion.

"You have a distant look in your eyes. What are you thinking?"

Carly sipped her drink and spoke softly. "Actually, I'm not very good company tonight."

"You're always good company. But what's on your mind?" Jennifer pressed.

Carly couldn't stop thinking of her conversation with Kolton. Her anger had subsided, but she was still confused over his hostility and accusation. She turned to Jennifer and blurted, "Kolton stopped by tonight right after I talked to you on the phone."

Jennifer's eyes widened. "Really?"

Nodding her head, Carly wrapped both hands around her drink and explained. "He brought over my parents' feed delivery. I took one look at him, and I got all tongue-tied. I acted like a teenager with a wild crush." Carly thought back to Kolton's rugged appearance and continued. "You should have seen the man, Jennifer. I never would have thought Kolton would have grown up to be so handsome."

Jennifer nodded her head in agreement. "He is handsome—and smart, too. He works hard to keep improving the feed store. His parents still help him occasionally, and his mom tells me that he's making a good profit. I doubt he'll ever be rich, but he makes a good living. Everyone in town buys their feed from Kolton, and his prices are always fair. I know it's old-fashioned to deliver feed these days, but he wants his regular customers to have that old-hometown service. Personally, I love the convenience, and since there are few working farms still in the valley, he makes most of his profit off of people like us that have small orders."

A brief silence ensued as Carly stared into her mug, deep in thought. After a few moments Carly noticed her friend was looking at her expectantly, so she explained, "He asked me if I had plans tonight, and I told him I had an invitation to go out." Carly lowered her voice almost to a whisper. "The truth is, he made me so nervous I couldn't think straight. But when I told him that you had invited me over tonight, he accused me of using you as an excuse."

"He asked you out on a date?" Jennifer asked incredulously.

"No, he just wanted to talk." Carly waved her hand. "You know, catch up on things."

"Would you rather be here than visiting with Kolton?"

Quick to answer, Carly replied, "No, not really. I would love to talk to him and see what his life has been like. It's just that I was so unprepared. I knew he might stop by with the delivery, but I didn't think he would ask to visit—at least not tonight." Carly remembered Kolton's anger and continued, "Anyway, I can't believe how rude he was. He didn't give me a chance to explain myself. I wasn't making an excuse to avoid him—it was the truth."

Jennifer said nothing in response, yet Carly could tell she was deep in thought. Her lips were tightly pressed together and her eyebrows furrowed. "What is it?" Carly questioned her friend.

"Perhaps this is all a misunderstanding. I'm sure that he didn't mean to offend you. You need to realize that because he's had a difficult life, maybe he's more defensive than most people. You shouldn't be so hard on him."

"Jennifer, I can't believe you're defending him."

She shook her head and insisted, "No, it's not that. I'd rather not gossip about Kolton's past, but if you knew some of the things that I know, I think you would be more understanding toward his behavior."

"Regardless, I still can't believe I said anything that would make him so angry."

"Well, from experience, the best way to find out is to ask him outright. You're just wasting time stewing over it."

"I know, but I somehow feel guilty for upsetting him, even though I don't feel like I owe him an apology. I didn't do anything wrong."

Jennifer smiled and consoled Carly. "I'm sure it will be easy to fix. Go talk to him at church tomorrow, and I'm sure it'll all work out."

Carly suddenly remembered. "That's right. He is in our ward."

Jennifer nodded, "The ward boundaries are the same as when we were kids. I think he's teaching the ten-year-old kids in Primary."

"Really?" Carly had a hard time imagining Kolton being good with kids. Recalling the displeasure and impatience she had recently witnessed in his blazing blue eyes, she couldn't imagine him being patient with anyone. She sighed heavily and wondered why she even cared what he thought. A brief thought of Adam rushed to mind, but she quickly dismissed it. Having a man in her life wasn't a priority right now. She had come home to be with her family and to start a new job.

She turned to Jennifer and changed the subject. "So, do you have any ice cream?"

Jennifer laughed. As girls they had always shared their troubles over ice cream. "Not only do I have ice cream, but I also have plenty of chocolate syrup hidden away."

As they ate, the girls discussed Carly's past with Adam, and Jennifer was a sympathetic ear. After two hours of girl talk, Carly went home. Her parents' car was parked in the driveway, and the front porch light was on. She entered the house quietly to avoid disturbing anyone and went to her room. She pulled her favorite dress from the closet, ironed it, and hung it on the closet door. After changing into her pajamas and washing up, she knelt down at her bed and said her prayers. Her mind was reeling with thoughts of Adam, Kolton, her new job, and living at home with her parents. Grateful for all her blessings despite her trials, she prayed for inspiration about her life and crawled into bed.

Before she drifted off to sleep, she decided to face Kolton the next day. She wasn't going to allow another man to treat her so disrespectfully. If she had the strength to leave Adam, she was certainly strong enough to let Kolton Raywood know how she felt about his behavior.

Chapter Four

The clouds had lifted overnight, leaving behind a warm, slightly humid spring morning. Carly wore a dress with a pastel floral pattern, the hem to the ground. She had slipped on a pair of sandals and wound her hair up, allowing the ends to fall softly out around her hair clip. Normally she wore little makeup, but today she wanted to look good—she needed a little extra confidence to face Kolton—so she selected light shades of eye shadow and lipstick and applied them carefully.

Taking a last glance at the mirror, she realized she was running late. She had taken so much time getting ready for church, she didn't have time to eat breakfast. She quickly grabbed her handbag and called out to her parents. She heard them answer from the front porch, and went outside to join them.

Her parents were waiting for her with their scriptures and Church books in hand. "Well," her dad exclaimed, "don't you look nice. I guess I can't reprimand you for making us late when you look so pretty."

"Thanks, Dad. Good morning, Mom."

"Good morning, honey. Could you grab my purse from the hall? We're going to be late if we don't hurry."

When Carly got back outside, they all climbed into the car and backed out of the driveway. "Oh, I see the feed delivery is here," Emma noticed. "Did Kolton stop by last night, Carly?"

Carly saw her father glance at her in the rearview mirror, but she managed to keep her composure steady. "Yes, he did. He dropped it off not long after you left."

"How was he?" her father asked.

"Fine. After he dropped off your delivery I went to Jennifer's house. It was really good to see her and Rich again." Carly silently congratulated herself on successfully changing the subject, since her parents immediately started discussing how cute Rich and Jennifer's boys were. The conversation lasted until they reached the church. As they entered the chapel, Carly kept her eyes open for Kolton. She didn't know exactly what she was going to say to him, or how she was going to say it, but she was determined to let him know that his behavior had been uncalled for.

As she looked around, she realized that in some ways it seemed like time had stood still in Bridger. The building was the same as it had always been. The people were pretty much the same too—just older. There were a few faces that she didn't recognize, but she knew they could easily become new friends and acquaintances. Before the first meeting started, she took a moment to visit with many old friends. As she walked down the hall after sacrament meeting she heard a familiar voice.

"Carly, is that you, all grown up and pretty?"

She turned around to find Sister Gayle, her old Primary teacher. "Sister Gayle, it's so good to see you." Carly hugged her warmly and noted how frail the older woman had become. She'd thought Sister Gayle had seemed old when she was a child, but now, as she looked sharply at the older woman's etched face, pure white hair, and stooped posture, Carly estimated that she must be over eighty years old.

"Carly, how are you?" The older woman's voice was slow and deliberate, and Carly noticed that her pale blue eyes were moist with emotion.

Carly's own eyes grew misty from seeing the older woman. Sister Gayle had always been a special person in her life, and she had always felt that the feelings were mutual. "I'm great. I'm living with Mom and Dad for a while, and I'm beginning work tomorrow at the elementary school. How are you?"

"Carly, I'm just fine. I still find time to do my genealogy. I don't teach in Primary anymore, but I still love to come to church and see all the children."

After talking for a few minutes in the hall they parted to go to class. Carly felt a warm, cozy feeling—it felt good to be home among all the people she had once loved. As she made her way to Sunday School, she passed Kolton in the hall. He was wearing a dark suit with a crisp white shirt and a forest green tie. His hair was combed back, and she noticed that he had recently shaved. Regardless of what he wore or how his hair was combed, Carly realized that he had a rough, masculine appeal that she admired. For an instant her anger dissolved and she felt her heart flip, and—involuntarily—she smiled warmly. Their eyes locked for a moment, but he didn't return the smile. He only nodded, turned, and continued walking away down the hall.

Carly's face reddened. Her anger resurfaced, and she felt infuriated that he would dismiss her with a casual nod after being so rude the previous night. It suddenly dawned on her that his opinion of her meant something. It also bothered her that she was allowing her emotions to surface so easily over Kolton.

She sat through Sunday School with Jennifer and Rich, trying to pay attention, but growing more and more annoyed with Kolton. When the meeting ended, another voice from immediately behind her asked, "Carly, is that you?"

Carly looked over her shoulder and recognized Sarah Raywood, Kolton's mother, and her husband, Mark. "Yes. How are you?" Carly smiled, genuinely pleased to see them.

"Good," the couple answered in unison. Mark put out his hand to Carly and she stood to shake it. Sarah gave her a soft hug and said, "You look great. It's so good to hear that you've moved home."

"Yes, I'm glad to be back." In Carly's view, Kolton's parents didn't seem to have changed much at all through the years. Kolton had always looked a great deal like his mother, but she could see a resemblance between him and his father now that Kolton was older.

"And we're glad to have you back," Brother Raywood responded. He turned to his wife and said, "I'm going to head into priesthood meeting. I'll meet you in the foyer after church."

Sarah nodded in agreement and turned her attention back to Carly. "I remember what a pretty voice you had. Will you be joining the ward choir?"

"Oh, yes. I'm glad that you reminded me. I meant to ask someone when the choir practices."

"Every Thursday evening. There are just a few of us. I wish we could get more people to come. Kolton used to come, but since Leann comes now—," Sarah stopped abruptly, then went on as though dismissing her slight slip. "Well, Carly, it's so good to see you. I hope you'll be at practice on Thursday at seven."

"Thank you. I'll try to be there." As they parted, Carly wondered what Sister Raywood had meant about Carly's sister-in-law and Kolton. *Why would Kolton care if Leann was at choir practice?*

She found her mother in the hall and followed her into Relief Society where they joined Jennifer. Carly smiled warmly at the people around her, exchanged hugs with old friends, and tried paying attention to the lesson, but now the *only* thing on her mind was Kolton—now that another mystery about his past had been hinted at. His story was beginning to intrigue her. Her mother, Jennifer, and now Sarah Raywood had all implied something odd about Kolton. Carly felt that their behavior was definitely strange. They all knew something that they didn't want to repeat.

She imagined him in the Primary rooms, teaching children, oblivious to the anxiety he was causing her. It didn't matter to her what secrets his past held, she decided she was going to have her say one way or another. He could try to ignore her all he wanted, but she was not going to be ignored. He had treated her with contempt last night, and had falsely accused her of avoiding him. Her tension was beginning to grow, and she was not going to relax until she told him exactly how she felt.

She realized her heart and mind were not on the lesson in Relief Society, so she politely excused herself and quietly slipped out the back door into the hallway. Deciding she needed to sort out her thoughts, she went outside to walk around the church grounds. She remembered that whenever she'd had problems as a child, she'd walk around the chapel until she could work them out. She felt bad that she'd missed so many classes as a kid, and when she realized she was doing the same now, she laughed and promised herself to concentrate more on the lessons from that point on.

The yards and flower beds surrounding the church building were full of life and free of weeds. Large trees were scattered around the building, providing large areas of shade. The clouds from the previous day were gone and the sun shone brightly, warming her skin. She could feel her tension begin to subside. The church had the only sidewalks in all of Bridger, and she walked peacefully along them, enjoying the time alone.

As she rounded the back corner of the church, she noticed a young boy and a man kneeling in the grass. The boy was crying, and the man was talking harshly. Carly looked closely and recognized the back of Kolton's head. She was unable to hear the words being spoken, but she caught a slight glimpse of the boy and noticed the shame on his face. She walked briskly toward them and asked in a stern tone, "Is everything okay?"

Kolton turned his head and rose when he saw her. He dropped his hand from the young boy's shoulder as she walked up to them. Although his face showed surprise, his voice was gruff. "We're fine, Carly. Thank you."

The boy hung his head, and Carly could see his lower lip poking out. He looked as though he were about seven years old. Ignoring Kolton, she kneeled down and asked the boy again, in a softer tone, "Are you okay?"

The boy kept his head down and didn't answer. Carly reached out to touch his arm, but Kolton stepped in closer, pulling the boy up by the arm and ordering him back to class. The boy answered, "Yes, sir," and took off at a jog toward the church doors.

Kolton's angry blue eyes locked with Carly's as they quickly got to their feet. "This is really none of your business."

She held her ground. "Oh, really? You're being unkind to small boys, and it's not my business?"

"Unkind?" He shook his head in disbelief. His voice stayed gruff yet controlled. "You don't know what you are talking about."

"Kolton, I know you teach Primary, and that is no way to handle a child."

Kolton put his hands on his hips and, in a mocking tone, replied, "And you have so much experience with kids that you're an expert on raising children."

Carly folded her arms to her chest and stood straight, leaning slightly toward him. "I'm sure I know more than you." Her anger with him surfaced, and it was obvious in her voice. "You are so impatient and hardheaded that you jump to conclusions and make unreasonable judgments."

"Really?" His voice quieted, his interest piqued. "How so?"

"You wouldn't even listen to me last night. I was trying to explain myself, and you accused me of doing something dishonest—and then tried to tie it to something in high school that I can't even remember."

Kolton's eyes expressed his renewed fury. His voice was bitter. "Then obviously, what happened in high school was of no significance to you. So, tell me, Carly, the child expert, how would you have handled the boy?"

"That depends on what he's accused of."

Kolton folded his arms to his chest, took a step closer to Carly and spoke in a hushed tone. "He pinched a girl in his class—then he laughed at her when she cried."

Carly was surprised that such a sweet-looking child could have done such a thing, but she had been raised with an older brother, and she knew how young boys could act. She firmly replied, "I would have talked to the child in a reasonable manner."

"Good," Kolton agreed. "Sister Conway, his Primary teacher, did just that. But he was still unrepentant and disrespectful to her." A sly grin etched his face. "So now what would the answer be, Carly?"

Carly shook her head in disbelief. "The parents should have been informed. You shouldn't take matters into your own hands. I've taught Primary before, and I always went to get a parent and let them handle it."

"Good. I bet you were a great teacher," he stated flatly. Kolton turned away from her and began to walk back to the church. Abruptly, he stopped midway and turned back, commenting loudly, "By the way, Carly, that's exactly what Sister Conway did. She brought me my *son*, and I handled it."

She watched him reenter the building, thankful that he couldn't see the crimson color creeping up her neck and into her face. His *son*. She hadn't gotten a good look at the child's face, but she realized now that his hair had been dark like Kolton's. The child was his son, and she had blatantly accused him of inappropriately reprimanding someone else's child. She took a deep breath and swallowed hard. She couldn't believe that she had made such a mistake. *I should have minded my own business and walked away.* All of Carly's tension returned and tears of humiliation sprung to her eyes. She had no idea he had a child. No one even bothered to mention that to her.

In order to avoid another possible encounter with Kolton, she walked toward her parents' car in the parking lot and leaned against it. Glancing at her watch, she realized there were only minutes left before the church meetings would end. She sighed and looked heavenward. *Am I destined to be alone forever? Why am I always attracted to the wrong type of men?* She leaned against the car and watched children run from the entrance of the church, waving papers and carrying their scriptures.

Families began to exit, and Carly watched with a forlorn gaze. All she had ever wanted was a family of her own. People of all ages left the building with their families and loved ones. Carly couldn't help but notice that there weren't many single people her age in this ward. Across the parking lot she noticed Jennifer trying to walk evenly next to Rich, her pregnancy making it difficult for her, and their little boys running ahead. She would give anything to have a slice of Jennifer's life—a loving husband, darling children, and a home. She longed for an immediate family of her own.

Carly noticed her parents exit the building. She waved, and they approached her at the car. "How was your first Sunday back?" her dad asked. "I bet it was good to see everyone."

Forcing a smile and holding back the tears, she replied, "It was great. It's just like it's always been."

Her mother handed over Carly's purse and scriptures. "You left these in the Relief Society room."

"Thanks, Mom," Carly said.

As her father pulled out of the parking lot, he noted, "Chad and Leann weren't here today. I hope Leann is feeling better."

"Has she been sick? Chad didn't mention anything to me," Emma commented.

"When we were over last night he mentioned that she hadn't been feeling well. I think that's why they haven't come over to see Carly yet."

Carly realized that she had been so immersed in her own problems that she hadn't even noticed Chad and Leann's absence from church. She and Chad had been close as kids, but they had never lived near each other as adults. She had only really spent time with Chad's wife, Leann, a few times, but she had really liked her. Now that she was home again she hoped to grow closer to her brother and his wife.

Emma suggested, "I'll invite them over for dinner. I'll make chicken soup, and she'll be better in no time."

Carly rested her head back on the seat and closed her eyes. *Chicken soup.* She wondered if that would cure a broken heart and keep her from making a fool of herself in front of Kolton. As soon as they reached home, her mother offered to make Carly some lunch. Carly declined and retreated to her room instead. She wanted to be alone and rest, hoping to escape all of the thoughts swimming in her head. After changing her clothes, she crawled into bed and drifted off to sleep.

* * *

Kolton's heart had raced as he'd walked away from Carly to follow his son into the building. He thought that Carly's shocked expression should have brought him great pleasure, but it hadn't. He'd assumed that her family or Jennifer would have told her about his son, but it was obvious that she'd been completely unaware of Kyle's existence. He'd wondered if, perhaps, no one wanted to speak of it because of the scandal surrounding the child's birth. When he saw an opportunity to embarrass her, as she had him, he immaturely took it. He thought Carly would have known Kyle was his son by their similar characteristics—the raven-colored hair, dark complexion, and, most of all, the same deep blue eyes. But she had been too angry with him to notice.

A small part of him wished to be spiteful and enjoy Carly's humiliation, but he couldn't. He knew he'd handled the situation with both his son and Carly wrong. It was clear that Kyle was becoming mischievous without a father who could always be there or a loving motherly influence to guide him, but regardless, Kolton certainly didn't want Carly to witness and critique his less-than-effective manner of discipline. Thinking back on his own actions, he regretted raising his voice at Kyle. He should have just sat him in the hallway until church was over, then given him the old lecture on respecting girls.

As soon as he entered the church building, Kolton immediately found his son crying in the hallway leading to the Primary room.

He gave his son a big hug, "I'm sorry, Kyle. I shouldn't have been so harsh."

Kyle had squeezed his father hard. "It's okay, Dad," he said as he wiped a tear off his cheek with his sleeve.

Kolton then held his son at arm's length and looked at him with the love and concern he felt he should have used in the first place. He wondered how he was going to raise this young boy to be a good man when he wasn't always sure how to handle disciplining him. "No, Kyle, it's not okay. I got angry at you, and that's wrong."

"It's okay, Dad. I'm sorry."

Kyle so easily forgave and forgot. He warmed at his father's attention, and it burned Kolton's heart to realize that he'd been neglecting his fatherly duties. He knew that his son was suffering from the lack of maternal guidance that could balance his father's inadequacies. But that wasn't a problem that was easily remedied— he couldn't change fate.

"Listen, Kyle. Do you know why I was mad?"

Kyle nodded.

"Do you remember the talk we had about pinching and teasing girls?"

"But they tease me, and—"

Kolton raised his hand and told his son, "Wait. This isn't about what other people do. This is about the choices you make. You need to keep your hands to yourself."

Kyle nodded in agreement. "I'm sorry, Dad."

"You need to apologize to the young lady you pinched, and to your Primary teacher."

Kolton was expecting Kyle to resist, but the boy nodded again in agreement. "I'll walk you back to class, okay?"

"Okay."

Kolton remained outside the classroom door, waiting for his son. It was hard to be there for Kyle all the time, run a business, and keep a household together. His parents had always been helpful, but they were getting along in years, and he didn't want to burden them with his responsibilities.

Kyle was smiling as he came out of the classroom, and Kolton let out a sigh of relief. He felt confident that he had handled the situation right that time. He took Kyle by the hand, and they walked out to their truck. Perhaps he could spend some quality time with his son that afternoon.

As they crossed the parking lot, Kyle pointed and asked, "Daddy, who is that lady over there? She looks sad."

Kolton glanced over to see Carly. He couldn't help but feel terrible about his behavior. She had been right on both accounts. He had not only been too harsh with his son, but he had been too short-tempered with Carly the night before. An apology was in order, but he didn't have the courage to deal with it right then.

Kolton answered his son, "She's an old friend from school, Kyle."

Thinking suddenly about his lunch, Kyle forgot Carly and begged excitedly, "Hey, Dad, can we have pizza for lunch? Grandma brought over four frozen pizzas yesterday." They climbed into the truck and buckled their seat belts, but Kolton's attention stayed riveted on Carly. She seemed totally immersed in her own thoughts as she leaned on her parents' car and stared out into the parking lot.

"Dad, why aren't we going? I'm starving," Kyle pressed.

Kolton pushed the key into the ignition, but didn't turn on the engine. "Hold on a minute."

Kolton sat motionless as he watched Carly's expression change from confusion to sadness, and then to envy. He'd followed her gaze across the parking lot to where Rich, Jennifer, and their boys were heading toward their car. The look on Carly's face was unmistakable—pure longing. His heart softened. He knew exactly how she felt. There was nothing more important in the world to him than his son. He had always desired a complete family, and at that second, he knew Carly did too. Perhaps he had been too hard on her. As usual, his temper had overridden his sense of compassion and understanding. He resolved to try to be more compassionate in the future.

He thought Carly looked beautiful in the sunlight. Strands of her golden hair waved in the breeze, and her cheeks were flushed. Perhaps she was more vulnerable than he guessed. She waved to someone, and he looked over to see her parents wave back. Although she'd offended him by accusing him of being too harsh with Kyle, he realized it was just like her to stand up for a child, especially if she thought he had been harassing someone else's child. As he turned on the engine, he remembered that in their youth Carly had often volunteered in the church nursery when many of her friends preferred to join in other activities. It was funny how he hadn't thought much of it then—he had simply assumed that all girls liked small children. But a reaffirming memory of one specific time came to him as he sat staring at her.

When Kolton was a teenager, the Simmons family had lost their house to a fire. It was a rare tragedy in their small town, and everyone from their ward had volunteered to help. Financial donations, food, and clothing had piled up at the bishop's house within the first few days. Reflecting back, Kolton remembered how Carly had been absent from school for two days to tend their small children so the parents could take care of business and get their affairs in order. As Kolton prepared to leave the parking lot, he wondered if she still had the same caring heart, or if time had changed her. Judging by her recent actions, he had to assume she still cared a great deal for children.

He wrenched his gaze away from Carly and turned the truck around. He truly admired Carly, but he realized he'd probably have to settle for admiring her from a distance. He had offended her the night before, and at the church, to the point where she probably wouldn't have anything to do with him ever again. Sighing heavily, he shook his head and wondered why he had been so insensitive.

Then, with more than a little regret, he recalled how, during his marriage, his wife had always gently tried to help him understand how abrasive his actions were. She had pointed out where he was too judgmental with other people and how he would always assume the worst before listening to their point of view. Perhaps she was right, he thought. The realization of what his inability to control his anger had cost him was disheartening.

He watched Carly's parents join her and waited for their car to leave. After they were gone, he pulled out of the parking lot and tried to turn his attention fully to his son, his mind still jumping occasionally to thoughts of Carly.

* * *

Carly snuggled tight under the covers and yawned. She was so warm and relaxed that she didn't want to acknowledge the distant sounds of voices. Glancing at her alarm clock, she was surprised to see it was almost 5:00 P.M. She had napped much longer than she had intended. Knowing her mother's strict dinner schedule, she figured that dinner must be ready and her family was probably waiting for her to wake and join them. Sounds of laughter led her to believe that Chad and Leann had already arrived. Carly yawned again and pushed back the covers.

She sat on the edge of the bed and tried to clear her head. She tried to stop worrying about her personal life and think about her new job. Tomorrow would be her first day at work, but she noticed that she didn't seem to have that nervous feeling that usually accompanied the start of a new job. Her own school years had been spent at the same elementary, so she knew the school well. Mr. Stout was the current principal, and she had known his family for many years. He was older and, contrary to the image his name might suggest, he was quite tall and thin. He had a smile and a kind word for everyone, and Carly assumed that his demeanor would be similar at work with the children. She was excited about her new job and not in the least apprehensive.

But as hard as she tried to think about her new job, she couldn't deny that recent memories of Kolton occupied most of her waking thoughts. She closed her eyes and recalled the events from earlier that morning. She couldn't believe that she had really made such a fool of herself with Kolton. She didn't want to be at odds with him, but she wasn't sure how to remedy the situation. Just then a strong voice rang out. "Carly, dinner's ready."

Her father's voice and her own hunger pangs motivated her to get up and brush her hair. She smoothed her wrinkled clothes and ventured out to the living room. Her father stood by the unlit fireplace visiting with Chad and Leann.

"Hey, Chad." She greeted her brother with outstretched arms and was surprised how strong he was as he pulled her close. She also noticed his mustache and how grown-up he looked. Leann came over and offered a hug too. Carly's eyes moistened and she was instantly aware of how familiar this seemed, although it had been ages since she had spent time with Chad or Leann. She had missed her family more than she'd thought.

"You both look great," Carly complimented them.

Leann had been in school with Carly and Chad, but she had been a few years younger, so Carly had never been well acquainted with her.

"You look great too, Carly," Leann responded as she took a step back to look at Carly. "I love your hair."

Carly ran a hand through it and smiled. "Thanks. I had it lightened a few days ago."

"The golden hues really look natural," Leann added, studying her sister-in-law's new style.

Chad said, "It's good to have you home, Carly, and—"

Their father rested a hand on both of their shoulders and gently nudged them toward the kitchen, interrupting whatever discussion Chad had been about to launch into. "Let's eat before it gets cold," he suggested.

Seeing Chad made Carly realize that she had been negligent in maintaining her relationship with her brother. She wanted a close adult relationship with him. As children they had fought and teased one another in the usual manner that siblings did, and they'd never really grown close as adults. She decided to make more of an effort now that she was back home.

"Mom, do you need some help?" Carly offered as she entered the kitchen.

"Sure. Get me the salad dressing, and Leann, could you please grab the salt and pepper shakers off the stove?"

Before Leann could respond, Chad jumped at the opportunity to help and quickly reached for the shakers, nearly knocking his mother over in the process. "Chad, there's no hurry," Emma commented. "It's not a race." All eyes looked at him, and he blushed.

"Sorry, Mom. I didn't want Leann to have to bother. She hasn't been feeling well and all." His voice trailed off, and Leann blushed along with her husband.

Raymond winked at his daughter-in-law and teased, "Well, her color looks better all of a sudden. She's not so pale anymore."

Everyone sat down to a curiosity-filled silence as Leann continued to blush to a deeper shade of red. It was obvious to Carly that Chad and Leann were being peculiar. "So, how have you been feeling, Leann?" Carly asked. Everyone looked at Leann as she turned to her husband—looking for support.

Chad reached for his wife's hand. "Actually, we can't keep it a secret any longer." He admitted. "Leann is expecting."

Happy voices suddenly filled the room as everyone began talking at once, expressing their happiness and congratulations. Emma cried, and Raymond smiled proudly, both excited to have a grandchild. Carly could also sense the genuine love between Chad and Leann and their excitement over this new experience they would have together, and a small part of her couldn't help but feel jealous. But, she decided, she was excited to have a niece or nephew to spoil. For an instant she wondered if Adam had ever looked at her the way Chad was looking at Leann right now. She doubted it—she couldn't remember a time that she had ever seen his eyes filled with the level of love Chad had for Leann. It was obvious that Chad cherished Leann with all his heart.

After all the congratulations had begun to die down, Carly raised her water glass and proposed a toast. "I wish you both the best with your new bundle of joy, and I hope that it's a boy just like his father. Paybacks would make me a happy aunt!"

Emma and Raymond both laughed and raised their glasses in unison, and Emma chimed in, "I will agree with that."

"As long as the baby is healthy, I don't care about anything else," Chad commented.

"I agree. But I would love to have a son with his dad's gray eyes," admitted Leann.

"Well, I'd like to see a little girl with your red hair and green eyes," Chad countered. "But like I said, it doesn't matter to me as long as it's got all its fingers and toes."

Dinner went by pleasantly, the hour filled mostly with talk about the new baby. They were finishing the last of their meal when Carly turned to Leann and asked, "Have you been sick much?"

Leann wiped her mouth with her napkin and shook her head. "No, surprisingly I haven't been. I'm only a few weeks along—seven at the most, but I haven't been sick. I've been really tired though."

"That's good. Some women stay sick for the entire pregnancy," added Emma. "I was just a little sick in the beginning of both of my pregnancies."

Leann set her napkin on the table. "My cousin Stacey was really sick with Kyle. She complained nearly every day about not feeling good, right up until she had him."

Carly took the last bite of her chicken soup and laid the spoon in the empty bowl. "Stacey? I don't remember your cousin. Did she go to school here?" Carly noticed her parents exchange a concerned look, but she focused on Leann's response.

"No, she moved here after she graduated from high school. She was at our house so much she practically lived with us before she got married, and we became very close. She had a son, Kyle, and then she passed away. Her parents moved away right after her death. Her father has since died, but my aunt is still alive." Leann paused, remembering, then continued briskly, "Our family doesn't get along well with her husband, so we don't see much of Kyle."

"How tragic," Carly sympathized. "So the husband and son still live here in Bridger?"

Leann's jaw tightened and her voice turned icy. "Kolton Raywood was her husband, and I can't stand the sight of him. If you ask me, he's to blame for her death."

Carly wasn't aware that her mouth was hanging open until her mother nudged her under the table. Carly began, "So Kolton—" but her mother cut her off.

"Carly, would you please help me clean off the table? Perhaps Chad and Leann would like to get ready for the fireside tonight. I heard the speaker is really good."

Raymond hastily agreed, "Yes, he is." He motioned for Chad and Leann to follow him into the living room. "Let's grab our jackets—it's a bit chilly out."

Chad took his wife by the hand and followed his father out of the kitchen. Carly sat quietly, patiently waiting for everyone to exit the room. As soon as they were alone, she pressed her mother for information. "What is she talking about? Kolton killed his wife?"

Emma sat down and looked into her daughter's eyes. "Kolton Raywood is a sensitive subject with Leann's family. There were a lot of rumors and some bad gossip spread about Kolton and Stacey after she died. I don't think it would be right for me to repeat any of it."

"But Mom, if everyone already knows, then it's okay for you to tell me."

"No it's not," Emma insisted. "Keep your voice down. I don't want to discuss this around Leann. Besides, all I've ever heard was rumor. It all happened when we were back in Maine with your grandma. I have never talked to Kolton about it, and I don't intend to. I have always cared about him and his family. Almost eight years have passed, and I think it's a subject that shouldn't be discussed. His personal life is none of my business."

"But Mom," Carly pleaded, "I want to know." She paused and leaned toward her mother, "I need to know, Mom."

After a moment's hesitation Emma firmly answered, "I've seen the way Kolton's face lights up when your name is mentioned, and I've seen that same smile form on your face when you hear his name. I also know the damage that can come from gossip. If you truly want to know what happened, then you need to go to the source."

Carly leaned back in her chair, disgruntled. "After today I doubt Kolton will ever talk to me again. If I ask him about his dead wife, he'd probably be done with me forever. I think I've offended him enough for one day."

"Really? What happened?" her mother asked with concern.

She listened intently as Carly quickly related her recent experiences with Kolton. When Carly was finished, Emma held her daughter's hand tightly and said, "That certainly explains your mood after church today. Don't judge Kolton, Carly. Be open-minded and forgiving. I think that you're upset about how things are going because you're sensitive right now."

"Maybe you're right." Carly reflected on her feelings. "I think I'm still not completely over Adam."

"That's not exactly what I meant. I think there is a chemistry between you and Kolton. Why else would you be so sensitive?"

Carly acknowledged her mother's perceptiveness with a sheepish smile, which soon faded. "Then why won't you tell me what Kolton's been accused of, so I can decide what to do about pursuing him?" she persisted.

In a hushed yet serious tone, Emma answered, "I've heard Leann's family talk about this scandal, and—between you and me—I don't think that Kolton is responsible for what they've accused him of. But you must understand," her voice grew more firm, "that I cannot get involved in this. I love Leann, and I love Kolton and his family. I will not jeopardize my relationship with the people I care about over gossip that is none of my business."

"I understand, Mom." If there was one thing Carly was sure of, she knew her mother held tightly to her own convictions. If she said she wouldn't speak of it, she would honor her word.

Carly's father yelled from the adjoining room, "Let's go, honey, or we'll be late."

"Leave the mess, Carly," her mother said as she glanced at the messy kitchen. "We'll clean up when we get home."

Carly obeyed her mother and quickly ran to her room to change back into her dress and brush her hair. Chad and Leann decided to take their own car and Carly rode with her parents. They arrived at the church just in time for the fireside to begin.

There was a large attendance for the fireside and the pews were filled. Since they were some of the last to arrive, they had to sit near the back of the chapel. As Carly listened to the spiritual messages about the importance of home teaching and visiting teaching, she kept an eye on the congregation. She didn't see Rich and Jennifer, but that didn't surprise her. They were probably spending time with their children at home. She spotted Kolton sitting only a few pews directly in front of her family, and she was positive that he hadn't spotted her yet. She noticed that his parents weren't in attendance, so she figured that his son was probably with them.

As she thought about Jennifer's earlier comment that Kolton's life had been difficult, and how angry Leann had become at the mere mention of his name, she realized how curious she had become about the mystery surrounding him. But at the same time, she was more interested in him than in his infamous past. She was curious about him as a person. He had changed so much since their childhood and she wondered if he still had the good heart that she remembered.

Heeding her mother's advice, she decided not to judge Kolton on what others said or her first impressions of him. She wanted to believe

that the harsh words she and Kolton had shared were a misunderstanding. Perhaps she would be able to talk to him tonight and clear
the air.

As the meeting came to an end, their bishop announced that
there would be refreshments in the cultural hall and all were invited
to stay. Chad and Leann decided to leave, and said good-bye to Carly
and her parents as they left the chapel.

As Carly entered the cultural hall she scanned the room for
Kolton. He was standing in a corner talking to a few men. They were
laughing and seemed to be having a good time. Her parents soon
went their separate ways to visit with friends and left Carly standing
alone.

She wanted to talk to Kolton and apologize for her rude behavior
earlier that morning. If she apologized first, maybe it would open the
door for him to explain his behavior toward her. She definitely
intended to discuss his memory of her using Jennifer and Rich as an
excuse for something, and although she was dying to know more
about Leann's accusations, she decided that she wouldn't broach that
subject with him just yet. She watched him from a distance, waiting
for him to move away from the group of men he was standing with.
However, before she had a chance to approach Kolton, a stranger
walked up to her. "Excuse me," he said.

Carly smiled. "Yes?" She looked more closely, but he didn't look
familiar.

The man extended his hand, "I'm Brother Cowell. How are you?"

"Fine, thank you. I'm Carly Weston. Please, call me Carly." Carly
noticed that his handshake was firm.

"Very well, I will. Please call me Stan, then." He leaned toward
Carly and asked, "Are you new here?"

"No, I'm actually from this area. I've just recently moved back,"
she explained.

He nodded, then said, "I'm new to the area. Did you buy a home
here?"

"No, I'm living in my parents' home."

"Are you renting from them?"

His questions were beginning to make Carly uncomfortable. "No,
I'm just living with them for a while."

He stepped slightly closer, causing her to stiffen, "Do you have any children, Carly?"

She shook her head no, and casually glanced down at his left hand. She noticed that he wasn't wearing a wedding band.

Unable to discern the man's intentions, she glanced around the room hoping to make eye contact with her parents. They were both engaged in conversations, but she did meet Kolton's gaze. He was staring at her from across the room with a mischievous grin.

Carly wondered about Kolton's expression, but turned back to the man. Before she could speak he asked, "So, what kind of work are you in?"

"Actually, I'm starting a new job tomorrow. I'll be working at the elementary school."

"How are the benefits there?"

Hesitant to answer any more personal questions, she hedged, "Well, actually, I really don't know all the details. I suppose—"

Before she could finish her sentence, Kolton walked up with a wide smile and a sparkle in his eyes. He extended his hand and said, "How are you doing, Stan?"

Carly gave Kolton a relieved smile, appreciating the interruption, but he didn't acknowledge her.

"Great, Kolton. I was just chatting with Carly Weston here."

"Oh," Kolton said as if surprised to hear that information. "It's nice to meet you, Sister Weston."

Carly's smile faded. Kolton was obviously well aware of how uncomfortable she was with Stan, and found pleasure in the awkwardness of her situation.

"Well, you two are probably deep in conversation, and I wouldn't want to interrupt. It was nice seeing you both, but I should get going."

"No," Carly said quickly. "You don't need to run off."

Kolton gave her a sly smile and said, "Oh, I need to get home. You know, I have a *son* at home."

Carly's temper flared, but she maintained her composure. His tone was teasing, but she thought he might be intentionally trying to provoke her.

She smiled wryly. "Yes, I know."

Kolton slapped Stan on the back and said, "It's always nice to come to these ward gatherings and meet new people."

Stan nodded in agreement as Kolton continued, "Sometimes the best opportunities in life are through people we interact with at church. You never know when you'll make a new friend."

Carly resisted the urge to roll her eyes. She wondered if Kolton was implying that she and Stan could be a couple.

Kolton seemed to be only encouraged by her expression of disbelief. "Yes, I believe that fate is always around the corner. You need to take advantage of life's opportunities." Then he wished them both a good evening and walked away.

Stan seemed to stand a little taller and smile a little broader. He turned to Carly and said, "Well, like I was saying . . ." But Carly had stopped listening. She was fuming.

How dare Kolton try to set me up with a complete stranger! Her angry thoughts continued until she realized she wasn't even listening to Stan's ramblings as he handed her a business card.

She took the card without reading it and Stan offered, "So, like I said, give me a call anytime."

"*Call you?*" she asked incredulously.

"Sure, call anytime you need something—especially if your situation changes."

"My situation?" Carly was becoming more confused.

Patiently, he explained, "Yes. We offer great renter's insurance. Surely your parents have insurance on their home. But if you rent a place after you move out, it's a great insurance policy to protect your belongings."

Carly quickly read over the business card. It finally dawned on her that he wasn't hitting on her, but that he was an insurance salesman. "Well." She smiled, relieved to know that she had misunderstood the man's intentions. "I will definitely keep you in mind."

"And if you marry, it's a really good idea to buy life insurance. We have great policies for children, too. You know, the earlier you buy it, the cheaper it is in the long run."

"Well, thank you. I appreciate it." She slipped the card in her purse. Changing the subject, she asked, "How well do you know Kolton?"

"We met a few months ago, and he just purchased a couple of policies from me. He's really been a lot of help."

"How so?"

"My business is just getting started, and he's been helping me meet new people. Actually, he'd seen you walk in and encouraged me to come over and introduce myself. He's really a great guy."

Carly politely nodded in agreement, but was uncertain whether she truly agreed. Stan shook her hand again, and she promised to call if she had any insurance questions. They parted and she crossed the room to find her parents. She found her mom and stood by her as her mother talked with a small group of friends.

Many people had already left when Carly's dad approached them. "Are we ready to go?"

Emma said good-bye to her friends, and the three of them made their way out into the hall. As they were leaving, Carly looked back over her shoulder to see Kolton helping other men in the ward take down the refreshment tables. He looked up, gave her a wink, and smiled complacently. Her anger began to subside. She realized that he was probably justified in teasing her to get even for her rude behavior earlier in the day. If nothing else, at least she knew he still had the same sense of humor that she remembered. She wanted to smile back at him, but she decided against letting him off the hook just yet.

When they arrived home, she and her mother quickly cleaned the kitchen, and then her parents went to bed. Not feeling sleepy, Carly stepped out the back door and sat on the porch swing. As a child, she used to sit in the same swing daydreaming or thinking through her problems. She folded her arms and rocked gently as she admired the sunset. Summer was approaching, but the nights were still cool. A soft breeze played with her hair, and goose bumps formed on her bare arms.

None of these pleasant distractions could compete with her thoughts of Kolton, however. She pictured his face—his laugh lines and piercing eyes. The sun had tanned his skin, and she thought it gave him character—a rough, cowboy quality that she liked. Her attraction to him was natural and hard to ignore. Then she remembered the hurt and impatience in his face when she had apparently offended him at her house and at church. His actions proved him to have a short temper, and she wondered about Leann's accusations against him. But his manner had completely changed at the fireside. He apparently found himself to be quite funny, and looked well pleased with himself when Carly left. She had to admit that she too found some humor in his actions, even though she had been Kolton's target.

Carly wondered if it was possible to be attracted to a man who was somehow accountable for his wife's death. After all, she had been attracted to Adam, and he obviously hadn't been right for her. She didn't want a husband just for the sake of being married—she wanted a potential soul mate to share every aspect of her life with. In her heart she needed someone to connect with spiritually, physically, and mentally. She wondered why it was so difficult for her to find the right man to do that with.

Her thoughts strayed back to her past with Adam. Although she hadn't been making progress in teaching Adam the gospel, she had, perhaps unwisely, continued to date him, hopeful that her example would somehow influence him. She wondered how it was she could have kept dating the wrong man. Within six months of dating they had become inseparable, and after eight months of dating, Adam had confessed his love to Carly. It was on a Saturday evening. They had gone out to dinner and returned to Adam's apartment afterward for dessert and were cuddling on the couch, eating cheesecake and talking.

"Someday, I am going to get my mom's recipe for cheesecake," Carly had said between bites.

"Oh, yeah? Is it better than this?" Adam teased.

Carly grinned. "Well, it's different."

Adam had clapped his hands over his heart. "I'm hurt. I spent hours slaving over a hot stove, grating cheese, and slicing strawberries."

"Really? Was Miss Sara Lee standing alongside you?"

Adam laughed, "Did I leave the box on the counter?"

Carly nodded. She pointed her fork at him and said, "My mom makes the best cheesecake from scratch. It's a family tradition to have cheesecake every year on my birthday."

Adam had set his empty plate on the coffee table, leaned back against the cushions, and pulled Carly in next to him. "Well, perhaps you can keep the tradition alive by making cheesecake for our kids someday."

Carly swallowed hard. The room had become silent. "Our kids?" she whispered. Was this the proposal she had been waiting for?

Adam had pulled back a little so he could look her straight in the eyes. "I'm falling in love with you, Carly. I want to be more than just a couple." He'd paused briefly, then said, "I think you should move in with me."

Carly hadn't known what to say. She had allowed cuddling and kissing in their relationship, and Adam had always respected her values. She didn't think she had ever given him the impression that she would have a sexual relationship outside of marriage. She'd tried to think of a response to his proposal that wouldn't hurt his feelings.

When one didn't come to her immediately, Adam continued. "I can tell by the look on your face that you're surprised, Carly. And I know how you feel about the whole sex issue, but I want to be with you. We're together all the time at work, afterward, weekends—it makes sense. I couldn't bear the thought of you with someone else. I want to make you mine." He ran his hands through her hair and pulled her face close to his.

She'd looked into his eyes, and her heart had melted. *Why do you have to be so handsome and irresistible?* she thought painfully. "Adam, I'm falling in love with you, too. But this is a big decision, and—"

Adam had cut her off with a deep, passionate kiss that made her slightly uncomfortable. She knew that this was an important choice that could determine her entire future. She gently pushed Adam away from her. "We need to talk, Adam."

He leaned into her neck and kissed her softly. Again, she gently pushed him away. "I'm sorry, Adam, this is just moving too fast for me." Her voice wavered as she tried to compose herself.

"Carly," he'd growled impatiently, "this is not fast. We've been seeing each other for months. You don't know what you do to me. We can't just go on dating forever and never get any further."

Suddenly Carly felt young and naive. "I know," she said, trying to sound convincing. She'd wanted their relationship to progress, but she had hoped that he would accept the gospel in his life. She knew that if they both shared the same religious views they would both desire a temple marriage. "It's just that I've always wanted a temple marriage. It means so much to me."

Adam had shaken his head in disbelief. "It's not the eighteenth century, Carly. You're a mature woman. People don't get married to have sex anymore."

"You don't understand." She'd spoken carefully. "When I go to the temple to be married, it will be forever. We will be married here on earth, and also hereafter. I want us to go someday."

Adam had stood and put both hands on his hips. Softly he said, "I love you, Carly, but I'll be honest with you. I don't have plans to join your church. I can respect your wishes, but I'm not ready for marriage. My career is still growing, and I'm not sure I'm ready for that step. Don't question my love for you—it's genuine. I just don't see things the same way you do."

Carly hadn't believed what was happening. She didn't want to lose Adam, but could she make him understand? "It's not an option for me, Adam. I really want to be married in the temple. If you would just take the time to talk to our missionaries or come to church with me you might understand why being married in the temple for time and eternity is so important to me." From his expression she could see that his heart was not responding to her words.

Carly had felt the tears swelling in her eyes. She'd known in her heart that the moment was a turning point, that if he didn't agree to investigate the gospel she would have to break off their relationship. She knew that she had to make the choice, but it had seemed so difficult to love someone and let him go.

Adam had rejoined her on the couch and pulled her into his arms, cradling her gently. "I'm sorry, baby. My offer still stands. I'll give you some time to think it over."

Carly had pressed herself into his chest and tried to blink away the tears. There was nothing to think over. She hadn't waited all these years for a temple marriage to throw away her dreams, even for someone like Adam. In silence, he'd driven her home. He'd walked her to the door of her apartment and kissed her softly. "I'll see you Monday morning."

Without a word, she'd nodded and gone into her apartment, locking the door behind her. She then went to her room and sobbed into her pillow. *Life is so unfair*, she'd thought. *Why haven't I met any active Mormon men who have the same effect on me that Adam does?* It had made her furious and frustrated to be so drawn to him once she knew that she couldn't be with him. But in her heart her choice was already made. She wouldn't sacrifice her beliefs to live with Adam.

As she'd sat on her bed, she'd remembered a conference talk that she had heard when she was younger, wherein the prophet of the Church had warned the youth about dating the right people. There had also been a special Young Women's leader that Carly had greatly admired. She once told Carly about her own experiences in dating men who wouldn't respect her beliefs. She had taught Carly that she should respect herself enough to be selective in her dating choices. These loving yet forgotten words of advice suddenly had direct application to her life. When dating Adam, Carly had felt that an adult relationship would be different, and that the advice from her younger years was somehow less applicable. But Carly was beginning to see the mistakes in her actions.

She'd slept restlessly that night and woken early, then skipped breakfast and called her mother. "I truly have feelings for him, Mom. But I just can't marry outside of the temple," she'd finished explaining.

"Carly, you are the only one who can make this choice. No one else can live with the consequences of your choices but you. And all of our choices have consequences—good and bad."

Her advice was exactly what Carly had expected, but it felt good to hear her mother's comforting words. "I know, Mom. I guess I just wanted to talk to someone."

"We are so proud of you, and your father and I both trust that you will make the right decisions for your life."

"Thanks Mom. It's just so hard to let go."

"I know, honey. But it sounds like you've made your decision." Her mother wished her well and told her to pray often for guidance.

Carly knew that agreeing to live with Adam would be solely her decision to make. If for no other reason than her own self-respect, Carly knew she couldn't possibly accept Adam's proposal. She went to church that morning, prayed about her dilemma, and felt confident that she was making the best choice. But she felt inclined to discuss the gospel with Adam again, hoping his heart would soften.

As soon as she arrived home from church, she called him. He'd picked up the phone on the first ring.

"Hello."

"Hi, Adam, it's Carly. I wanted to talk to you about something." She'd kept her voice hopeful and cheery.

"What's going on?"

"I went to church today, and I had a feeling that I should share something with you." She took a breath and summoned her courage to continue. "I want you to know why I can't move in with you."

"Carly, we've been over this—"

"I know, but I don't think you fully understand my point of view. I want to explain the gospel perspective."

Adam responded angrily. "I will not have some priest telling me to feel guilty or telling me I'm going to hell for having a physical relationship with the woman I love."

"No, Adam, it's not like that." Carly sighed heavily. "There is so much to understand. I just want to give you a better explanation—"

"Carly," he'd interrupted, "it doesn't matter. You could be any religion, and it just wouldn't matter."

She felt a sudden flash of anger. *Why is he so unwilling to listen?* In all the time that they had dated, he had never had such a cold attitude toward her. She spoke sharply, "Fine, Adam. I need to go. I guess we'll talk later."

"Perhaps we need to cool off. I'll call you in a few days."

"Fine," she'd agreed, and hung up the phone.

At work the next day the tension had been thick and they had little to say to one another. Unexpectedly, that same day, Matthew had another stroke. He'd passed away in his sleep soon afterward, and the office was left stunned. Carly was so full of emotion that she'd slipped out of the office without notice and gone home. She had been lying on her bed resting when the telephone rang.

"Hello?"

"Hey, Carly. It's Adam."

The sound of his voice had brought tears to her eyes. She wished that he was with her to hold and comfort her.

"How are you?" she asked.

"Good," he answered flatly. "I looked for you at work, and I couldn't find you. You didn't tell anyone that you were leaving. I wanted to make sure you're okay."

"I'm okay." Her voice trembled. "I finished my work early, and I felt like coming home." She propped herself up on her pillows and talked in low tones. "I can't believe that Matthew is gone."

"I know." Silence ensued, and Carly didn't know what else to say. She wanted to talk things over and share her concerns about Matthew's family and their own relationship, but he quickly ended their conversation.

"I just wanted to check on you, but I can't talk right now—I'm in the middle of something here at work."

"I understand," she said trying to cover up the disappointment in her voice.

"I'll call you tomorrow if I hear anything from Matthew's family. The office will be closed for the rest of the week, so you don't need to worry about coming in. Angie will come by daily to check for messages."

"Good. I really don't feel like going to work."

"Me neither. Take care, Carly." He hesitated a moment and then added, "I love you."

"I love you too. Good night."

The phone clicked, and the line was dead. Carly had set the phone back in its cradle and curled up in bed, hugging a pillow. She did love him. She wanted to be with him. *If only he could be with me now.* Closing her eyes, she imagined that he was with her, stroking her hair and whispering in her ear that he would always be there for her.

Thoughts of Matthew and his grieving family had also plagued her thoughts. The children ranged in age from ten to sixteen. She couldn't imagine the horrible hopelessness and sorrow they were experiencing. Carly made a mental note to call Jean soon. Then, thinking of the many disappointments in her own life, she quietly cried herself to sleep.

Carly and Adam had spoken little the rest of the week. They attended the funeral services together and tried not to act awkward during their short phone conversations, but their disagreement was too big an obstacle to overlook for long. After they returned to work, Carly suggested that they go to lunch together. As they ate in a neighborhood café near Carly's apartment, she couldn't take the silence any longer. They had hardly said more than a few words to each other, and their meal was almost over. "Adam," she started, "I think we should talk."

He wiped his mouth with his napkin and laid it back in his lap, taking a sip of water. "About what?"

The tension and uncertainty had been taking an emotional toll on her patience. "About what?" she repeated curtly. "Us, Adam. About us."

"Relax, honey, we're fine. Don't worry so much," he'd assured her. "Keep your voice down."

Ignoring his request, she said, "No, Adam, we are not fine." Tears began to surface, and she tried to hold them back. She'd wanted to control her emotions so she could have a mature conversation. "I can't sleep, I can't eat, and I don't know how to fix this problem between us."

He looked her directly in the eyes. "I do," he stated firmly. "Move in with me and get over this silly self-righteousness."

"What?" she exclaimed. "I told you how I feel about that, and I thought you understood."

"Of course, Carly," he said nastily. "It's all about your feelings. I need to be the one to change." He shook his head in disgust. "I'm tired of this whole religious setback in our lives. The world is not going to come crashing down because we sleep together without a piece of paper to make it legal. Carly, up to this point I have respected you and your wishes about our relationship, but I just can't keep going like this."

Stunned, Carly didn't know how to respond. She had thought he was compassionate about her feelings because he valued her opinion. She had never suspected that he found her feelings so trivial.

Adam gave her a hard glare and warned, "I will not let you guilt me into marriage."

Carly's temper began to flare. "Are you accusing me of holding out on you for a marriage proposal?"

Adam's voice turned smug. "I bet if I had a ring right now, and I proposed marriage to you, you would accept."

"Try me," she goaded.

"See," he concluded, "that proves you want me to."

"I can't believe you." Carly was shocked. "I have never tried to manipulate you. How dare you suggest that I would—"

"Hold it," he interrupted. "You were the one who started all this nonsense. I refuse to be labeled the bad guy. I'm the one planning for our future. There are going to be some big changes at work, and if you just do as I ask you, we will have the biggest, most lavish wedding you could ever want."

"What are you talking about?"

Adam had leaned in over the table with a dissolute grin. "I have a feeling that I'll be a senior partner soon."

"How do you know that?"

"I called Williams yesterday to see if he would consider me as a partner, and he said he would get back to me."

"Matthew has been dead for ten days, and you're already out for his job?" Carly was furious.

"Don't make it sound ugly, Carly," Adam had said defensively. "Business goes on. With the money that I'll make we'll be able to afford a wedding and a honeymoon anywhere you want. It might take us a year to save for it, but I know we can do it. Especially with the rent money you'll save by moving in with me."

Carly was stunned. All she desired was to be loved and valued for who she was. The worldly offerings were of no concern to her. Incensed, she responded, "Money and lavish weddings mean nothing to me. Obviously you don't even know me, Adam." She tossed her napkin on the table and said, "I would rather have a honeymoon in a hay barn than be married to a selfish, ego-maniacal jerk like you!"

She grabbed her purse and rushed out of the restaurant. Her urge to cry had diminished as her temper had risen. *He is unbelievable!* she thought. She wondered how he could have possibly thought that she was trying to manipulate him. He was the one making self-serving plans with a total lack of compassion about Matthew's death, or her goals and values.

Carly realized that she had thrown a tantrum in public, and she laughed at herself for her childish behavior. Now that she was away from Adam, other profane names for him, more serious than "jerk," had popped into her head, but she dismissed them. He really wasn't worth it. Seeing this selfish side of Adam had been surprising, but now she knew that it was better for her to leave their relationship. She had sensed he could be selfish when he refused to even discuss her religious views, but now she knew for certain that he wasn't the type of person she wanted to be with. A part of her had felt sad, but another part of her felt free. Free to move on with her life without the temptation to make a bad decision.

Now, sitting in the porch swing a few weeks later, Carly wondered what her life would be like if she had stayed with Adam and tried to work out their differences. She couldn't deny that she was physically drawn to him, and she did admire his work ethic, despite his aggressiveness toward partnership in the company.

After the incident, she had prayed for direction from her Heavenly Father, and she'd felt at peace with her decision to leave Langdon and move home.

She wondered if she truly missed Adam, or if she just missed having a boyfriend. Her emotions were so conflicting, and thoughts of him had occupied her mind almost constantly. She didn't ever want to make the same mistake of getting involved with the wrong man again.

Continuing to rock in the swing, she realized that although she had prayed for happiness with Adam, her prayer wasn't answered in the manner she had hoped for. She had expected Adam's heart to soften, and for him to show an interest in her religion. But no matter what she said to Adam, he wasn't willing to listen. In fact, as she recalled their last conversation, she realized he had mocked her views and moral standards. Her feelings were reaffirmed that she had made the right choice to leave Adam, no matter how much it still hurt, and she wasn't going to make the same mistake twice. From now on she would put more thought into her prayers and actions.

It's not easy following through on tough decisions, she reflected. She remembered an argument with Jennifer as a child, after which they hadn't spoken for a week. Years had passed since that quarrel, and Carly couldn't remember why they had argued, but she remembered how she had felt going to Primary and seeing Jennifer talking to another girl and ignoring her. Jealous and sad, Carly had begun to cry, and Sister Gayle had pulled her into the hallway. When her teacher asked why she was sad, Carly was too embarrassed to admit her troubles. Sister Gayle simply told her, "You are never alone, child. Take your problems to your Heavenly Father, and He will help you."

"He can't make people be nice to me," Carly had sobbed.

"No, He can't. But Carly, He can help you. If you did something mean to someone, you need to ask their forgiveness. If they did something mean to you, you need to forgive them. Heavenly Father will help you be strong enough to do these things."

Tears had run down Carly's cheeks, but she'd nodded in acceptance. Sister Gayle put an arm around her shoulders and squeezed. "Carly, your Father in Heaven wants to help you. Think about what you want. Pray sincerely, and He will help you make your choices."

Carly realized that she had been too young at the time to fully comprehend Sister Gayle's wisdom. But by now Carly had learned the objective, and was not going to make any more tough decisions without guidance.

Her first week of work passed in a blur, and by Friday Carly was exhausted. She hadn't anticipated the demands of being an elementary school secretary. The school brought back a lot of childhood memories, but she had underestimated how time-consuming the work would be. Every day after work she had stayed late trying to acquaint herself with the computer programs and office equipment. Her co-workers and teachers had been helpful, but Carly was feeling overwhelmed.

Carly was looking forward to the weekend. After lunch she went to give a message to the school janitor and deliver some mail. Arriving back at the office, she told Laura, the other secretary, "I can't believe someone had the time to write all that in marker on the wall, and no one saw them do it."

Laura laughed knowingly. "Just you wait. That's nothing compared to the lunchroom incident last week. It took the janitor two hours to clean up that mess."

After talking for a few minutes about what an exhausting day it had been already, Carly sat at her desk and began to shuffle through some papers. Laura approached her and apologized. "I really have to get going. I'm sorry to leave early today and leave you here alone." She handed Carly a file, a lunch box, and a bandage. "This file is for Jimmy Marlin. His mother wants to pull him out of school and homeschool him. Make a copy of everything for her. She'll be in first thing Monday morning to pick it up. This lunch box was found in the hall, and the little girl in the chair needs a bandage on her arm." Carly sighed and took a mental note of her instructions.

"I really am sorry to leave you alone, but I think everything will be okay," Laura reassured her with a wink. "You're doing a great job. You'll get the hang of everything in no time."

Carly fought the urge to groan and forced a smile instead. "I know, Laura. It's just a bit overwhelming right now."

"It's only your first week. A couple more weeks, and you'll know as much as me. Just keep working and everything will be second nature to you," Laura encouraged.

Carly seriously doubted that. She glanced at the clock and noted, "There are only two hours left. I think I'll be fine."

"Oh, and I almost forgot. There is a boy in the principal's office. He was kicked out of class again. You'll have to figure out his punishment since Mr. Stout won't be in for a while." Laura lowered her voice and confided, "I seriously doubt that child is going to make it through the year without being expelled. Oh!" She glanced at her watch. "I have to go—I'm late."

The phone rang, and Carly grabbed it while waving good-bye to Laura. "Good afternoon. Bridger Elementary, Carly speaking."

The caller asked about bus schedules, and, luckily, Carly knew where to find the needed information. After she hung up the phone she bandaged the little girl, sent her back to class, set the lunch box in the lost-and-found box, and made a copy of the papers in the file. She realized now that this job was going to require more effort than she had anticipated. There were so many unexpected tasks to keep her busy that she felt as though she were neglecting her main job requirements.

Nonetheless, there were great aspects of her job as well. Her boss, the school principal, Mr. Stout, was wonderful. On her first day he had lunch and flowers brought in to welcome her. And Laura Cross, the other office secretary, had helped her with her duties and explained how the office was to be run. Laura knew everything there was to know about running the school office, and she was kind and patient. Carly felt instantly that Laura was going to be a great co-worker. They had chatted briefly about each other's lives and interests, and Carly appreciated Laura's spunky style and attitude toward life. Laura was in her early forties and had two boys in high school. Her dark hair was cropped short and she wore thin wire-framed glasses over her dark brown eyes. Both of her sons were

competing in a track meet in a nearby town later that afternoon—
the reason Laura had left early.

Carly didn't mind Laura's absence too much. She realized that she
was going to have to learn how to occasionally manage the office
without Laura's assistance. Both of Laura's boys played sports year
round, and she liked to follow them to all of their activities. Besides,
Carly expected everything to go smoothly since it was Friday and
everyone was more relaxed at the end of the school week.

When the office was finally quiet, Carly sat at her desk and took
care of some work. She had just finished enrolling a new student in
the computer system when she thought she heard someone enter the
room. She looked up, but saw no one. Resuming her typing, she still
felt as though she wasn't alone. Finally, she turned around and
looked behind her. She was startled to see two deep blue eyes staring
back at her.

"How did you get there?" she asked. Suddenly she remembered.
"Oh, you must have been in the principal's office. I got busy and
forgot you were in there." She turned her chair to face the young
man. It took her a few seconds to figure out why the child looked so
familiar. "You're Kyle Raywood, aren't you?"

The boy nodded in the affirmative. He stood facing her with his
hands in his pockets. Carly appraised him, noticing his ruffled hair,
worn T-shirt, and jeans. His shoes appeared to be relatively new and
both laces were untied. She remembered the comment Laura had
made about him, but he didn't look like a troublemaker to her. She
asked, "Do you know who I am, Kyle?"

Again, the boy nodded. "You're the lady my dad was staring at on
Sunday."

Carly smiled—it pleased her to know that Kolton was watching
her. "I think you and I are going to be good friends, Kyle." She
motioned for him to sit in Laura's chair opposite her own. He took a
seat and looked at her expectantly.

"So tell me, Kyle, why are you in the principal's office today?"

The boy's countenance changed, and he looked guiltily at the
floor and shrugged his shoulders.

"Come on, Kyle, there must be a reason your teacher sent you here."
She kept her voice soothing, in hopes that he would confide in her.

"Well, there's this boy in my class named Aaron, and he's always picking on me. He called me stick-boy because I'm littler than him. So I called him a fart head, and my teacher sent me here."

"Your teacher sent you to the principal's office just because you called him a name?" Carly asked skeptically. "You didn't do anything else?"

Kyle smiled and admitted, "Well, I did tell the class that he still wets the bed."

Carly frowned at him. "That wasn't nice, Kyle. I'm sure you embarrassed him."

Kyle argued, "I know he does because Tom spent the night at his house and he told me."

Carly narrowed her eyes and scolded him. "That wasn't nice, Kyle. It may be the truth, but it wasn't nice to tell everyone. Even the truth can be embarrassing, Kyle." Remembering Laura's comments about Kyle's behavior, she asked, "Do you get in trouble a lot, Kyle?"

"My teacher says I dist . . . destr . . . dismiss . . ."

Carly broke in, "Disrupt?"

"Yeah. I do that to the class too much."

Carly didn't think the boy looked particularly remorseful. He looked sheepish, but not scared of being in the office. She remembered that Mr. Stout had gone to a meeting and wouldn't be returning soon. Laura had told her that his punishment would be her responsibility, but she wasn't sure how to react in this situation.

Kyle had begun to fidget. "Can I go to recess now?"

Carly gave him a stern look. "Kyle, when you do something wrong you need to face the consequences."

The boy rolled his eyes and slumped down in the chair.

He may look like his father did when he was young, but he certainly doesn't behave like Kolton did, she thought. Kolton had been quiet as a child, and a bit reserved even later in his youth. She never remembered him getting into trouble—even his occasional pranks were good-natured.

She sighed heavily and decided on his punishment. "I want you to write a letter to your teacher and a letter to Aaron, apologizing for your rude comments and disruptive behavior."

Kyle suddenly became angry and glared at her. "I don't have to. You're not the principal."

His outburst surprised her, but before she could respond, a stern voice filled the office. "You will do as you are told, young man, or you'll face a worse punishment when you get home."

Carly and Kyle both jumped at the masculine voice and were equally surprised to see Kolton standing at the office counter. "Furthermore," Kolton added, "you will offer Miss Weston an apology also."

Kyle straightened up in his chair and quickly responded, "Yes, sir." Without making eye contact, he mumbled an apology to Carly.

Carly was rattled. She hadn't expected Kolton to appear—especially while she was reprimanding his child. Avoiding his gaze, she opened her desk and pulled out some sheets of blank paper. She handed Kyle a pencil and told him to stay at Laura's desk until he was done writing both letters. Under his father's watchful eye, Kyle obediently went to work.

Kolton watched with interest but remained quiet. Carly walked over to the counter, her arms folded tightly against her chest. "I'm sorry about Kyle," she apologized. "He said some mean things in class. Usually Mr. Stout would have handled it, but he's not here. I know it's not my place."

Kolton smiled, "Don't worry. Mr. Stout and Kyle are well acquainted with each other." He pushed his thumbs into his front pockets and lowered his voice. "Truthfully, it doesn't surprise me to find Kyle in the office. He seems to be a regular troublemaker lately. He doesn't do anything too terrible—just a lot of teasing and disrupting the class. I'm convinced that he's only reaching out for attention, but I haven't figured out how to deal with it. I'm sure that you handled it well. After all, you are an expert when it comes to raising children."

She stiffened, but when she looked him in the eye she could see that he was teasing her. Carly returned his smile. He wore the same red T-shirt that she had seen him in the week before, and his work jeans were dirty from a day's work. His tousled hair wasn't much different than his son's, but his blue eyes sparkled. Carly also liked the rough look of his face with a few days' scruff.

She could feel a faint blush rise to her cheeks. Their eyes met for a moment, and she wondered if he felt the same about her. She had no words to explain her feelings; she just felt drawn toward him.

Breaking the silence, she said, "I've been meaning to talk to you about that day outside the church. I'm sorry how I treated you—I was wrong to intrude on you and Kyle."

Kolton shook his head and leaned on the counter. He was so close that she could faintly smell his cologne. It was already becoming recognizable to her. She noticed how rough and dry his hands were, and thought about his work ethic.

"Actually, I came down to the school to talk to you," he said. "I've wanted to talk to you all week."

"Really?"

"Carly," his voice was a mere whisper since Kyle was in the room, "I am sorry I was so rude to you last week at church. I have no excuses. I sometimes get angry, and I don't keep my anger in check. Occasionally I say things that I regret later." The hope in his eyes raised her interest. "I'm also sorry about interfering with you and Stan. I thought I was being funny, but I shouldn't have done—"

"No," she interrupted, "you did me a favor."

"Really?" he questioned skeptically.

"Yes. Stan has convinced me to buy a million dollar life insurance policy and name him as the beneficiary."

The smile on her face made him laugh. Knowing that she was finally kidding him back, he explained, "Stan is harmless, but I know how hard he's trying to get his business going. You looked uncomfortable, so I purposely tried to make it worse for you. I'm sorry, Carly. At the time it seemed like a funny thing to do, and I guess I thought that if I could make you laugh, it would be easier to approach you. I hope we can start over and become friends."

"It's fine." Carly lowered her own voice. "I shouldn't have interfered with your business on Sunday. I really didn't know Kyle was your son. I'm the one who should apologize."

"Thanks, Carly." He kept his eyes locked on hers for a moment before he finished. "It's good to see you again." He straightened up and glanced past her. "Kyle, get that done and get back to class. I'll talk to you when you get home after school."

Kyle mumbled a low, "Yes, sir."

Kolton turned to leave. "I need to get back to work." As an afterthought he offered, "Oh, and I'm real sorry about the other night at your house. I shouldn't have spoken to you the way I did. Once again, I overreacted."

Carly remembered his harsh accusations. "Kolton, what did you mean about my using Rich and Jennifer as an excuse?"

He shrugged uncomfortably. "You know. When I asked you to prom and you said you had a date, but then you went with Rich and Jennifer. I guess I was a little offended that you'd rather go alone than with me. When you said you had plans, I felt as though you were avoiding me and using them as an excuse again."

Carly unfolded her arms and relaxed. She looked up at him, embarrassed. "Well, I did lie to you about prom. But not because I didn't want to go with you."

"Carly, you don't have to say that to make me feel better."

"No, I want to tell you the truth. I should have told you the truth that day at my locker."

His interest piqued as she continued. "I was in trouble, and my Dad wouldn't let me go to prom. I didn't want anyone to know, because I felt stupid that I was grounded, so I pretended that I was going already. But at the last minute my dad had a change of heart. I didn't have a new dress or a date, but I went with Rich and Jennifer anyway. I promise I wasn't blowing you off. I always liked you, Kolton. You were one of the nicest boys in school."

He seemed relieved. "Well, now I really look like a jerk. I seem to owe you a lot of apologies."

Carly laughed. "No, you don't. I'm glad you came down to talk to me." He looked doubtful, but she continued, "Really, Kolton. I'm glad we settled this."

"Me too." Again, he pushed his thumbs into his pockets, a habit she was beginning to like. "Well, I better get going. I need to finish some deliveries."

"Okay. I'll see you later."

"See you around, Carly." He leaned over the counter and spoke to his son. "Shape up, Kyle. I'll see you when you get off the bus."

Kyle mumbled, "Good-bye, Dad."

Carly watched him walk out of the building, feeling as though a weight had been taken off her shoulders. It felt good to be at peace with Kolton.

"Is this alright?"

The small, hopeful voice broke into her thoughts, and she turned to see Kyle holding up his letters. She skimmed over them and gave him a smile of approval, "Very good, Kyle. You can go now."

Without a word he headed back to class. Carly watched him walk off and sighed. She wondered what life was like for Kyle without a mother's influence and love. She began to think of Leann's accusations against Kolton and then tried to dismiss the thoughts. Without knowing what really happened, she wasn't going to allow herself to form any rash judgments. She liked Kolton, and she wanted to form a friendship with him.

* * *

The weekend had come so quickly that Carly didn't have any plans for Saturday. Because the week had been tiring, all she really wanted to do was relax. Her parents had decided to take Chad and Leann to do some shopping. Emma was anxious to begin shopping for the new baby, and they were going to pick out some baby furniture. Although they'd invited Carly, she had declined. She wanted to spend some time at home.

Her family had all departed by seven in the morning and Carly was grateful to have the house to herself. She had spent the early morning unpacking a few remaining odds and ends in her room. She had left most of her household items boxed in her parents' garage along with her furniture. She assumed that she wouldn't be living with her parents for long, so there was no point in unpacking them. She really wanted to be back on her own, but it was convenient to stay with her folks for at least a couple of months, and that way she could spend quality time with them and save up some money for an apartment or a down payment on a small home.

Once her inside tasks were completed, she went outside and admired the yard and flower beds. She had always liked gardening with her mother, but it didn't appeal to her today. She checked on the chickens in the henhouse, and noticed a new shed built around the well. Curious, she walked out to the back of the property to inspect the shed. The paint looked fairly fresh, and Carly assumed it must be a project her dad had completed in the past month or so.

She opened the door to peek inside. Most of her mother's gardening tools were stacked neatly against one wall, and her father's lawn mower and edger were against the other wall. In the middle of the shed were two bikes. One bike was hers and the other was Chad's. She had completely forgotten about her old red mountain bike. She'd never been interested in competitive sports, but she had always enjoyed athletics, so as a child and in her teens, this hobby had filled that interest.

Carly pulled the old bike out and examined it. The tires were flat and cracked, and the bike was covered in dust and cobwebs. A ride sounded nice, but she wondered if the tires would hold air.

Remembering that her father had an air compressor, she walked the bike into the garage. Surprisingly, the tires did hold air. The gears looked a bit rusty, so after she had briskly hosed down the bike to get rid of the cobwebs, she sprayed them with some lubricant. She decided to go for a short ride and enjoy the nice weather.

The day was clear, but a bit cool. As a teenager, she and Jennifer would usually ride together to Main Street to meet up with friends or hang around, but she decided on a more scenic ride today.

She headed east toward an undeveloped part of Bridger on a gravel road. After three miles of riding her legs were beginning to ache a bit, but she was enjoying the ride too much to turn back. She continued at a steady pace and came upon some open fields and homes scattered out across the desert. There was very little traffic and the ride was quite peaceful. As she rode down a slight embankment, her back tire made a low swishing sound. Applying the brakes, she noticed the sound become deeper.

Assuming that she had a flat, she completely stopped the bike and inspected the tire. It had completely cracked opened along a half-inch gap. She looked around and figured she was at least five miles from home, and the closest house was about a half mile away. Taking a deep breath, she figured her only option was to walk the bike home. There was no use in going to a stranger's house when there was no one at home to call. She thought to call Jennifer, but remembered that they were going to Rich's family reunion for the weekend.

Heading for home, Carly soon realized that it was more work to push the bike than it had been to ride it before the flat. After walking a mile she began wishing she had thought to bring a water bottle. She noticed an approaching cloud of dust and moved to the side of the road to avoid it. She immediately recognized the truck as it pulled alongside her. She stopped and waved to Kolton and Kyle.

Rolling down his window, Kolton lifted his sunglasses and said, "A damsel in distress. Are you waiting for a knight to come save you?"

Kyle laughed, and Carly couldn't help but smile. "I'm always waiting for a prince, but all I ever get are toads."

He countered, "Careful, we toads get offended easily." He got out of his truck and assessed the damage to her bike. "Well, it looks like you're going to have to replace that tire—and the other one too. I'm surprised it hasn't split yet."

"I shouldn't have taken it out," Carly admitted, "but I wanted to go for a ride. These are the original tires from fifteen years ago."

He whistled, "You're lucky you got this far from your house."

"Well, I guess I shouldn't have gone for a ride. I should have waited and replaced the tires before I rode it."

Kolton looked back at Kyle and offered to Carly, "Well, let me load it in the back of the truck, and I'll run you home."

"Dad," Kyle whined. "We're supposed to be going shooting."

"Kyle," his father explained, "We can't leave her stranded. Now mind your manners."

"It's okay," Carly said. "I don't want to ruin your time with Kyle. If you have plans I can walk it home."

Kolton had grabbed the bike and was lifting it into the back of his truck as she spoke. "No. Kyle will just have to be patient. It's a good lesson for him."

Kyle folded his arms and gave Carly a brooding look. "But Dad," Kyle reminded his father, "we only have an hour."

"I have to get back to work by noon," Kolton explained to Carly. "My mom is watching the store while I take Kyle shooting."

Not wanting to impose on Kyle's time with his father, she leaned into the driver's side window and said to Kyle, "If you don't mind, I could come with you, and then your dad could run me home afterward."

Kyle looked hopefully at his father who was standing behind Carly. "Sure," Kolton agreed. "Jump in." His eagerness to have her join them made her believe that he wasn't just being polite. Carly felt that he was as willing to start a friendship as she was.

She walked around the passenger side of the truck and climbed in while Kyle scooted closer to his father. Kolton jumped in and they were on the road headed out into the vacant desert.

"Where do you go shooting?" Carly asked.

"Remember where the old silver mines are, at the base of the hills over there?" Kolton asked, pointing.

Carly remembered that the mines had all been filled in years ago, but that most people still avoided them just in case an open ground mine had been overlooked and unfilled. "All the way out there?" She pointed out the windshield.

"In that direction, but it's not too close to the mining area. There are some big rocks that stretch in a line, and we bring cans for Kyle to shoot with his BB gun."

Kyle was becoming excited and talked rapidly. "Last week I shot four out of five. My dad only hit two out of five."

"Really? I guess you're a better marksman than your dad," Carly complimented him.

"A what?" Kyle asked.

"A marksman. That means that you're a good shot. You can hit almost anything you want."

Kyle smiled proudly and nodded in agreement.

Kolton glanced at Carly and smiled. "There's no need to swell his head, he already thinks he's better at shooting than his old man."

Kyle looked at Carly and whispered, "I am better than my dad."

Kolton lightly jabbed his son in the ribs with his elbow, tickling him and making him laugh. "You think you're a better shot, huh?"

Kyle continued to laugh and nod his head up and down, anticipating more tickling.

"We'll see," his father said. "I bet Carly could outshoot you."

"No way," Kyle said loudly. "I can shoot better than any girl."

Carly joined in. "Really? You'll have to prove it."

"Okay. I'll beat you both," Kyle challenged.

Kolton continued to jab his son until all three of them were laughing. Carly enjoyed seeing Kolton interact with his son. She could sense what a close bond they shared. They soon came to a dirt road off the main gravel road, then drove about fifty yards before parking the truck at the end of the line of the large boulders Kolton had described. She and Kolton helped Kyle set up twenty cans and then they walked back behind him. Kolton reached in the cooler in the back of his truck and offered Carly a soda. She appreciatively accepted, and they both sat on the tailgate to watch Kyle.

"Remember, son, keep it pointed at the ground when you're not shooting."

Kyle's first shot knocked a can over, and he smiled back at Carly.

"Good job," she encouraged.

Kolton shook his head. "I'm warning you, you're creating a monster. Look at him showing off for you."

"I think he's cute. You've done a good job with him."

Kolton smiled, but looked doubtful. "I hope so. My parents help me out a lot."

"It would be very difficult to be a single parent. I admire you."

"It's not by choice, but I guess you handle what life brings you. His mom would have done a good job raising him." Kolton usually never discussed Stacey, and he surprised himself at mentioning her. But he couldn't deny that he felt comfortable with Carly—he figured she would be an empathetic listener.

Carly was anxious to know about Stacey's death, but she knew better than to ask. Although Kolton had mentioned Stacey's name, she could see that he was a bit uneasy, and she wasn't sure how to address the topic without hurting or offending him. Still, she really wanted to set her concerns about Stacey out of the way.

"I didn't know your wife, but I'm sure she was wonderful," Carly ventured. She noticed Kolton suddenly looked very uncomfortable, so she quickly dropped the subject. Instead, she observed, "Kyle is doing really well."

"Yeah, we come out here almost every weekend. There isn't much else to do in Bridger. He has friends he hangs out with, but I don't let him troll all over town on his bike like I used to do when I was his age."

"Why not? Don't you think Bridger is safe?"

"Yeah. I guess so. When I was a kid, I'd ride my bike all over town with my older brothers, but now . . . I suppose I'm just overprotective."

"I don't blame you," Carly agreed. "Times have changed. You never know what could happen to your kids."

Kolton agreed with Carly's thoughts, but those types of dangers weren't his real concern. Bridger was a safe town. He didn't want to admit his worries were different, that he didn't want his son to be approached by any of Stacey's family. He wanted to keep Kyle close and protect him from their beliefs about his father—as much as he could, anyway.

He looked at Carly, and she was biting on her lower lip. He chuckled, and it caught her attention.

She turned to him, "What? What's so funny?"

"Nothing," he lied. He didn't want to tell her the truth.

"What?" she repeated. "Tell me."

He squished an empty soda can in his hands and shook his head. "It's nothing."

She reached over and softly shoved his shoulder. "Tell me, Kolton. You're laughing at me, aren't you?"

"No, of course not." He smiled innocently.

"What's so funny, Kolton?"

"Okay," he relented. "It's nothing. I just saw you with your lip tucked in, and it reminded me of elementary school."

Uneasily she said, "Please tell me you don't really remember me sucking on my lip."

"Actually, I remember you sucking on your thumb."

She smiled ruefully through a faint blush of embarrassment. "Oh, I can't believe you remember that. I suppose you remember that rotten Walter Davis boy, too."

"I'd totally forgotten about it until I saw you biting on your lip. How old were we? Eight or nine?"

Carly remembered well. "We were eight. It was in the third grade."

"That's right. We were in Mrs. Grey's class."

Carly nodded, and admitted, "I only hit Walter because he made fun of me. And I didn't suck my thumb *all* the time," she defended herself. "I only did it when I was really upset."

"Well, Walter must have really upset you," Kolton teased. "That poor boy had a shiner for a week."

"That boy was just mean, and he got what he deserved."

"I only remember the rumors. Do you want to tell me your side?" Kolton prodded.

Carly shook her head in mild disgust, but she smiled at his teasing. "I was upset about something—I don't remember what—and I started sucking my thumb. So, on the playground at recess, Walter starts making jokes and singing songs about me. He had some other kids joining in, and I went home all upset. My dad said that if I stopped sucking my thumb, he wouldn't be able to tease me. So I stopped."

"But you started sucking on your bottom lip, right?"

"Yeah, I started sucking my lip, and he still teased me. He came up to me on the playground and asked me if I needed a pacifier. So I hit him."

Kolton's laugh deepened. "I never knew exactly what happened, but everyone figured you had done it, even though Walter wouldn't tell anyone who had hit him. I guess he was embarrassed that a girl left such a mark on him."

Carly smugly said, "I don't think he talked to me for the rest of the year. And since he wasn't talking to me, he wasn't teasing me. My life was good."

Kolton laughed, "No one ever talked to you about sucking on your lip. We were all scared you would pound us."

Carly laughed along with him.

Then Kolton noticed that Kyle had shot down almost all of his targets. "Slow down, Kyle," his father kidded. "You're going to wear yourself out and I'll beat you."

"No way," Kyle insisted, and kept shooting. After all the targets were down, the three of them picked up the damaged cans and set them up as targets again. This time they took turns and Kyle proved himself the winner.

As they were getting back into the truck to leave, Kyle said to Carly, "You're not too bad for a girl."

"Thank you. I think that's a compliment." She grinned.

Kolton looked down at his watch. It was already twelve-thirty. He hadn't realized the time had gone by so quickly. "We better get a move on it. I told my mom I would be back at noon so she could go do her grocery shopping."

They rode to Carly's house listening to Kyle talk about his gun, his bike, and the new baby chicks he was getting soon. "I want a dozen baby chicks. And I'm going to pick them all out myself. My dad says the first shipment of baby chicks should be at the feed store any day, and I get first pick when they come in." Kyle's enthusiasm made Carly laugh. Despite his inappropriate actions at school, he really could be darling, she decided.

When they approached her house, Carly was disappointed to have to leave their company. But, thanking them both, she got out and waved as they left. It didn't dawn on her until after they had gone out of view that her bike was still in the back of Kolton's truck. She made a mental note to remind him about it the next day at church.

* * *

Kolton and Kyle were both silent as they arrived at the feed store. Kyle jumped out of the truck and went running into the store to see his grandmother. Kolton sat in the truck and reflected back on the morning spent with Carly. He had thoroughly enjoyed it and had felt somehow lonely after dropping her off at her house. Kolton had noted that Kyle had energetically talked nonstop while Carly was riding with them, but as soon as they'd dropped her off he'd quieted down. *Funny*, Kolton thought, *how her presence seems to lift both our spirits.*

He had lived alone with Kyle for so long that he'd almost forgotten what it was like to have a woman around. Spending time with Carly reminded him of the time he'd spent with Stacey. It felt good to have a woman to talk to. He was surprised to realize how much he truly missed having a partner to share his life with. He recognized his feelings of loneliness and wondered if they had taken a toll on his attitude and patience in the past eight years, and whether he'd be a different man now if he'd had a wife to confide in all those years. He also wondered about the future and his desires to change.

* * *

At breakfast the next morning, Carly's mother told her about the great time she'd had shopping for Chad and Leann's baby.

"What did you buy?" Carly asked. "If you don't know whether she's having a boy or girl, how do you know what to get?"

"Well, Leann was looking at cribs and furniture mostly. I told her that Dad and I would like to buy the crib for them."

Her father almost choked on his oatmeal. "What?" he stammered. "Did you see the cribs she was looking at? That white one was over three hundred dollars, and—"

Emma interrupted, "Relax. If I'm buying it as a gift, then I'll pick out something nice that we can afford. You need to get used to this, honey, I'm planning on buying a lot of things for our grandbaby."

Raymond rolled his eyes. "Just like you did for our kids, I suppose."

"You didn't like it when Mom spent money on us?" Carly asked her dad.

"Oh, you know, women and shopping. She was always coming up with an excuse to buy you something."

Carly was suddenly reminded of the Christmas she received her mountain bike. She had wanted one, but she hadn't thought that her parents would be able to afford it for her. They always seemed to have enough money to meet their needs, but they lived quite modestly.

Memories of the bike reminded her of her ride the day before. She decided to mention it to her parents. "I took my old bike out for a spin yesterday. I found it out in the new shed."

"Really?" her father asked. "I'm surprised the tires held up."

"They didn't. I got out about a mile past the Crockers' old house and I had a flat."

"That's at least five or six miles from home. What did you do?" her mother asked, concerned.

"I lucked out. Kolton Raywood and his son Kyle were driving out to go shooting, and they picked me up."

Her mother's eyes sparkled. "How convenient." Smiling, she added, "So can I assume that everything is cleared up between you and Kolton?"

"Yes, and actually, it was enjoyable." Carly smiled. "Oh, except I left my bike in the back of Kolton's truck."

"How is Kolton doing?" Raymond asked.

"Good. And Kyle is really cute. He beat us both at shooting cans with a BB gun."

"He's all boy," Emma commented. "But he is overall a good kid. I ran into Sarah Raywood the other day. She said that Kyle spends a lot of time with her, and she wasn't complaining. She loves the boy, and she told me she loves being a grandma."

"Is someone here?" Raymond suddenly asked.

"I didn't hear anything," said Carly.

"Me neither," Emma said.

"I'll go take a look." Raymond got up and put his dishes in the sink before heading for the front door.

"So," Emma pried, "what did you and Kolton do?"

Carly couldn't help but grin when she was talking about Kolton and Kyle. "We sat back and talked while we watched Kyle shoot his gun. We even shot with him. He's a good shot—better than his dad."

"Carly," her father yelled from the front door, interrupting them. "I think you need to come out here."

Curious, Carly hurried out of the kitchen with her mother following behind. As she walked out onto the porch she was speechless. Her mountain bike was parked in the driveway near the house, sporting brand new tires and scrubbed clean to a shine.

Emma exclaimed, "What a sweet thing to do—how thoughtful of Kolton."

Carly agreed, though somewhat in shock.

Later that morning after church, Carly caught up with Kolton and Kyle as they were walking out to the parking lot. "Hi Kolton. Hi Kyle."

"Hey, how are you?" They stopped at the edge of the sidewalk while she caught up to them.

"You'll never guess what happened at my house today." She smiled widely.

"Oh?" Kolton feigned innocence. "What happened?"

"The bike fairy came. My bike was on the front porch all shiny clean with new tires."

"No Carly, it was us," Kyle bragged loudly.

"It was?" she asked, pretending to be astonished.

"Yeah, my dad and I brought your bike back. Dad put new tires on it, and I washed it."

"The kid can't keep a secret," Kolton complained dramatically.

"Well, I want to thank you, it was very nice. You really didn't have to do that."

Kolton looked her straight in the eye. "I know. I wanted to—actually, we wanted to. I'm glad that you like it."

"Well, let me repay you. I'm sure tires aren't cheap."

"No, don't worry about it," he insisted.

Kyle put his hand out. "You can pay me," he said impishly.

Kolton lightly slapped Kyle's hand down, "No, Kyle. Knock it off—she's not going to pay either of us."

Carly squatted down facing Kyle. A thought flashed through her mind. "If I can't pay you in cash, maybe I could pay you in a different way. Would you like to come to my house for dinner sometime?"

Kyle nodded his head and looked at his father for permission.

"What's your favorite food, Kyle?" she asked.

"Pizza. And hot dogs. And cheeseburgers."

"Okay, would you like to come to my house next Saturday for pizza?"

"Sure. And hot dogs?"

"How about root beer floats instead of hot dogs?"

"Okay," Kyle agreed excitedly.

Carly stood and faced Kolton. "That is, if it's okay with you."

"Yeah, that would be great." Kolton agreed. "What time?"

"Around six?"

"Great."

Carly noticed her parents were already in their vehicle, waiting for her. "I better get going. I'll see you soon."

"Thanks, Carly. See you later."

"Bye, Carly," Kyle called as she walked away.

On the way home from church she wondered what she was getting herself into. Was she ready to get closer to another man? The more time she spent with Kolton, though, the more her fears and doubts about him were beginning to fade. Could she be so drawn to him if he had truly hurt his previous wife? She dismissed the thought from her mind. She decided to get to know him better herself and form her own opinions based on more objective information.

The week passed quickly for Carly. At work on Friday she had forgotten to do some of her simple daily tasks, and Laura asked, "Is everything alright?"

"Yeah," Carly answered as she searched over her desk for a student file. Unable to find it, she asked Laura, "Have you seen the file on the Larson boy?"

"You gave it to me twenty minutes ago and asked me to file it. Carly, are you sure you're okay?" Laura asked.

"Yes. Why do you keep hinting that I'm not?" Carly laughed.

"I just noticed that you seem to be distracted. I went to put the class folders in order, and I noticed you hadn't logged the attendance yet."

"Oh, I know, I'm sorry. I know I'm supposed to do it, but it hadn't even crossed my mind today. That reminds me, I also forgot to fax the papers for the Smith kid that just moved."

"Well," Laura prodded, "there must be something or *someone* on your mind."

Carly grinned mysteriously, to Laura's frustration, but she didn't want to admit to her co-worker that she was actually getting nervous for her date with Kolton and Kyle the next night. However, right before school let out that afternoon, a delivery man brought in a beautiful bouquet of yellow roses. Carly took the flowers and looked for a card. Her name was on the envelope.

Laura, standing right beside her, teased, "You have an admirer, Carly."

Carly smiled wide with anticipation. "I think I know who they're from." She was hoping they were confirmation that Kolton was as anxious to see her on Saturday as she was to spend time with him and Kyle. She carried the flowers to her desk and opened the card.

The note read, "Thinking of you." And it was signed by Adam. The surprise must have shown on her face.

Laura asked, "Carly, is everything alright?" Carly stuffed the note back in the envelope

"Yeah. The flowers are from an old friend." She waited until Laura wasn't looking and threw the envelope in the trash.

She busied herself with her work, hoping that Laura wouldn't try to discuss the flowers. *Adam*, she thought. *I haven't thought about him for days.* She pushed the floral arrangement back to the corner of her desk. *Why is he sending me flowers?*

She thought of how thoughtful Kolton had been to repair her bike. She wondered if Adam would ever have thought to do the same kind of thing for her. Adam had been thoughtful at times, but more on the conventionally thoughtful side—Like sending flowers, for instance. He never really did anything that only she would appreciate. There were also incidents when he hadn't been willing to help her. Once, her kitchen drain had clogged in her apartment in Langdon. She told Adam about it, and his advice was to call a plumber. Another time she was having car trouble, and she asked Adam to take a look at the car. He said he would, but she eventually took the car to a mechanic because Adam was too busy. She surmised that Kolton would have reacted differently—he would have at least taken a look at the problem, if not fixed it himself.

She picked up the bouquet of flowers and moved them across the office onto the filing cabinet in the back corner. She didn't want to think about Adam today.

* * *

Carly's parents left the house to visit friends just as the clock chimed six on Saturday evening. Carly ran to the mirror for one last look. She stood in front of her full-length glass and wondered again if she had made a mistake to invite Kolton and Kyle to dinner. She wore a simple white cotton dress with short sleeves. The hem was long, but she wore a gold anklet and sandals to dress up her appearance. Her hair was curled and fell in waves across her back and shoulders.

Feeling pressured for time, she rushed into the kitchen to set the table. The pizza had been delivered, and it was in the oven staying warm. Her mother had given her the recipe for cheesecake and Carly was well pleased with the results. It was in the refrigerator with a garden salad she'd made that afternoon. She had also picked up root beer and vanilla ice cream for Kyle.

She had wanted to dress the table up a bit, but she decided candles would be inappropriate, so she set the table with her mother's everyday stoneware and cloth napkins. Putting ice into the glasses, she hoped that Kolton and Kyle both liked lemonade. She wanted this evening together to be personal and comfortable. Carly took one last look around the kitchen; everything seemed to be in perfect order.

She entered the living room to check that everything had been straightened, and heard a knock at the door. Quickly she smoothed her dress and took a deep breath, opening the door for her guests.

* * *

Kolton had left the church parking lot in shock the previous Sunday. When he had fixed up Carly's bike, he had been aiming to improve their friendship. Asking her out for a date hadn't even crossed his mind—he had no intention of putting himself in a position to be shot down again. So she had completely knocked him off guard with her offer for a Saturday-night date, and he was determined not to say or do anything to ruin the night.

This might be his chance to get to know her better, to see if they were compatible beyond the attraction he felt for her. He was glad that she had included Kyle in on the plans. It made the date seem more comfortable for him to have his son there.

During the week, Kolton had tried to hide his excitement, but Kyle was more open with his feelings. He had told everyone he saw that week that he would be having pizza at Carly Weston's house. Whenever he'd passed the office at school he would smile shyly at Carly. And every day after school he would retell his grandmother about his pizza date on Saturday. Kolton's mother had asked her son about his date with Carly, but he didn't want to discuss it. He brushed it off as a thank-you dinner for the work he had done on her bike, and tried to make it sound like no big deal. But in his heart he considered it their first date.

Kyle came into Kolton's room while he was dressing. Like his father, he had put on a good pair of jeans and a T-shirt. "Are you ready, son?" Kolton asked him.

"Almost," Kyle said. He went into his father's bathroom and shut the door. When he came out, Kolton instructed, "Go lock the back door and get into the truck."

He suppressed a laugh as he watched his son leave the room. Kyle was wearing a bit too much cologne, but Kolton didn't have the heart to say anything.

They finally arrived at Carly's house and Kolton let Kyle knock on the door. When Carly opened the door, Kolton was speechless.

She was beautiful. Her golden hair shone and cascaded over her dress. His voice was deeper than he had anticipated. "Hello," he managed.

She could see the approval in his eyes, and it bolstered her confidence. "Hello, Kolton. You look really nice." Carly noticed that he had shaved and brushed back his hair. His deep blue eyes were fixated on her, and she relished the attention.

"Thank you," he said, "You really look beautiful, Carly."

"Thank you," she responded.

Carly gave Kyle a warm smile and said, "And you also look very nice, Kyle. I'm glad that you could come."

He smiled back at her but seemed suddenly too shy to say anything. Carly became aware that he was wearing cologne, and she glanced questioningly at Kolton, the smell strong between them. He shrugged, and they exchanged a knowing smile.

"Well, come on in." She led them into the kitchen. "Have a seat—dinner is all ready."

"It smells great," Kolton said, motioning for Kyle to sit at the table.

Carly nodded to the pitcher of lemonade on the table. "Go ahead and pour the drinks, and I'll serve up our plates."

Kyle watched her but still said nothing, and Kolton watched too as Carly picked up their plates and moved around the kitchen. He couldn't help noticing that she was a bit nervous. It made him feel better to know that he wasn't the only one. Carly set the plates down on the table and sat across from him. She asked him to bless the food, and he offered a prayer. Carly noticed Kyle's scrunched-up nose when he saw the salad on his plate. "You don't have to eat the salad if you don't want to."

Kyle immediately looked at his dad for confirmation.

"It's okay, son." Kolton agreed. "Just eat your pizza."

"I gave you pepperoni, Kyle, but I have supreme too if you want some."

Kyle shook his head and picked up the slice of pepperoni pizza.

"Do you like cheesecake, Kyle?" Carly asked.

He nodded a yes as he bit deeply into his pizza.

"I have everything for root beer floats too, if you'd rather have that."

Kyle's eyes remained fixed on his plate and he didn't respond.

"I think he's a bit shy all of a sudden," Kolton explained with a chuckle.

"Dad," Kyle complained. Carly gave him a reassuring wink, and he went back to eating his dinner.

Kyle ate quickly as Kolton and Carly began chatting. Their conversation was comfortable as they discussed how little their small town had changed over the past fifteen years. After three pieces of pizza it was clear that Kyle was done eating.

He had begun fidgeting in his chair, so Carly asked him, "Do you want to go in the living room and watch a movie?"

He nodded and followed Carly out. When she reentered the kitchen, Kolton had cleaned the dirty plates from the table and put the salad dressings in the refrigerator. He was refilling their glasses as she came back in and said, "I'm sorry about Kyle. I don't know why he's acting shy and not talking."

"It's okay. This is a strange house, and he still isn't used to me. He's watching a cartoon video, and he seems happy."

"Yeah, he'll sit in front of the television all night if I let him."

Carly sat down and faced Kolton. "I really appreciate what you did with my bike. I hope it wasn't too forward of me to invite you over."

Kolton took a sip of lemonade and set the glass down. "No, it's fine. Actually, I'm flattered. I've never had a woman ask me out on a first date, especially someone like you, Carly. But I hope that you didn't feel obligated to do this for me."

Carly lowered her eyes and felt her face flush. She hadn't been prepared for Kolton to talk so openly. Adam had never been good at expressing his feelings, except for the times that he was criticizing her standards. She could see, now that she had someone to compare him to, that he had rarely given her important compliments.

Determined to continue with the openness, she said, "Honestly, I wanted to see you. I didn't do this because I felt like I owed you something. I even wanted to see you the night you came over last week—I just came across wrong. Truly, I didn't mean to run you off, but I was nervous and a little scared."

"Scared of me?"

"No, not of you." She thought about how to correctly articulate her feelings. "I'm scared of having feelings for someone and not having the same feelings returned. Actually, it's not just that—I don't want to waste time dating someone who doesn't respect my values and ideals. And although I remember you from school, we really don't know much about each other."

Kolton nodded that he understood, but the discussion about their relationship was a little awkward, and he remained silent.

Carly quickly changed the subject. "Would you like some cheese-cake?"

"Sure. Do you need some help?"

"Yes, ask Kyle what he wants. I have either the cheesecake with strawberries, or root beer floats."

Kyle chose a root beer float, and Kolton and Carly worked side by side in the kitchen serving the desserts. Kolton carried the root beer float carefully to his son and warned him not to spill. He rejoined Carly at the table, and they sat down to eat their dessert.

Just then the phone rang, and Carly picked it up from the counter. "Hello."

"Hello, Carly."

Adam's voice surprised her. "Oh, hi, Adam. How are you?"

"Good." Carly could hear the uneasiness in his voice. "I was just calling to see how you're doing."

"I'm good." She looked over at Kolton, and their eyes met. "I'm sorry, Adam, but I have company right now."

Reluctantly, Adam said, "Okay—I'll let you go." A quiet moment passed, and he said sincerely, "Take care, Carly."

"Thanks, Adam. You too."

"Good-bye."

"Good-bye." She turned the phone off and returned to her seat. She wondered why Adam had called—*was there more to his call than he admitted? Was he still interested in working things out?*

Kolton noticed the perplexed look on her face and asked, "Is everything okay?"

"Yes. It was a friend from Langdon. We dated for a while before I moved here."

Kolton didn't say anything in response, and Carly realized she didn't want to give him the impression that she had a current boyfriend. "Actually, we broke up. I'm surprised he called."

"He must still be interested," Kolton remarked carefully.

"Our relationship didn't work. I don't think there's much hope for it to work out even if we tried again. We have very different values."

Kolton looked interested, and she felt at ease confiding in Kolton about her past with Adam. They both ate slowly, and Kolton listened intently as she explained how she and Adam had met, how their relationship progressed, and why it had ended.

By the time she had nearly finished, he was leaning on the table giving her his full attention. "Since he didn't want to even try to understand my desire for an eternal relationship, and all he cared about that day was money, I told him that I would rather have a honeymoon in a hay barn than be with him. I called him a jerk, and I left."

"A hay barn?" Kolton teased. "Remind me not to get on your bad side. I don't think I could handle the verbal abuse."

Carly laughed. "I can't believe I said that."

Kolton reached across the table and held Carly's hand in both of his. "From the gospel point of view, I think that you made the right decision. A temple marriage is worth the wait. His voice grew more serious. "It's so important not to rush into a marriage. It sounds like you have valid concerns. For me, I now have Kyle to think about. A mother would probably be a huge blessing for him, but I don't want him to ever be hurt. He is my number-one priority."

She smiled in response and felt the warmth of his hands around hers. "He's lucky to have a father like you. I think you've done a good job raising him, especially with your circumstances. He's a good kid," she said.

"He can be—when he's not into mischief."

Carly laughed and agreed. "He does seem to find his share of mischief at school."

"At home, too. He's on his best behavior tonight." Kolton sighed. "It's not easy being a father. I had no idea how difficult it was going to be, but it's also a lot of fun. The rewards are worth all the hard work. Kyle is everything to me."

Carly could feel the conviction in Kolton's voice and her heart warmed at his words. Then Kolton let go of her hand and finished the last of his drink. He set the glass down and stretched out his arms.

Feeling stiff herself, Carly realized that they had been sitting at the table for over an hour. "We could go sit outside on the swing if you want," she suggested.

"Sure. Let me just go check on Kyle first."

Carly put their glasses in the sink and waited for Kolton to return. He came back with the empty root beer glass. "Kyle fell asleep on the couch, so I turned the television off."

"Do you want a blanket for him?"

"No, he'll be fine. I won't stay much longer." He set the glass in the sink with the others.

Carly motioned for him to come outside with her and he followed her out the back door. As they sat on the swing, he put his arm on the back of the cushion behind her. It was a gesture that made her feel warm and cozy.

He commented, "It's so nice in the evenings. I remember when Stacey and I would sit out at night and look at the stars. I try to do that with Kyle now."

Carly's hopes rose, anticipating that Kolton would share stories about Stacey. "Did she like astronomy?" Carly asked.

"No, not really. She just always thought it was peaceful to watch the night sky. No matter how many shooting stars she saw, she was always excited to see another one." They fell silent, wrapped in their individual thoughts as they began to sway in the swing and look out at the stars.

Carly was experiencing a feeling of security and contentment that surprised her. If nothing else, she knew that she had found a friend in Kolton. She closed her eyes and savored the moment.

Kolton too felt secure. He wanted to tell Carly more about Stacey and everything he had been through since she'd died. The time they had shared this evening had been enjoyable, but something inside warned him to wait, to see how their friendship progressed before he discussed intimate details of his life. They continued to rock slowly in the swing, and neither one noticed someone come up behind them.

"What is going on?" a disapproving voice questioned.

Startled, they both turned and Kolton's arm fell lightly on Carly's shoulders.

"Hello, Leann." Kolton's voice was controlled, but there was an icy undertone.

Leann's eyes were blazing. "What are you doing here?" she spat at Kolton.

Alarmed, Carly faced her. "Leann, Kolton is my guest. What are you doing here?"

"Carly," Leann warned, "you have no idea what this man is like."

At that moment, Chad walked in behind his wife and assessed the situation. "Hey, sis. Hello, Kolton." His voice was noticeably more friendly than his wife's. Kolton nodded, but Carly only stared at Leann. She would never have thought her sister-in-law could be so rude.

Leann's stare was unforgiving. "You shouldn't be here, Kolton," she said with disdain.

Chad immediately pulled his wife's arm toward the back door to lead her into the kitchen. "Come on, Leann. They are obviously busy, and we are interrupting."

She hesitantly followed her husband, but the pitch of their voices from the kitchen made it evident that they were having a disagreement. Kolton relaxed his grip on Carly and sighed deeply. She reluctantly pulled away from him and stood up.

"I am so sorry, Kolton. I don't know why she acted like that."

His face was grim. "Leann and I have a history. She has an opinion of me that she won't let go of."

Carly looked at him expectantly, but he didn't continue his explanation. He stepped up to her, put his hands on her shoulders, and lightly kissed her cheek. "I think I should go. Thank you for a wonderful evening."

"No," she said, her voice rising in frustration. "There's no reason you should leave. This isn't your fault."

The voices in the kitchen were getting increasingly louder. He nodded in the direction of the kitchen and said, "I think I should go anyway."

She followed him around the house to the front door. He walked briskly into the front room and gently scooped Kyle off the couch.

"Kolton, you really don't have to leave."

He stepped out onto the porch and turned to her. His voice was almost a whisper as he explained, "I had a great time, Carly. Thank you for having us. I think it's better that I take Kyle home before he hears something he shouldn't."

Carly hadn't thought of that, and she nodded in agreement. She felt like begging him to stay, but stifled her impulses. "Good night."

He jumped into his truck and was gone in seconds. Carly watched from the porch until she could no longer see his taillights. *Why was Leann so angry?* she wondered, irritated. Her temper began to rise, and she decided to go back in the house and confront her sister-in-law. She had looked forward to spending time with Kolton all day, and Leann had ruined the entire evening.

As she entered the kitchen, Leann had tears streaming down her cheeks, and Chad was across the room with his arms folded. There was an uncomfortable silence, and Carly noticed Leann's chin quivering.

Carly's anger turned to confusion. Keeping her voice low, she asked firmly, "What was that all about?"

Leann avoided her gaze, and Chad shook his head, but neither one offered an answer. Carly spoke again. "I would like an explanation." Looking straight at Leann, she pressed, "You ruined my date, and I think you owe me an explanation."

Leann began to sob and dashed out the back door. Carly was amazed. "Chad, what is going on?"

"Calm down, Carly. You don't understand."

"I don't understand?" Carly became defensive. "*I* should calm down? Your wife is acting crazy. I don't think that I need to be lectured on *my* behavior."

Chad's eyes were dull. "Carly, all I can say is that Leann's family doesn't admire Kolton. When she saw him here, she was surprised. This is the last place on earth she thought she would see him, and she was unprepared."

"I know, Chad, but nobody was more surprised than me and Kolton."

He nodded. "I realize that. But you have to understand that Leann didn't mean to be so rude. There is just a lot of pain between Leann's family and Kolton, and she doesn't want to be around him."

Carly couldn't believe her ears. "You know, Chad, I know she's your wife, but these excuses are lame. Regardless of what she thinks of him, he's my friend, and he doesn't deserve to be treated like that."

"I agree, Carly. Leann let her emotions overrule her good sense." He thought for a second and suggested, "Maybe you could make it easier on everyone if you didn't have him over."

"What?" she asked in disbelief. "I live here, Chad. If your wife doesn't care for him, then maybe she shouldn't come here."

"Maybe you could see him other places."

"Chad, do you have any idea how unreasonable you're being?"

"I'm not saying you can't see him. Carly, you don't understand—"

Carly cut him off. Shaking her finger, she said, "No, you don't understand. I will not have Kolton treated this way by my family. I've heard the rumors, and if Leann has a problem, then it's her problem. She can keep her big mouth shut and stay away."

Chad gave his sister a look of surrender. "Carly, I'm sorry," he said apologetically. "I'll talk to Leann, and I'm sure this won't happen again. Actually, I'm tired of her attitude toward Kolton. I've tried to discuss it with her, but we always end up in an argument. With Leann's condition, the last thing I want to do is upset her more tonight." Chad sighed heavily. "I need to find Leann and make sure she's okay. Tell Mom and Dad we stopped by, and I'll see ya tomorrow at church."

Disgruntled, Carly was left alone as he walked out the back door. She still had unresolved aggression, but there was no one left for her to take out her frustrations on. She looked around at the mess from their dinner and decided to take it out on the dirty kitchen.

As she wiped the counters and began to load the dishwasher, she wondered about Leann's reaction to Kolton. She had been so hateful, and Carly had never seen her treat anyone that way. She didn't know Leann very well, but she was pretty sure Leann's actions were out of character. Thinking back, she remembered that Jennifer had mentioned that Kolton had a tough past, and her own mother wouldn't speak of Kolton's marriage or his wife's death. Leann had made a comment last week at the dinner table about how Kolton had been responsible for Stacey's death. And even Sarah Raywood had made a remark about Kolton not wanting to be in the church choir because of Leann. Could Kolton really be guilty of such a hideous crime as causing his wife's death? Surely Stacey's death had been investigated, and if Kolton had been guilty of murder, he wouldn't be free to live in Bridger.

Doubts began to surface, and Carly wondered what had really happened in Kolton's past. She finally decided that if he was a dangerous man, surely she would have felt apprehensive to be with him. She remembered how she felt with Adam when he was pressuring her to move in with him. She had known in her heart that it would be a wrong choice, and she had immediately begun to feel awkward around him. With Kolton she didn't have the same feeling—she looked forward to spending more time with him. She wanted to know about his past and understand why there was still speculation and gossip about his circumstances after all these years.

She kept replaying the evening in her mind. Kolton couldn't be the person that Leann thought he was—Carly's heart wouldn't let her believe it. She changed into her pajamas, ironed a dress for the morning, and retired to bed before ten o'clock. As she lay in bed, she decided to speak to Kolton at church the next day. Perhaps he would finally explain Stacey's death and the events that seemed to haunt him.

* * *

Kolton drove home in silence, his thoughts thick with memories. Once home, it didn't take him long to get Kyle ready for bed and under the covers. They said their prayers, and Kolton turned off the light.

"Daddy?" Kyle spoke into the darkness.

"Yes, son?"

"I had fun."

"Me too Kyle. Go to sleep." Kolton gave his son a kiss on the forehead and turned to leave.

"Is Carly going to be my new mom?"

Kolton stopped and took a deep breath. He turned back into his son's room and sat on the bed that had once been his as a child. "Carly and I are friends from school. We used to know each other when we were your age."

"I know, but is she your girlfriend?" Kyle persisted.

"No, Kyle. She's just a good friend." Kolton paused, then asked, "Do you wish you had a mother?"

"Sometimes," he replied. "All of my friends have moms."

Kolton had explained to his son before how he was sealed to Stacey, but he doubted that he fully understood what it all meant. He said, "Your mom loves you very much. I wish she were here with us, Kyle. But I can't change anything."

"I know, Dad. It's okay." Kyle yawned and softly said, "But it would be cool to have a mom like Carly."

Kolton ruffled his son's hair, "Good night, son."

"Good night, Dad."

Kolton decided he needed to continue the discussion later. He wondered if Kyle would really be happy to have a stepmom, and how difficult adjusting would be for him. Every time Carly and Kyle had been together, Kyle was always on his best behavior. Tonight, Kolton knew he was excited to go to Carly's house, yet he had acted quiet and shy once he was there. Kolton thought perhaps that proved that Kyle had wanted to impress her by being good.

But after the evening's mishap with Leann, Kolton didn't know where he stood with Carly. He didn't think it would be long before all the old familiar gossip circulated through their small town again—and, of course, stories always became more dramatic with time.

Kyle snuggled in his covers as Kolton rose and took a last look at his son. Kyle was all he really had in life. As he walked out, he left Kyle's bedroom door ajar so the hall light could filter into the room. He entered the master bedroom across the hall, unbuttoning his shirt as he went. Pulling it off, he flung it on the dresser and sat on the edge of his bed to take off his boots. He casually tossed them to the side of the bed and lay back.

He rubbed his hands over his face before crossing them under the back of his head and staring at the ceiling. He thought of how pretty Carly had looked. After spending the evening with her, he was positive that time hadn't changed her personality—she still had the same qualities that he had always liked. Their conversation had been great, and he had sensed that she enjoyed his company as much as he enjoyed hers.

He closed his eyes, recalling the scent of her hair. She was definitely attractive, but he felt that there was more to it than just the physical chemistry. He was glad she had felt she could open up to him about her feelings and her past. The best part of the evening had been listening to Carly. He admired the strength of her convictions. He now knew that they both shared the same ideals and love of the gospel. And selfishly, he was glad Adam was no longer in her life. He wanted to talk to her about his own past, but now he was glad that he hadn't. It would have been horrible to be discussing his past with Stacey when Leann had turned up.

This had been his first date since Stacey's death, and it had felt right. He was actually surprised at how right it had felt. He thought about Stacey, and how different she was from Carly, yet they shared some similarities. When he had first met Stacey Powers, he had been immediately smitten. He was twenty-four and working for his parents at the feed store. She had just moved to town with her family and had recently celebrated her eighteenth birthday. Physically, she was the total opposite of Carly. Her hair was short and dark, her eyes a deep brown, and her stature very petite. Even standing on her toes, she was barely as tall as his shoulder. He wouldn't have described her as classically beautiful, but she was very cute with her wide eyes, little upturned nose, and big smile.

Like Carly, Stacey had been caring and kind. The people in their ward adored her, and she loved to serve in the Church. The gospel had meant a great deal to Stacey, and she'd tried to live it in all aspects of her life. Their courtship only lasted four months before they were married and sealed in the temple. At the time it had felt like the right thing to do, and Kolton had no regrets. He had loved her with all his heart.

She was young, and her family didn't approve of such an early marriage, so their marriage had been difficult, even tumultuous at times, but he had been loyal and committed. He remembered that there had also been many good times that now seemed overshadowed with the sad memories of the past.

When Stacey was alive, he had felt he was making the correct decisions for their lives. He had no regrets about their marriage, but as he thought back to the sad details of the weeks before she gave birth to Kyle, and her ultimate death, he realized that he had probably been too stubborn at times and not empathetic enough to his wife or her family. His heart filled with remorse and guilt, and he wished he had behaved differently. He also struggled not to feel hate and anger toward the Powers family.

Stacey's family had disliked him when she was alive, and they still despised him today. They felt he had ruined her life, and—to some degree—he agreed. He opened his eyes and blinked away tears. He didn't want to relive the past. He wanted to move ahead with his life and start fresh, but he wondered if that would ever be possible. As long as the Powers family hated him, he would never truly feel released from the guilt he harbored over Stacey's death.

He pictured Carly in his mind. She was the kind of person who could help motivate him to turn his life around and help him find greater happiness. Unfortunately, he was sure she would soon be hearing all about Stacey and how he had killed her. Despite the rumors, everyone knew that he hadn't physically killed his wife. But he had shown poor judgment and it weighed heavily on his heart.

At Stacey's funeral, Leann had outright accused him of killing Stacey emotionally—by not being supportive and sympathetic to her worries. He would never forget seeing Stacey's mother Annette crying outside of the church. In his heart he thought maybe he had contributed to Stacey's death. He had definitely upset and hurt her before her death, and his actions still haunted his dreams. It didn't matter that the Powers family didn't know the whole truth about Stacey. Now, after all the years that had passed, it wouldn't make any difference anyway. Someday he would tell his son the whole story, and hopefully Kyle would understand what happened between his parents, and not blame his father for his mother's death.

He rose from the bed, opened the door to his closet, and fumbled around near the back wall until he found a flat, rectangular package. Pulling it out from behind an old suitcase, he carried it to his bed and laid it down. He carefully unwrapped the old floral-patterned blanket and stared at the contents. No one else had ever seen this. It was a reminder of better days, and of worse days. Someday he would share it with his son. Tears welled up in his eyes, and after a few minutes he put it back in its place.

Throwing himself on the bed, Kolton closed his eyes tightly and tried to fight off the old memories. He slowly drifted off to sleep, trying to focus on Kyle and their possible future with Carly.

Chapter Six

The morning was warm and beautiful. A slight breeze played through Carly's hair as she walked out of church. It felt good to be out in the sunlight and fresh air. The meetings had seemed long and dull since she hadn't been able to concentrate on the messages that were shared. Kolton had never arrived at church, and Carly wondered if his absence had anything to do with the incident during their date last night. She couldn't help but feel somehow responsible.

Chad and Leann weren't in attendance either. She hoped that they had worked out their differences, but she was still determined to get an explanation from Leann. She knew that she would have to be careful. She didn't want to hurt her relationship with them. But she wasn't going to stand back and allow them to hurt Kolton either.

Jennifer had been at church, but her Relief Society calling and her children absorbed her time, and she hadn't been able to have a private moment with her friend. During the sacrament meeting, Carly stole glances at Jennifer's family. The boys were adorable, and very busy with their toys and books. Rich and Jennifer both appeared to be tired, but Carly could see the visible enjoyment on their faces as they tried not to laugh at their children's antics. Carly felt like she ought to learn more about motherhood, even if she wasn't a mother now, and she made a mental note to call Jennifer soon and chat with her.

As soon as all the meetings were over, Carly picked through her purse for her keys and strolled out to her car. Her parents both had meetings to attend after the church services, so she had driven herself to church. She wanted to confide in someone about Saturday night's occurrences, but she hadn't had the opportunity yet to speak with her mom.

As she unlocked her door, a woman approached her. "Carly Weston? Can I speak to you a moment?"

The woman appeared quite familiar, but Carly couldn't place a name with the face. "Sure."

"You probably don't recognize me," the woman said. "I'm Leann's mother, Katherine Powers."

"Oh, yes, I remember." Carly hadn't seen her for years.

"It's been awhile. We are certainly glad to have you back home." Her southern drawl sounded condescending to Carly.

The Powers family was wealthy from cattle ranching, and Katherine wore her wealth abundantly. Her dress was a dark blue silk, her hair and nails were obviously salon-cared-for, and she wore sparkling gold jewelry on her neck, wrists, and fingers. Although her hair and skin coloring were darker than Leann's, they shared the same features, and Carly could see the resemblance between mother and daughter.

Carly had always wondered why the Powers family bothered to grace the town of Bridger when they appeared to consider the country atmosphere beneath them. Carly remembered her mother once commenting on her own frustration with Sister Powers's lack of regard for others, and Carly had personally found the woman a bit uppity.

Carly bristled a bit at the too-sweet welcome but politely asked, "What can I do for you?"

"Well, Sister Brown, our Relief Society president, talked to you today about becoming a visiting teacher." Katherine's voice was well trained. She spoke confidently, as though no one would dare question her words.

Carly had been so absorbed in her own thoughts during the church services that she had forgotten that Sister Brown had approached her in the hallway. "Yes." Carly remembered now. "I told her I would be happy to do visiting teaching."

"That is wonderful," she drawled. Reaching into her bag she pulled out a piece of notebook paper and explained, "I'm the visiting-teaching coordinator, and I would like you to visit these sisters. We don't have a companion for you yet, but we're working on it. It's better that you take someone with you, so if you could ask your mother or a good friend from our ward, that would be great."

Carly glanced at the paper and recognized both names. "This will be easy," she told Sister Powers. "Jennifer Parker lives next door, and I would love an excuse to visit Sister Gayle."

"Good, dear. I knew we could count on you. I will get you a computer printout as soon as possible." Sister Powers raised her bag strap over her shoulder and stepped closer to Carly. She lowered her voice and placed her hand on Carly's arm. "I'm not one to pry, dear, but I also feel that I must warn you about your choice of friends. You have been gone for so long, and I'm sure you're still innocent when it comes to affairs of the heart."

Carly's mouth opened in shock but no words came out. The woman continued, "I'm sure that you've found a friend in Kolton Raywood, but I must warn you about him. He is an undesirable person, Carly. I know he seems to be fine, upstanding, and well liked, but he has done things to our family which are unspeakable."

Carly cocked one eyebrow and glared at the woman. "Sister Powers, I think that you may be mistaken—"

Sister Powers's voice instantly became stern and she took her hand off Carly's arm. "You have no idea, Carly. You were not here when my niece, Stacey, died, nor did you witness the hell he put that poor girl through before she gave birth to Kyle. And, Kolton will not even let us speak to Kyle."

Due to the intensity of Sister Power's words, Carly chose to keep her mouth shut. The woman was obviously convinced that Kolton had done something horrible.

"Carly, you come from a good family. We love Chad, and we're only concerned for you. Please be careful in your choices and know that we wouldn't want you to make any decisions that could cause you grief or heartache."

"Thank you. I'll take your advice into consideration." Carly offered the words, but she was only being polite. Sister Powers smiled and gave her a brief, stiff hug before she walked off.

Carly wished she had spoken her mind, but, truthfully, the woman had intimidated her. She settled into her car and sat still, thinking over what she'd just heard. She didn't want to believe the things that Sister Powers had said, yet she didn't get the feeling that the woman had been lying, so she could only assume—or hope—that there was a possibility that whatever had happened in the past with Stacey had been a huge misunderstanding.

Only Kolton had the answers she needed. The rumors were nagging at her, and she knew that she wouldn't have any peace of mind until she had resolved some of her concerns with him.

Making a quick decision, she pulled her car out of the church parking lot and headed toward Kolton's house behind the feed store. It took only minutes before she arrived, and she hoped that she hadn't made a mistake in dropping in to see him.

She parked her car in front of the house and waited for a moment as she took in her surroundings. The store and house had changed dramatically since she was a child. White vinyl siding had been installed on both. The wood-shake roof was gone, replaced with brown tile. The feed yard had been extended, and chain-link fencing had replaced field fencing around both buildings. A huge sign read "Raywood Feed," with the days and hours of store operation listed. The yards were immaculate, and Carly wondered how Kolton was able to take care of the store and house so efficiently.

Kolton's truck was parked by the side of the house, which confirmed that he was probably home. She took a quick glance in the rearview mirror to check her appearance and got out of her car. A cement walk led the way to the front porch, and the tap of Carly's sandals was the only sound she heard. Smoothing the front of her shirt and skirt, she tossed her hair back over her shoulders and knocked at the door.

A surprised and bedraggled-looking Kolton pulled open the door. His hair was a mess, he hadn't shaved, and he was dressed in a worn white T-shirt and faded jeans. Her heart flopped anyway.

"Well, hello," he said, raking a hand through his hair.

"I know I shouldn't have just dropped in on you like this," she apologized, "but I was worried when I didn't see you at church."

"I know," he answered as he glanced back at the couch. "Kyle woke up with an upset stomach, and I didn't think he should go to church."

Carly could see past Kolton to a blanket-covered figure on the couch. "Oh, is he sleeping?" she asked in a hushed tone.

"Yeah, he's a little weak from being sick." He stepped back and welcomed her in. "You're okay. Come on in."

"No, this isn't a good time. I hope it wasn't anything he ate at my house," she said.

"Probably not. I think it's just a bug."

"Well, I should go. We'll talk later," she decided.

"No, wait." Kolton ran a hand over his stubble and looked at his sleeping son, then finally said, "Hold on, I'll grab some shoes and come on out."

She nodded in agreement and he closed the door. She stepped out to the porch railing and studied the yard. There were no flower beds or hedges, but the lawn was beautiful. A big willow to her left gently swayed from the breeze, and a tire swing hung from the mulberry tree to her right. Kyle's bicycle had been dumped in the middle of the lawn, and she noticed a half-eaten apple on the table next to her. *What a peaceful, homey place,* she thought. There were two rocking chairs near the wooden table, but she chose to remain standing.

Kolton appeared, and she smiled inwardly at his appearance. He had apparently taken a brush to his hair and now wore brown leather slippers. There was something intimate about seeing him this way. "Is Kyle feeling better?"

"Yes. I called my mom this morning, and she told me to give him some apple cider vinegar in water. He pitched a fit about drinking it, but it really helped. He fell asleep just before you got here."

Carly made a face. "My mom used to make me drink that. If you put a little honey in it, it's not as bad."

Kolton nodded and looked out across the yard. He leaned against the railing, and Carly casually stepped a little closer to him. For a moment neither one spoke. Carly was first to break the silence. "I wanted to talk to you about something."

"I know," he said. "I figured that we'd eventually have to talk about it. You probably want to know about Leann and her ugly accusations against me."

"I'm sorry Leann treated you that way last night," she apologized. "You were a guest in my house, and she had no right to talk to you like that. I told Chad how I felt, but Leann was so upset she wouldn't talk to me. They weren't at church today, so I haven't talked to her about it."

Kolton didn't answer, so she continued. "I know it's your private business, but I don't understand why her family hates you so much—and nobody else will tell me anything about your past." The last statement fell out of her mouth before she could stop it. She regretted it immediately.

Kolton raised both eyebrows at her. "So, you've been snooping around asking about me?"

Nervously, she waved her hands as she spoke. "No, not like you think. I've just picked up on some comments made about you and, well, I just want to know more about what really happened. I've really enjoyed spending time with you, Kolton. And I've had fun getting to know Kyle too. I guess I just want to understand why Leann has a problem with you."

Kolton returned his gaze to the yard. He hated being in this position. He had been here many times before with other friends and family. His decision, from the time that Stacey had died, had been to keep his mouth shut. There was no one besides his parents that he had talked to about the events before and after Stacey's death. His mother had thought he was being childish not to share his side of the story, but Kolton firmly disagreed.

He had convinced himself that only guilty people defended themselves, and—knowing that Stacey's family still thought him guilty—he didn't want them to know how guilty he really felt. He knew that they had said their share of nasty things about him, but he had decided that he wasn't going to jump on their hate wagon and make the same bad decisions they had. From the very beginning he'd never talked in a negative manner about the Powers family or his wife. If he was successful in keeping Kyle away from them, he wouldn't have to. Some things were better left unsaid. Right or wrong, that was his decision, and no one—not even Carly, he decided—was going to convince him to deviate from it.

Without looking at her, Kolton asked, "Does our relationship hinge on me telling you my side of the story right now?"

Carly thought for a moment. "I don't know."

He faced her and locked eyes with her. "Yes, you do know, Carly. You wouldn't be here asking if it didn't mean something to you."

The lines in his face were taut and his eyes piercing. She grew defensive at the accusing tone in his voice. "Kolton, I didn't mean to imply anything. I simply want to understand what hap—"

Interrupting, he remarked, "I know, I know. You want to know if the rumors are true. Did I really kill my wife? Am I a terrible monster who is going to sweep you off your feet and then harm you? I don't know exactly what you've heard, but I have a good idea."

Carly folded her arms and retorted, "You don't need to be so dramatic."

"Dramatic?" Kolton raised his arms up in mock surprise. "Me?" Seriously, he went on. "You have no idea what my life has been like or the trials I have had to face since my wife's death."

"Kolton," Carly's said, trying to let go of her own defensiveness. "I'm not here to judge you. I realize there are always two sides to every story." He didn't comment, so Carly probed further. "I want to help you. You should have a chance to express your feelings about what really happened."

"You don't understand, Carly. I don't have a 'side.'"

Confused, she asked, "What do you mean? The Powers family is telling the truth?"

"What do you think, Carly? Do you think I'm capable of *'killing'* my wife?"

Carly shook her head and looked down at her feet. Kolton shook his own head in disbelief. "Well, judging from your expression, you have doubts," he charged.

She didn't like the increasing level of conflict between them. She had gone over there intending to discover some truths that would help her develop her relationship with Kolton. Her intentions had backfired. Kolton was agitated, and she was more confused now than ever.

Choosing to be blunt, Carly began, "I want to believe that you're the person that I remember you being. I want to think that you're not capable of the things people are saying."

"But you obviously don't believe I'm the person you remember me being, or you wouldn't be here now," he concluded.

"I will admit that there does seem to be some sort of dark cloud hanging over your head. If we are going to be friends, then I think you should be honest with me."

Kolton controlled his temper. He felt like lashing out at her, but he realized that it wasn't really her that provoked his anger. It was the entire situation, and the fact that it was still forefront in his life after all these years.

But Carly did need to respect his feelings now, and if she couldn't understand him or accept who he was, then their relationship wasn't meant to be.

Kolton spoke firmly. "Carly, think about what you're saying. You think I owe you an explanation for something that doesn't involve you. You're asking me personal questions that I don't feel obligated to answer. I don't owe you or anyone else an explanation for my past. Right now, you act like I have to admit something in order for our relationship to progress. But I don't feel that my choice not to discuss the past has anything to do with me being honest with you now, in the present."

Carly simultaneously felt ashamed and indignant. She knew she didn't have any right to ask about his personal affairs, but she also disagreed intensely with his last statement. A friendship required different levels of honesty than a dating relationship, and she wished she could make him understand that she felt their relationship had possibilities of growing beyond friendship. She had assumed that the comfortable and secure way she had felt the previous night was an indication that their relationship had potential. She thought she'd sensed that he felt the same way before Leann interrupted their night, but perhaps she had jumped to conclusions.

"Fine. I think I understand," she said dully.

"Carly, you don't. I can tell that you're offended." Kolton pushed his thumbs into his pockets and walked the short length of the patio away from her. He reached the end and stopped. He didn't feel like he was very good at expressing his emotions, but he wanted to clearly explain why he didn't believe that all relationships he started should focus on resolving this one element of his past.

He turned around slowly to face her and explained, "I don't want to be judged for my past. And I don't want to be condemned for something I didn't do. My policy is to forgive and forget. But nobody else seems to share my opinion."

"I do want to understand, Kolton, and I'm sorry that you have had so much turmoil in your life," she said sincerely.

"Thank you," he acknowledged her honesty.

Silence followed. Neither one knew what to say next. Kolton didn't want to lose his chance to get to know Carly, but he wasn't prepared to delve into the past just yet. He didn't know how to express to her how painful the past was for him.

Carly felt uneasy. She realized she had moved too fast, assuming that Kolton would confide in her concerning the most intimate details of his life. She offered him a weak smile. "Well, I guess I better get home. I'm sorry I was so rude, Kolton. It wasn't my intention." Nervously, she began to talk more rapidly. "I hope Kyle gets better soon. Don't forget to try the honey with the apple cider vinegar."

She moved to escape down the porch steps, but in two swift strides Kolton was next to her, gently holding her arm. "Carly, don't leave like this."

She looked into his eyes and wished he would pull her into his arms, that the comfortable feeling between them would return. But instead, she hid her vulnerability and gave into her pride. Looking downward, she solemnly said, "I'm sorry, Kolton, but I really should go."

He released her arm and stood aside. He paused for a slight moment and then said, "Alright. I'll see you later?" There was a hopeful, questioning look in his eyes.

Without another word she hastily stepped down the walkway. She got halfway to her car before turning around. Kolton was watching her intently. She spoke carefully. "You may think that this is all your private business, Kolton. But it does affect the people that care about you most. And you don't have to go through all of this by yourself." For a moment they looked at each other, but when Kolton didn't respond she turned and walked out to the driveway. Then she slid into her car, feeling his gaze still on her.

Kolton didn't know what to say—she sounded like his mother, and he resented it. He didn't want to be saved or told what was best for him. He didn't expect her to understand his wishes concerning sharing his past, so she would have to make her own choices and follow her heart. If she decided to believe the gossip rather than trust her heart or the Spirit, then he was resigned to facing the consequence of losing her. As her car left his property, he prayed that she would give him the chance to prove that he was a better man than she'd ever hoped.

* * *

Carly could feel Kolton intently watching her as she pulled out of his driveway. She didn't want him to know how upset she was. She felt as though something had just changed between them. A rift had formed, and she wondered how they would ever find enough common ground to continue the relationship.

To an extent, she could understand Kolton's reasoning. If he wasn't guilty of what the Powers family accused him of, then he surely didn't owe an apology or explanation to them or to anyone else. But something nagged at her. He had been more stubborn about his views than she had expected, and she felt he wasn't being totally honest. She couldn't explain how she knew it, but she sensed that he was hiding something. Whatever it was, he had made it clear that he didn't think it concerned her. But it did. It meant a lot to her to have total understanding and honesty in a relationship.

She drove home slowly. She needed a few minutes to herself to think about her life and the choices she was making. Taking a detour, she guided her car toward the Ballards' open fields. There were a dozen head of cattle grazing in the field, and Carly remembered how she used to watch them as a child.

She parked her car near the fence line and got out. Carefully stepping through the brush, she found a large rock to sit on. The breeze had picked up, and she tucked her hair behind her ears and looked out onto the field. The cattle grazed lazily. They had watched her intently at first, but now they realized she was no threat and continued browsing for lunch in the meadowlands.

Carly stared past the field, consumed with doubts. Her life had not progressed the way that she had hoped. When she was a young woman, she had thought that she would finish high school, go on to college, meet a handsome returned missionary, and be married in the temple. She would be able to stay home with her family and have her own house and yard. As a youth she had always wanted to live on a farm, and she still hoped that she could give that country lifestyle to her children someday.

But fate had taken a turn in her life, and her expectations had not been met. Instead of her life falling in place, step by step, she seemed to encounter road blocks and sharp curves, constantly knocking her off course. There were no guarantees in life and too many difficult choices. But she wryly concluded that the only bad thing about being in control of her choices was living with the consequences.

At one time she had thought that Adam was the perfect, ideal man. As a potential husband he was handsome, successful, and attentive. Perhaps Adam would have accepted the gospel someday, but it had been too big of a chance to take. She had lived a worthy life, and in her heart she knew that she deserved a temple marriage, and the blessings that it would bring to her family.

But there was always the nagging possibility that Adam would have changed if she hadn't left. She had truly loved Adam. It had only been a few weeks since she had left him, and she still wondered what might have happened if she had stayed with him. Perhaps he would have softened his views about her religion. Maybe she could have convinced him to come to church and investigate the gospel after all, if she had continued to press the issue. But, she really didn't know, and what if he'd simply done what she wanted to please her—without truly converting?

Kolton, on the other hand, already had the gospel in his life. There was something special about Kolton that she couldn't quite put her finger on. He wasn't as sophisticated or financially successful as Adam, but she was somehow more drawn to him. Carly had noticed from their brief encounters that he did have a problem of being impatient at times, but everyone had faults, she realized.

And his strengths seemed to outweigh Adam's. She loved how caring and loving Kolton was with Kyle; she felt that his actions with his son spoke volumes about his character. When he told her that Kyle was his first priority, she knew it was true. And she firmly believed that Kolton was more thoughtful and less self-absorbed than Adam would ever be.

When she looked deep into Kolton's eyes, she could sense the goodness of his spirit. Yet, the speculations and rumors that seemed to surface every time his name was mentioned were daunting—especially when there was so much that Kolton wouldn't tell her about his past. She didn't dare put her guard down when she was still so uncertain about what Kolton was hiding from her.

There were other obstacles with Kolton. He had been married before and had a son. That certainly hadn't fit into her life plan. She hadn't imagined herself being someone's second wife or becoming an instant stepmother. The role of mother was something she longed for, but she also knew that being a stepmother could be a huge responsibility. There would be so many challenges and adjustments to make, even if they got past the issues at hand. Carly sighed heavily. She was getting ahead of herself to even imagine that she and Kolton would marry, but she couldn't help it—the thought was intriguing.

The breeze began to blow harder across the fields, and a gust of wind pulled at her skirt. She smoothed it down and decided to go home before her parents started worrying about her. The drive home was quiet, and her parents' car was parked in the driveway. She stepped cautiously into the house in case her parents were resting—it was common for them to have lunch and nap afterward. Then she shut the front door softly behind her and walked into the kitchen to get something to eat.

There was a ham sandwich on the counter covered in plastic wrap, and a note beside it. The note was in her mother's handwriting:

> *Carly, a young man called for you. He didn't leave his name. We had sandwiches for lunch. Love, Mom.*

Carly instantly wondered if perhaps Kolton wanted to talk to her and make amends. Maybe she had been worrying too much. She should have more faith in Kolton and her own intuition. She smiled, grabbed her sandwich, and headed to her room to rest.

After a bit, she realized she couldn't sleep, so she ate, changed clothes, and read awhile, waiting for her parents to get up. She was anxious to finally talk to her mother about the incident with Kolton and Leann. Finally she heard muffled voices, so she came from her room, calling out, "Mom, are you up?"

"In the kitchen, Carly," her mother called back.

Walking into the kitchen, Carly began, "You will never believe what happened Saturday night. Leann and Cha—" Before she could get the words out, she nearly bumped into her parents and Chad standing close together near the door. Chad's face was drawn, and his eyes were swollen and red. Carly's parents looked shocked and sad.

"What is it?" Carly asked, suddenly concerned.

Her parents looked at Chad, and her father said gravely, "Leann had a miscarriage this morning."

The room fell quiet. *No wonder they weren't at church,* Carly thought, guilt sweeping over her. "Is she okay?" Carly asked.

Chad swallowed hard and explained in low tones, "Her mom is at the house with her. We figured something might be wrong yesterday when she began to spot, so we came over here to ask Mom about it. When she wasn't here, we decided to go back home. Leann was okay until she woke up this morning with some cramps."

Carly's anger at Leann had quickly dissolved, replaced with compassion for her sister-in-law's loss. Raymond put an arm around his son and offered what comfort he could. "Chad, the Lord knows what you and Leann are feeling. He loves you, and He is aware of your pain, and—for whatever reason this happened—be assured that He is looking after you and Leann."

Chad's voice cracked. "I know, Dad. It's just so hard." Chad took a deep breath and fought back his emotions.

"Honey," Emma tried to console him, "your father is right. But it's okay to mourn over loss. There is no way to replace your baby." She hugged her son, and they both cried.

Carly couldn't help but feel choked up. As angry as she had been at Leann, she would never have wished this on her. Her eyes filled with tears. "I'm so sorry, Chad. Is there anything I can do?"

Before Chad could answer, their mother said, "Why don't you fix some dinner, Carly, and we'll follow Chad home to check on Leann. If she doesn't feel like coming over to eat, we'll send some dinner over for her." They all nodded in agreement.

"Do you have my keys, dear?" Raymond asked his wife.

"They're on the kitchen table. Oh, and don't forget to change your shoes. You still have your slippers on," Emma said.

As their parents prepared to leave, Chad slipped by Carly and went out the front door to his car. Carly followed him to the porch. "Chad," she started, "I am so sorry. Please tell Leann that I'll be thinking of her."

Chad gave her a weak smile. "I'll let her know. Thanks, Carly."

She knew this wasn't the time to discuss last night's scene, but Carly felt as though she should say something. Chad noticed the concern on his sister's face and reassured her. "Don't worry, Carly. We'll talk later."

Carly's parents left quickly, following their son down the driveway. Carly stood on the porch momentarily, and then went in to start dinner. It didn't seem overly helpful, but she wanted to do something. Any service she could do for Leann would help to ease her own conscience.

Carly realized that if Chad and Leann had thought there was something wrong with the pregnancy Saturday, it would explain why Leann had been so sensitive and moody, and therefore so prone to take it out on Kolton with his unexpected presence. Her words and actions had still been hurtful and unnecessary, but what Carly knew now did clarify why she overreacted and confirmed Carly's thoughts that such behavior had been out of character for Leann.

Hurriedly, Carly grabbed some chicken out of the fridge and some salad ingredients. She could whip up a chicken salad and possibly have time to make some quick brownies. The phone rang as she was washing her hands, and she hoped it was Kolton. It would be good to be able to explain Leann's behavior of the previous night, and once they discussed Leann's condition, she hoped it would open the door to resolve some of their contention over Kolton's silence.

Anticipating Kolton's voice, she answered cheerfully, "Hello?"

"Hello, Carly."

For a moment she was startled. The voice was familiar, but it obviously wasn't Kolton.

"Carly, this is Adam."

"Adam." Carly's voice wavered. "How are you?"

"I've been thinking about you, and I thought we could talk. Did your mother tell you that I called earlier?"

"Yes, I was out. She left me a message."

"Did you get my flowers?" he asked.

"Yes, I did." Remembering her manners, she said, "Thank you."

"There's something that I wanted to tell you."

"What is it?" she asked pointedly, searching for a bowl to mix the brownies in.

"I have some good news to share with you. I was made partner." He paused a moment, as if waiting for Carly to comment, but her only response was silence. Adam continued, "It's been great, but very time consuming."

"I'm glad for you, Adam." Carly was sincere. "I know how much you wanted it, and I think you'll do a great job. How is Jean and the rest of Matthew's family?"

"Good. The office is doing great. We've been just as busy as always. I have more responsibility now, but it's worth it."

Carly shook her head at his own self-absorption. Adam was obviously still the same man. His lack of concern for others was more apparent to her now than ever. He had a one-track mind—focused on his career and his own aspirations.

Carly continued to prepare dinner as they talked. She decided to pin Adam down on his reason for calling. "Adam, surely you didn't track me down just to tell me about your job."

"No, I didn't," he admitted. "There is something else I think we should discuss."

Carly remained silent and waited for him to continue.

"I've been thinking about you a lot lately. I guess I still miss you, and I wanted to make sure that you were okay."

"I'm good," she said. "I have great job, and I'm spending time with family and old friends." She was slightly tempted to mention Kolton, but she disregarded the somewhat immature impulse.

"Good. How's work?"

"Great. I love being the secretary for the elementary school. I've had a lot to learn. I still haven't mastered the whole routine, but I have great help."

"You know, the firm is still looking for another secretary. If you ever want a job here, there will always be an opening for you."

Carly was perplexed by his offer. "Adam, you know why I left. I assumed you would realize why I couldn't come back." Her voice was firm, but not angry.

Adam paused. "I miss you," he admitted. "Everyone in the office misses you. They all tell me I was a fool to let you go. At first I decided that you were right, that we didn't have enough in common, but . . . Carly, I could never find anyone to measure up to you." Adam's voice was soft and caring. "Carly, I'm sorry. Really, I am. I didn't want this to happen to us."

Carly didn't like the emotional turn this conversation was taking. She didn't want to discuss her feelings with Adam now, not when she was already confused about her relationship with Kolton.

"Adam," she responded, "I can't talk right now. My sister-in-law just had a miscarriage, and I'm making dinner for her. Maybe we can talk later."

"When?" he questioned.

"She lost the baby this morning. My brother came by a little while ago to tell us."

"No," Adam explained, "I meant, when can we talk? I would like to talk to you as soon as possible."

The extent of his insensitivity was unbelievable to Carly. Her tone became short and tense. "Well, I don't know. Tonight will probably be bad. Perhaps we can talk in a day or two. I'm usually home in the evenings."

"Okay. I'll give you a call tomorrow night."

"Fine," she said flatly.

"Good-bye, Carly."

"Good-bye." She quickly turned off the phone and laid it on the counter. Her disgust with Adam eventually faded and curiosity replaced it. *Now he wants to talk about our relationship?* She really didn't feel as though she owed him anything, but she wondered why he was having second thoughts about her. She also wondered if she had enough regard left for him to have second thoughts about their relationship. Either way, she couldn't deal with one more emotional ordeal tonight. Their conversation had only confirmed her conclusion over the past few weeks that Adam was a selfish man, and she no longer wanted to waste her time thinking about him. She put more effort into finishing the salad and concentrated her thoughts instead on Chad and Leann.

Chapter Seven

Carly's parents didn't arrive home until after dark. She was pulling brownies out of the oven when they entered the kitchen, looking tired.

"So, how is she?" Carly asked.

Her father was the first to answer. "She's pretty distraught. She's weak too. Her mother is trying to convince her to go to the doctor in the morning, but she's refusing to eat anything tonight."

Emma filled in some details. "Chad and Leann decided to stay home since Leann's mother is there. Leann wasn't feeling up to coming over and insisted she wasn't hungry. We talked to Chad for a while and then decided we should give them some privacy. They'll need some time to get over this. So I guess it's just us for dinner."

"I made enough salad for an army," Carly said. "I guess we can take some over tomorrow."

"I'll do that," Emma offered. "Thanks, dear. I'm sure you wanted to go over and see Leann, but we appreciate you doing this."

Carly was silent. She really hadn't wanted to go and see Leann, but she knew it was her own guilty feelings keeping her away. She had been harshly judgmental, and she knew that she would eventually have to talk to Leann and completely resolve the anger that had begun to fester in her heart.

They sat down and ate dinner with little conversation. The usual teasing and joking at the table was absent. No one had much to comment on. After dinner Carly offered to clean the kitchen and wrap some of the leftovers for Chad and Leann. Her parents accepted gratefully and went to bed. As she washed the dishes she called

Jennifer to chat. She needed to vent her feelings, and she needed someone as a sounding board.

Jennifer said she was grateful for the distraction. Her older boys had given her youngest son a red marker, and he, in turn, had colored himself and two of her kitchen cupboards before she discovered the weapon of mass destruction. It had taken some time, but she was finally able to scrub the cupboard doors and her son clean. She was exhausted, due to her pregnancy, and needed to rest. So she'd curled up on the couch to talk to Carly while her husband read bedtime stories to their boys in another room.

"So catch me up on your life, Carly. I wanted to talk to you at church today, but I was so busy I didn't have time."

Carly realized church had been only that morning. She couldn't believe that so much had happened since she had talked to Jennifer last. She began with her date with Kolton, and told Jennifer everything from Leann's intrusion to her warning from Sister Powers, the conversation she had with Kolton, Leann's miscarriage, and then the phone call from Adam. Jennifer listened intently and didn't comment until Carly was finished.

"I am so sorry for Leann. I'll have to call her tomorrow. Tell your mom that I'll call and have the Relief Society arrange to take some meals in."

"My mom said Leann doesn't have an appetite tonight, but I'm sure she'll feel better tomorrow."

"I'm sure that she's depressed right now. I know that they were thrilled to have this baby. They've been trying since they got married."

"I am so glad I chose to come home. I want to be here for my family when they need me."

"I'll definitely go and visit tomorrow." Changing the subject a little, Jennifer commented, "I wouldn't judge Leann too harshly for her words to Kolton—especially now that you know why she was already upset when she got to your house."

"I know, Jennifer, but you should have seen the hate in her eyes. It disturbed me that she was so upset. From her reaction, you would have thought that Kolton was a dangerous criminal."

"I know that there are bad feelings there, Carly, but I don't think you should make any judgments based on that. I certainly can't."

"Do you believe the gossip about Kolton?" Carly questioned.

"No, of course not. I've known Kolton as long as you have, and I don't think that he's a bad person. But I do think there's been some sort of terrible misunderstanding. Leann has a good family, and I don't think that they would say those things unless they really believed them."

Carly agreed, "I've had that thought too." Inquisitive as to how others perceived Kolton, she asked Jennifer, "What do you really think of Kolton?"

"Well," she mused, "I like him. He's appealing in a rough sort of way. He's always very polite and sincere. Kyle can be a handful at times just like my own boys, but I see Kolton really trying to be a good dad. It would be hard to be a single parent. But you know, Carly, it doesn't matter what I think of Kolton," Jennifer said. "What matters is what you think of him."

"I know," Carly admitted. "But I don't understand why he won't confide in me. I want to be with him more, but after our talk today, I have even more doubts."

"Well, don't forget to consider Kyle. He's a big part of the package."

Carly had thought about Kyle a hundred times over. She thought he was generally darling. Sure, he was naughty sometimes, especially at school, but she felt that he acted up for attention. She didn't believe he was malicious or mean.

"I know," she agreed, and then changed her mind. "Actually, I don't know. I don't know how to raise a child, and I don't even know if I'll see Kolton again. How do I have a relationship with someone who won't open up to me?"

"Carly," Jennifer reminded her, "you had one date. You certainly can't expect Kolton to act as though you're a couple. It takes time to build up trust and confidence."

"You're right. I know I'm jumping the gun." But when she was with Kolton it didn't feel as though their relationship was new; it was exciting, but comfortable.

"What should I do now?" she asked Jennifer.

"I don't know," Jennifer laughed. "I'm not a relationship expert—I married the only boy I ever dated."

Carly sighed wistfully. She wished that her life was simple enough that she could say the same. "Thanks, Jennifer. It always makes me feel better to talk to you."

"Call me anytime you feel like it. Your life is far more interesting than mine. What are you going to do about Adam? Do you think he'll call?"

"Truthfully, I don't know." Carly realized that she wasn't focused on his call. Weeks ago his voice alone would have given her hope. Now, it only added to her confusion over men, and she didn't know if she even wanted him to call back. She wasn't sure what Adam really wanted, and she wasn't sure that she wanted to know.

After saying good-bye, Carly hung up the phone and finished cleaning the kitchen before retiring to her room to reflect on the day's events. She prepared her clothes for the next day and tried to read, but she couldn't stay focused, so forcing her mind to relax, she finally drifted off into a restless sleep.

The entire week turned out to be exhausting. Carly couldn't sleep well, and work was tiring. There were so many little things to learn, and she still hadn't figured out the school computer program. Laura was a huge help, but Carly was growing frustrated. By Thursday, although she hadn't heard from Kolton, she had dodged several of Adam's phone calls by checking the caller identification and letting the answering machine pick up the messages. The messages were short, and simply said he would call back the following night. Tonight she knew she would have to answer the phone when he called. She couldn't avoid him forever.

She had a feeling that Adam wanted to discuss their past and possible future relationship. But she didn't want to discuss it—at least not now. There were too many other things in her life to worry about. The previous night she had gone to visit Chad and Leann. Both were still hurting over the loss of their baby, but fortunately they were leaning on each other to get through the difficult time, as opposed to other couples Carly had known who drew apart when experiencing pain.

The three of them had talked for two hours about the baby and their hopes that they would still be able to have a family in the near future. Carly was grateful to be a part of their life. It felt good to be home and support her family in their problems. She didn't realize how much she had missed living away from home. Before she left their home, Leann gave her a reassuring hug, and Carly instantly felt more at ease. She hoped they could work out their differences and become close friends.

Apart from the problems of her brother and sister-in-law, Kolton was on her mind constantly. She tried to not spend every waking moment thinking of him, but it seemed she couldn't help herself. She remembered every facet of their date and how good it had felt to talk and share her feelings with him. The image of how disheveled he had been on Sunday made her smile. Somehow, although she still didn't really know him, he had worked his way into her heart. She was still trying hard not to jump to conclusions about him one way or another, and she was hoping he'd call to talk.

The work day finally ended, and Carly was grateful there was only one more day in the work week. The last bus had left and teachers were beginning to leave also. Laura had already gone home, but Carly still had to file some papers and make a couple of phone calls to the district office. As she shuffled through her papers, Kyle suddenly appeared at the front desk.

Worried, Carly asked, "Kyle, what are you doing here? Did you miss your bus?"

The boy looked around nervously and nodded his head.

"What happened?"

"I lost my new lunch box and I couldn't find it. I looked in the lunch room, and I looked on the playground . . ."

"And when you couldn't find it, it was too late. Your bus had already gone," Carly finished for him.

"Yeah," he mumbled. "I still can't find it."

"Well, I guess you'll have to call your dad."

"Or you could take me home," he suggested.

"I think we should call home first." Carly motioned for him to come around the desk. "Do you know your phone number?"

Kyle nodded. She handed him the phone, and he punched in the numbers. Carly noticed his hair was ruffled and his clothes were dirty from playing on the playground. The knees in his pants were worn and covered with dust. Carly smiled at the thought of him playing at recess with his friends. They both waited, but Kyle replaced the receiver without speaking. "He's not answering," he explained.

"Do you have any idea where he is?" Carly asked.

The boy shrugged. "Maybe he's out delivering stuff."

Carly smiled warmly. She thought all children could be adorable, but Kyle's mannerisms were especially endearing to her. "Do you know your grandma's phone number?"

"Yeah." He dialed the number and waited. Again, there was no answer.

"Don't worry about it, Kyle. I'll take you home myself." Carly was glad for this opportunity. She could drop Kyle off at the feed store and maybe coincidentally run into Kolton.

"Okay," Kyle said cheerfully.

Then she said, "I need to finish some work first, but it should only take me a few minutes. Would you like some quarters for the soda machine?"

Kyle smiled widely and put out his hand to accept her offer. Giving him the money, Carly instructed, "Get me a Sprite, and then you can have whatever you want, okay?"

He dropped his backpack where he stood and ran out of the office. Carly glanced down at the open backpack and noticed what looked like a lunch box inside. She picked up the bag and pulled out the box, examining it. *Why did he lie about his lunch box?* It suddenly dawned on her that he had wanted her to take him home. She smiled, put the box back into the backpack, returned her attention to her filing and tried to finish her work quickly. Kyle brought her soda back and sat on an empty chair in the office. It was the same chair he often sat in to wait for the principal. He sipped his drink politely, and his legs swung in the chair.

"So, Kyle, how have you been?"

"Good."

Fishing, she asked sweetly, "How is your dad?"

"Good."

"Do you think your dad will be upset when you don't get off the bus?"

"No."

Concerned, she asked, "Why not?"

He sighed and shrugged his shoulders. "He's busy working."

Carly finished straightening the office and quickly made her phone calls. Lastly, she called the feed store and waited for the answering machine to pick up. She left a brief message that she would be bringing Kyle home, just in case Kolton heard the message before he began to worry.

Carly grabbed her purse and dug around in it for her compact and lipstick. Kyle watched her intently as she straightened her hair and touched up her makeup.

"I have a mom in heaven," he said, softly and simply.

She was caught off guard. Replacing her things in her purse, she asked, "What?"

Clearly, he repeated. "I have a mom, but she can't live with us."

Carly felt a bit awkward and at a loss for words, but gave him a reassuring smile. "I know, Kyle. And I'm sorry that your mother can't live with you."

Kyle nodded and then said hopefully, "Are you going to marry my dad?"

Again, Carly wasn't sure what to say. "I like your dad, Kyle. But right now we're just friends." Kyle nodded that he understood and gave her a smile. She smiled back and grabbed her belongings. "Get your backpack so we can go."

Kyle rose and did as she said. He followed her outside and jumped into the front seat of her car. At first they rode in silence. Carly wasn't sure what to think of his question, and she was beginning to wonder if she was making a mistake by taking Kyle home. She felt uneasy, so for lack of anything else to say she asked him about his BB gun. He told her that he hadn't been shooting for a while, and then began to tell her about his new baby chicks. The rest of the way to his home he chatted and kept Carly entertained. By the time they neared the feed store, she felt comfortable with him again.

As she drove closer to the feed store, she noticed a cloud of dust on the gravel road in front of her. She recognized the speeding vehicle as Kolton's delivery truck just as she pulled into the feed store driveway after him. He parked next to the store, and she parked in the adjoining gravel parking lot. He jumped out of the truck and approached her car. She could see the obvious concern on his face.

"What's going on?" he asked as his son crawled out of Carly's car.

Carly rolled her window down but stayed seated. She turned the engine off. "Hello, Kolton," she greeted him warmly. "How are you?"

With a polite nod, he answered, "Good." He looked hard at his son. "Why weren't you on the bus? I rushed home to meet you."

Kyle pointed at Carly. "She gave me a ride home. I lost my lunch box, and I missed the bus looking for it." Kyle turned to Carly and waved. "Bye," he said, and headed to the house.

Kolton called after him, "Hey, young man, what do you say?"

Kyle yelled back, "Thanks."

"You're welcome. Bye, Kyle," Carly yelled back.

Kolton watched his son enter the house. He looked slightly embarrassed. "Sorry about his manners. I'll catch up with him later."

Carly waved her hand dismissively. "It's no big deal. We tried to call you, but there was no answer."

Kolton pulled off his baseball cap, ran a hand through his hair, and replaced the cap. He hooked his thumbs in his front pockets and squinted in the daylight. "Sorry about that. I'm a bit shorthanded right now. I usually make my deliveries by three, so I'm home when Kyle arrives at the bus stop. I can't afford to pay someone to answer phones right now."

Carly nodded understandingly. She caught herself admiring his features and deliberately looked away.

"Thanks for bringing him home."

"You're welcome. It's no problem." Carly debated whether she should tell Kolton about the supposedly missing lunch box, and decided to mention it. "I have to tell you that Kyle's lunch box is in his backpack."

"What?" Kolton thought for a moment, and then he guessed, "Do you think he purposely lied to get a ride with you?"

"I don't know for certain," she said. "He may have overlooked it. I really don't know."

"I'll have a talk with him. I don't want him to think he can deliberately lie just to get his way. I know he enjoys spending time with you, but he can't get away with being sneaky and dishonest."

Carly nodded her approval, although she was a bit flattered to know that Kyle liked her enough to want to spend time with her.

Kolton took a step forward and smiled down at Carly. "I'm sorry we disagreed on Sunday. I've been meaning to call you, but I thought you might need some time to think things over."

She had been hoping that he was thinking of her as much as she was thinking of him. "I'm sorry we argued too. I didn't mean to pry into your life. As a friend I had no right to assume that you owed me an explanation."

"Carly," he began, but she interrupted him.

"Kolton, I want you to know that I'm really sorry that I doubted you. I usually don't listen to gossip."

"Thanks Carly. I'm sorry if I was overbearing." He looked out across the yard and said thoughtfully, "I get a little defensive and argumentative sometimes."

"Well, I get pushy and a bit too nosy. Actually, you handled yourself great. Leann is in the wrong. I haven't had a chance to discuss it with her since her miscarriage, but I—"

"What?" Kolton broke in. "She miscarried a baby?"

"Yes, she lost the baby Sunday morning."

Kolton's face turned white. "I didn't even know she was pregnant."

"She was only a few weeks along. She and Chad are handling it pretty well. My folks have been going over every night to visit with them."

Kolton's jaw was set tight, and his eyebrows were drawn down. He listened intently.

Carly continued to explain, "I can't imagine how difficult it would be to lose a baby. Chad and Leann both have strong testimonies of the gospel, and it has to help them put things into perspective."

Kolton asked, "Is Leann okay? I mean health-wise, is she going to be alright?"

"Yeah, she seems to be. She finally went to the doctor yesterday. I think she was putting it off because she was so upset." Carly noticed Kolton's worried expression. He seemed so genuinely concerned— almost overly upset. "She's going to be fine," Carly assured him.

But Kolton seemed to be consumed by his own thoughts, so Carly asked, "Are you okay?"

"Yeah," he answered abruptly. "I have to go. Thanks for dropping Kyle off. I have to help him with his homework and get back to work."

He stepped back from the car. Surprised at his sudden shift in mood, Carly smiled hesitantly. "Alright. I'll talk to you later," she said hopefully.

Kolton waved and turned. He walked briskly to his house. She watched him as she started her engine and backed out of the driveway. He jumped the porch steps two at a time and didn't look back again to wave before slipping inside the house. Carly felt a sudden loneliness creep into her heart.

Her heart and mind didn't agree. Her heart felt impressed to pursue Kolton and give him a chance, but her head told her to avoid the heartache of trying to date someone with so much emotional baggage. She just couldn't tell what haunted him or how serious it was. Finally she left and drove home.

Her mother was in the kitchen preparing an early dinner. "How was your day?"

"Alright. How was yours?"

Emma took a quick glance at her daughter and noted, "Judging by the look on your face, I think my day was better than yours."

Carly sat down at the table and leaned her arms on the tabletop. "It's been a long day."

Emma grabbed some vegetables off the counter, a bowl, and her cutting board. She sat at the table across from her daughter to chop vegetables for a salad. "How do you feel about spaghetti and salad for dinner?"

"That's fine," Carly answered absently.

Emma raised an eyebrow at her daughter, "Well, you must have too much on your mind. I thought spaghetti was your favorite dinner."

Carly wanted to express all her fears and doubts to her mother. She wanted someone to understand how lonely she was with everyone around her being married and content. But the words wouldn't form, and Carly just stared blankly out the kitchen window.

Emma waited patiently, but when Carly didn't speak up, she shared some news instead. "Sarah Raywood called today and invited you to choir practice. She said that you had shown some interest."

"I did," Carly admitted. "And I do want to join, but I just haven't had the time. They practice on Thursday nights since there are four wards using the building on Sundays. But I've been staying late every day at work trying to redo some of the old files and introduce a new filing system. It's a lot of work now, but it will make everything easier next year. Once I get a handle on it I'll try to be at practice."

Emma nodded her head and changed the subject. "I went to see Leann today."

"How is she?"

"She's doing better. Her mother took her to the doctor yesterday, and he confirmed that she's going to be okay. She and Chad are already talking about trying to start a family again in a few months."

Carly nodded. "I was over last night," she explained. "She looked good, and she and Chad didn't seem so upset."

"It takes time, but you eventually come to terms with life's disappointments," Emma said as she sliced an onion and had to dab at her teary eyes with her sleeve. "Oh, that's a strong one."

Carly chuckled. "I can tell from here. Remember when I was a kid and I rubbed onion juice in my eyes accidentally? It stung so badly I thought I was going to go blind."

Emma again used her sleeve to wipe a tear from her cheek. "With all things that are terrible, we eventually find relief." Her mother smiled, adding, "The pain in your eyes eventually went away. And the pain of losing a baby for Chad and Leann will eventually dwindle. It will always be a sad memory, but they will move on and things will look brighter."

Carly remained quiet, so Emma tried again to get her talking. "Leann and I had a good discussion about last Saturday night."

Carly's eyes widened. "What did she say?"

"She said that she was really upset to see Kolton here. I honestly didn't realize how bitter she was toward him."

"You should have seen her, Mom. She was so rude. I've never seen her that upset before."

Emma looked her daughter straight in the eye. "Don't you think some of her emotional intensity was from the fear of losing her baby?"

"I do," Carly assured her mother. "I don't want to be overly judgmental. I'm sure that Leann wouldn't have treated Kolton so badly if she hadn't already been upset."

"Leann told me that she feels bad about her behavior. She wants to apologize to you and Kolton. Chad has convinced her that she needs to be supportive of your relationship regardless of her own feelings."

Carly thought for a moment, wondering what Leann knew, or what she thought she knew, about Kolton. "Well," Carly confided, "it doesn't really matter. Kolton is hardly talking to me. I went over on Sunday to talk to him about Leann's accusations, and he became defensive. I guess he's pretty tired of having to face it, year after year."

"I can't blame him. Unfortunately for Kolton, he seems to be a bit ostracized—although I think he does bring some of it on himself."

"What do you mean?" Carly inquired.

"When Stacey died, Kolton was heartbroken. But he wouldn't let anyone help him. The entire ward wanted to comfort him, help with the baby, and befriend him, but he wouldn't allow it. He just stayed with his folks and pulled away from Stacey's family."

"Yeah, but weren't they accusing him of her death?"

"Yes, but everyone knows enough about Kolton to know that he didn't kill Stacey. Her family would like to blame Kolton for her unhappiness, but I think even they know it's not entirely true." Emma developed a serious, thoughtful expression. "Kolton was so doting on her."

"Do you know anything else?"

"Oh, I remember some of the things Stacey's family said, but I've forgotten most of them. It wasn't my place to judge. As you know, your dad and I were away in Maine with you helping to take care of Grandma for a while, so there were a lot of things that I didn't hear until after we returned to Bridger. I do remember how devastated he was at the funeral—we were here visiting Chad at the time." Emma finished slicing the last of the vegetables and wiped her hands on a dishtowel. "He had a new baby, no wife, and a business to run. He had already taken over the feed store by then, and he didn't have much help."

"I've noticed that he does a lot on his own." Carly observed. "He still doesn't have any employees at the store."

"He is fiercely independent," Emma confirmed. "Sometimes his parents help out, but they're getting along in years. He's the baby of the family and all of his siblings live out of town. He acts as though he has something to prove. I don't know if I'm right or not about his personality, but I know he won't accept any assistance. Sister Gayle used to be a part-time cashier for his parents and for him, but even she's not working there anymore."

"Sister Gayle?" Carly asked, surprised.

"Oh, yes. Sister Gayle practically raised Kolton. In their early years she babysat all of the Raywood kids whenever their mom needed a sitter. Even now he sometimes sits with her in church, especially since her husband died a few years ago. I think Kolton was always her favorite Raywood child."

Discussing Sister Gayle reminded Carly of her Church assignment. "Sister Gayle is on my visiting teaching list. I really need to give her a call and go visit her."

"Oh, you should," Emma encouraged. "I'm sure she would love to have you over anytime."

Emma rose and put the salad bowl on the counter. She began to clean up her mess and asked, "Carly would you mind watching this sauce? I'm going to lower the heat, but I don't want it to boil over. The pasta is already cooked. I just need to go out to the garden and move the sprinkler."

"Sure, Mom." Carly rose and took the wooden spoon her mother handed her, gently stirring the sauce. Carly figured if anyone knew Kolton well, besides his family, it would be Sister Gayle. *Perhaps she could shed some light on the truth of Kolton's past,* Carly thought, feeling guilty about talking to anyone but Kolton, but also annoyed by his stubborn refusal to defend himself. As soon as her mother walked out the back door, Carly grabbed the phone and the ward directory.

* * *

Sister Gayle was thrilled to have Carly over. She had insisted that Carly come to visit as soon as possible, and they set a time for early Saturday morning. Friday seemed to be the longest day in history for Carly, but Saturday morning finally dawned. The day appeared to be bright and warm, so Carly put on a pair of denim shorts, a pink T-shirt, and a pair of leather sandals. She wore little makeup and had pulled her hair back into a ponytail.

Her parents were both up early to work in the yard, so Carly ate a quick breakfast alone before she left the house at nine. She had a million questions she wanted to ask Sister Gayle about Kolton. She had lain in bed until after midnight, wondering how she was going to work such delicate questions into their conversation. There were so many details she wanted answered, but she also didn't want Sister Gayle to feel like she had to betray any confidences.

The ride to Sister Gayle's house was refreshing. Carly rolled the window down and let the warm air blow through the car as she turned up the radio. As she directed the car into Sister Gayle's gravel driveway, she felt as though she were ten years old all over again. The little neighborhood was older, but most of the houses on the lane were still well kept. Sister Gayle's small, stucco house was familiar, as was the yard. Her lawn was neat and tidy, and cottonwood trees surrounded the house. There were a few shrubs along the front of the house and some decorative rocks, but not much else had changed.

As Carly walked up to the chain-link fence, a small white poodle jumped off the front step, barking wildly. Unsure whether she should venture into the yard, Carly held her ground. The dog was small, but her bark was fierce.

"Don't mind Pumpkin, Carly," a quavery voice came around the side of the house. "Come back here. We'll visit in the backyard."

"Good morning. She sure is a spunky little thing," Carly observed. The dog continued to bark, following Carly along the fence to the side of the house. At the corner of the house the chain-link fence ended, and the backyard was fenced separately with four-foot field fencing attached to railroad tie posts.

"Oh, that old rascal is more bark than bite. She's just like me—she has no teeth. We're a fitting pair, the two of us." Sister Gayle held the gate open, and Carly walked through, laughing.

Sister Gayle's voice was a bit slower than Carly remembered. She wore a pale mint housedress, dirty white tennis shoes, and pink plastic curlers in her hair under a light pink scarf. "She's my watchdog, and she keeps me company. She earns her keep."

Carly was amused by Sister Gayle's appearance—she reminded Carly of her own grandmother who had died many years before. She thought it was endearing how older women were so comfortable wearing curlers when most women her own age probably didn't even know how to wind their hair around them. Despite the age gap between them, Carly felt completely relaxed with the older woman. She slowed her pace to keep in step with Sister Gayle and followed her to the back patio where there was a covered porch with a wooden picnic table that was lined with seed packets, vegetable starts, and gardening supplies.

"Are you planting a garden?"

"Well, it's about that time, I suppose." Sister Gayle approached the table and picked up a rake that was leaning against it. "I was just going to go out and rake up the ground."

"Here," Carly offered, "let me get that for you. Would you like me to help with your garden?"

"That would be wonderful, Carly. Thank you." She handed Carly the rake and pointed to a pair of gloves. "Go ahead and put those on. That old rake has been left in the sun so often it's full of splinters."

Carly obediently did as she was told and asked, "What's first?"

Sister Gayle started walking out to the back of the property. "Well, let's prepare the ground." They crossed a small lawn and more gravel driveway that led to her deceased husband's workshop. Toward the back of the property there was a small orchard and a garden space that appeared to have been recently tilled.

"Your soil looks rich," Carly said in approval. The natural soil of the valley was known to be slightly sandy and lacking in nutrients. But Sister Gayle's soil was dark and moist. *Unfortunately*, Carly thought, *it also smells like fresh manure.*

"We just tilled it up earlier this week after we put down some fresh compost, manure, and grass clippings." Carly wondered who the "we" she referred to was, but didn't interrupt, as Sister Gayle had more to say. "All we need to do now is rake it smooth. I have a bundle of soaker hose to lay down afterward, and it works just fine. We'll plant everything in rows, going north to south. I'll set the taller vegetables in the back, and the smaller ones in front." She motioned with her arm where the plants were to be set in the ground. "I'd like to get the tomato plants in, but I worry about a late freeze."

Interested in the garden, Carly forgot her question and began to smooth out the soil with the rake. Dirt filled her sandals, so she shook them off and worked barefoot. As she worked, she spoke, "My mom just put her tomato plants in this week. Today she and my dad are going to plant the rest of the summer garden and get started on some bedding plants for the front beds."

"Your folks have always had a beautiful yard. I never cared too much to work outdoors. All of this was my husband's hobby. If Paul wasn't in the workshop, he was in the garden. Of course, it's a lot smaller than when he was alive. I just can't keep up with it anymore."

Carly looked at the garden boundaries. "It's still pretty big. You could probably cut it in half for just yourself."

"Oh, I'm sure I could, but I share it with Kolton Raywood."

Carly's heart skipped. "With Kolton?" she asked, trying to sound casual.

"We have a deal," Sister Gayle explained. "Kolton and Kyle till the ground, plant the plants, and help keep the weeds pulled. I do the watering, some weeding, and the harvesting. We share the bounty, and we're all happy."

Carly smiled. "That sounds like a good arrangement." She kept working as Sister Gayle looked on.

"Oh, yes," Sister Gayle agreed. "But I know what he's up to. He plants this garden just so I have to come outside and busy myself. But I pretend to go along like I don't know. He's a good man."

Yes, he is, Carly thought. Turning to face the older woman, she inquired, "If he usually does the planting, then why are you doing it?"

"Well, Carly, I'm not." She smiled slyly. "You are."

Carly laughed. Sister Gayle had planned this visit well. Taking advantage of the opportunity, Carly asked, "Do you know Kolton well?"

"He's like a son to me—he and Kyle are both like family."

"Kyle is a character, isn't he?" Carly prodded.

"Oh, he's a good boy," Sister Gayle answered in a grandmotherly tone. "Kolton does his best with the boy, but it's difficult to grow up without a mother. Of course, the boy can be a rascal, but he has a good heart like his father."

Sister Gayle watched Carly work in silence for a few moments, and then mentioned, "If Stacey were alive today, I think that Kyle might be better behaved. But there's no use wondering what might have been. We all have to move on."

"Did you know Stacey well?"

The older woman shook her head and frowned slightly. "No, unfortunately, I didn't. I know she was having a bit of trouble adjusting to life here. She spent most of her time with her aunt and cousin, Leann. She was from the city, and I understand that the only reason she agreed to live here was because Kolton was here. She knew that he loved this town and he wanted to raise a family here. I believe that she would have liked to go to college, but she loved Kolton and was willing to sacrifice her own plans for him and their family, even though the rest of her family seemed to think she should follow her dreams."

Carly took a break, leaning on her rake as Sister Gayle continued, "She would have done anything for Kolton. Even at the end—when they were arguing—I think she wanted things to work between her and Kolton, and she would have loved Kyle. Her untimely death was a great tragedy."

"How did she die?"

Sister Gayle thought for a moment before continuing. "She died in childbirth—there were complications due to her early labor. No one knows the whole story, Carly. I suppose that in time the hard feelings between Kolton and Stacey's family will dissolve. With good friends and a new start someday, I think Kolton and Kyle will be fine."

Carly wanted to ask more questions, but Sister Gayle changed the subject. "You're doing great, Carly. I think we are ready for planting."

"We could bring the plants and seeds over now." Carly agreed. "We'll need a hoe for the seed rows and a small shovel. Do you have a wheelbarrow that I can use to move all the plants at once?"

"I do. It's over by the shed, but you can wait for that." She turned to walk toward the house, saying, "I can hear the dog barking. Kolton and Kyle must be here. They were going to come to help with the planting."

Carly froze. *Kolton is here? Now?* With an effort, she resumed raking and wondered if Sister Gayle had purposely arranged her visit so that she would be there when Kolton arrived.

She worked quickly, waiting for Sister Gayle's return. The entire area was finally smooth and ready for planting after another ten minutes. Carly looked toward the back porch, but no one was there. She decided to go knock at the back door and tell Sister Gayle that she needed to leave.

Leaning the rake against a fruit tree, she gathered up her sandals and walked barefoot to the back porch. As soon as she stepped onto the cement patio, the back screen door opened, revealing Kolton with a large glass of lemonade.

Carly's heart tumbled at the sight of him. She looked for a welcoming sign from him. His eyes revealed nothing, but a faint smile graced his lips.

Carly was the first to speak. "Hello, Kolton."

"Carly." He nodded politely.

He reached out to hand her the drink, and she gratefully accepted. She didn't realize how thirsty she was until she took a sip. "Thank you. This is great," she said taking a long drink.

"Thank Sister Gayle. She's in the house making more with Kyle."

Carly held onto the glass and nervously traced a finger around the rim. Kolton moved to the edge of the patio and looked out toward the garden.

Carly joined him and explained, "I came to visit and offered to help. I didn't mean to take over your garden—Sister Gayle told me that you share it with her."

"Yeah, it works out for both of us."

"I think it's really nice of you to do so much for her."

"Well, Kyle really likes to come over. It's like having an extra grandma."

"I always loved her when I was little too." Carly felt like he was being humble. Not many men would do so much to help an elderly widow, she realized.

Kolton continued to stare out into the yard, but said nothing. His mind was racing to find the right words to say to Carly. He had made a decision about their future the night before, but he realized it was going to be difficult to follow through with it. He had a strong urge to gather her in his arms and hold her, instead. He tried not to look at her for fear that his resolve would weaken.

Carly's face was flushed and smudged with dirt. Her hair shone in the sun, and her eyes were bright. He knew it was going to be difficult to ignore his attraction to her, to avoid her—but he had to. He should have found a way to make peace with Stacey's family years ago, but he had allowed the bitterness to linger, and now it was affecting the one person that he was beginning to develop deep feelings for. He thought of Carly every day and night—her sweet personality, the slight tilt of her nose, the way her hair swung across her back when she walked, and the way she bit her lip when she was nervous.

He had to be careful. He didn't want to hurt her. If he made her a part of his life, he would be making his problems hers. It would cause conflict between her and her brother's family, and she would be a target of gossip and speculation. He cared for her too deeply to cause her such pain or grief. She deserved better in her life.

Carly was becoming uncomfortable in the long silence. She looked at Kolton's profile and yearned to reach out and hold his hand, to tell him how much she cared, but she resisted the temptation and made small talk instead. "It's beautiful weather we're having."

Kolton nodded in agreement and folded his arms to his chest. "Carly, there's something we need to talk about."

Carly waited anxiously, but Kolton kept his gaze outward. Prodding him, she said, "If it's about your past, it's okay. I won't bother you about it anymore." Feeling courageous, she suggested, "I think we should start over."

This is going to be more difficult than I'd thought, Kolton realized miserably. Forcing out the words, he announced bluntly, "I don't think it's a good idea that we see each other anymore."

Carly's heart sank. *He can't be serious,* she thought. Disbelieving, she asked, "What do you mean?"

Never looking at her face, he explained, "I just want to make sure that we're on the same page. We are friends, and I think things would get too complicated if we pursued any other relationship."

"Oh."

Carly moved to a post on the porch and leaned against it to put on her sandals. She remained silent, but her mind was reeling. She knew that she had felt chemistry between them and that they had a chance for something more. She hoped maybe he was teasing or just protecting himself and that maybe he would reconsider.

She stepped over to him and faced him toe to toe. He glanced at her face briefly, then looked away. He gave no indication of wavering in his decision. She reached for his hand and held it in hers. "I'm sorry for the trials in your life, Kolton. I'm sorry about what happened at my house with Leann, too. But it shouldn't affect you and me."

Kolton pulled his hand away gently and avoided her eyes. His voice was sincere but cool, "I'm sorry, Carly. I think it's best that we stay friends. I just think you deserve better than the problems a relationship with me would bring you."

Carly shook her head. "No, Kolton," she protested. "Your past doesn't need to be an issue."

"But it is, Carly. I'm serious about this. I want to be friends, but I can't offer you anything more."

Embarrassed, Carly bit her lip to hold back the tears. She nodded that she understood. "Are you sure?"

Without hesitating, he answered firmly, "Yes."

"I guess I'll see you around then," she said uncertainly.

Kolton nodded curtly and Carly asked, "Will you please tell Kyle and Sister Gayle good-bye for me? I need to get going."

"Sure."

"Good-bye, Kolton."

"Good-bye, Carly."

She held her head high and walked away. Hot tears threatened to surface but she fought them back. These feelings were familiar, but stronger. She had been heartbroken to lose Adam, but deep down in her heart she had known all along that Adam wasn't right for her. Kolton was different; she was so drawn to him physically, emotionally, and even spiritually. She knew that he was a strong member of the Church and lived the gospel worthily. The more time that she spent with him, the more she looked forward to seeing him again. There was so much she wanted to learn about him. All she wanted was for him to let her into his heart and open up his feelings to her. She wanted to share his problems. She had prayed about his past and his problems, and she felt at peace that Kolton was a good person. She knew they had the potential to be a great couple, if he would give them a chance.

Carly was even becoming willing to let his desire not to discuss the past slide. She wouldn't judge him or condemn him—she would even be willing never to ask about his past again. She just wanted to be a part of his life. The realization that he wasn't willing to allow her that chance was devastating.

Kolton felt the same pain he could see in her eyes. He watched her slim frame as she walked around the edge of the house and waited to hear the gate shut. The sound of metal hitting metal confirmed that she was gone. The sense of loneliness that overcame him was unsettling. He said a prayer in his heart for strength in his decision. He had made the move to give her up, and he would now have to face the consequences. Kolton knew it was going to be difficult, but he felt it was best for her sake.

Chapter Eight

Carly drove around town, unwilling to go home. If she was home she knew that she would just hide in her room and let all her bottled-up emotions escape. She didn't want to wallow in self-pity. She was too angry at Kolton to cry over him. He was being selfish, and she couldn't understand why. She sensed that he had deep feelings for her, but if so, why was he denying those feelings?

Was he worried about her finding out the truth of his past? What was he hiding? She had spent her whole life preparing herself spiritually for marriage, and she was ready. The only problem now was finding the right groom. She had truly hoped that she and Kolton could spend time together to see if they were compatible. She gripped the steering wheel hard and drove around the valley for an hour before she felt calm enough to go home.

As she drove up the gravel road to her parents' house, she noticed a strange black car parked in her spot. She parked next to her parents' sedan and walked over to inspect it. It was a new BMW with Nevada plates. She didn't know anyone who owned such an expensive car—except one person, she thought. She frowned, hoping that her suspicion was wrong.

Stepping cautiously into the house, she heard laughter from the kitchen and called out, "I'm home."

The laughter subsided as she entered the room. Her parents and a guest were seated around the kitchen table finishing lunch. It was Adam.

"Hello, dear," her mother greeted her. "We just had lunch. We saved you a turkey sandwich and some potato salad."

Carly's eyes locked with his. He was confident and handsome as usual, but her gaze remained indifferent and steady. Ignoring her mother's offer, she looked at their guest and questioned, maybe a bit too harshly, "What are you doing here?"

Adam wiped off his mouth and, using all his charm, grinned at her. "You haven't been available for my phone calls, so I thought I would drive out for a visit."

If I'd known you were going to come out here, I would have just answered the phone, she thought dully, but said aloud, "Well, I've been really busy."

Adam said, "Your parents have been very friendly. I had a nice tour of your mother's beautiful garden. She has exquisite flower beds."

Emma blushed, and Carly resisted the urge to roll her eyes. Adam continued, "Then your dad showed me around the house, and we had a good debate about ever-increasing gas prices."

"It's a crime," her dad stated. "This country is being robbed. The oil manufacturers are holding us hostage and getting richer every day at our expense."

Adam sympathized, "It's a shame you have to pay more for gasoline when you live in such a rural place. But this is a wonderful town. I can understand why you chose to raise a family here."

Her parents nodded in agreement. They both appeared to be quite taken with Adam, despite everything she had told them about him.

Carly stared at him in disbelief. She recognized a con when she saw one. Carly couldn't think of one past conversation with Adam where he had shown even close to this much concern for someone else. Adam only put on this face when he had something to gain. *What is he trying to pull?* she wondered.

"Also, your parents were telling me more about the gospel. They have cleared up a few misconceptions that I had. I'm impressed— they're well versed."

Carly's father instructed him, "Keep reading the scriptures and you'll be amazed how easily you develop a love and understanding for them."

"Thank you, sir. That's good advice," replied Adam.

An uncomfortable silence ensued. Picking up on Carly's indignation, Emma announced, "I need to get back out to the garden. No use wasting such a lovely day." Raymond noted his wife's cue and picked up his empty plate, reaching out to take hers. They both left the table, and he deposited their plates in the sink. Emma refilled their glasses with water, and they both headed to the back door.

"Thank you for a lovely lunch." Adam smiled widely at Emma.

"You are more than welcome. It was a pleasure to meet you."

"Yes," Raymond agreed, "it was a pleasure."

"Thank you, sir."

Carly threw her parents a hard glare. As soon as they were gone and the door securely shut, she allowed her displeasure to creep into her voice. "What are you doing here? You have no right to show up at my house and intrude on my parents unannounced."

"Carly," he said soothingly, "I'm sorry. I just felt I needed to come see you. At the least we can be friends. I have some good news to share with you."

"Really?" she asked sarcastically. "Did another senior partner die and you moved on up the totem pole another notch?"

Ignoring her cutting remark, he tossed his napkin on his plate and rose. In a few steps he was standing face-to-face with her. She couldn't help but notice his designer jeans and well-tailored button-down shirt. He did know how to turn an eye.

His voice was solemn. "I've made a decision to investigate the Church."

"My church?" she asked incredulously.

"Of course. I've had a change of heart." His voice turned smooth as satin, and his eyes softened. "You were a good influence on me." He reached out and held her shoulders in his hands. She stiffened, but he continued. "I'm sorry I made fun of your religion. I told you on the phone that I missed you, and I really do, Carly. I would do anything to prove that to you."

He leaned down to kiss her, but she turned her head away. As he brushed her cheek with his lips, she challenged him, "Even join a church?"

He dropped his hands and faced her with a scowl. "I'm hurt that you would think that, Carly. I really am sincere. I've given it a lot of thought, and I'm willing to learn about your church."

Carly rested her hands on her hips and decided to call his bluff. "Have you had the missionaries over yet?"

"I haven't taken the opportunity yet since I've been so busy at work. But I'm willing to have them over at their convenience."

"Have you attended a church service yet?" she continued.

Adam looked away and licked his lips nervously—a gesture Carly had seen a million times. It was an idiosyncrasy that came out when he was upset or trying to think fast.

She looked at him expectantly, and he explained, "I've only recently experienced this change of heart, Carly. I was hoping that you could guide me and help me understand all my options. I knew that you could give me solid advice since your convictions are so strong."

She marveled at how smooth he was—too smooth. In an instant, she realized that she had reacted just like her parents when she first met Adam. With all his charm, funny comments, gracious compliments, and apparent tenderness, he had appeared to be a perfect man. It wasn't until they had a major disagreement on their living arrangements that she had felt uncomfortable around Adam. He didn't share her moral standards, and there was something else about him—an emotional dishonesty she couldn't quite pinpoint before. He didn't have a strong spiritual strength or a compassion for others. He was always putting himself first, no matter what the cost to other people involved.

Witnessing his demeanor around her parents had confirmed her suspicions. She could now see through his facade. He was purposely endearing—when he had a goal to accomplish. Now that he was reconsidering his feelings for her, she had become his target of interest. His goal was to impress her parents, and apparently he had achieved his aim.

"I hope you wouldn't fake an interest in the Church just to win my affection," she said. She couldn't believe he was being honest.

Adam flinched slightly at her bluntness. "I told you on the phone how I feel, Carly. I miss you. I was hoping that you felt the same."

For an instant she doubted her own judgment. He did appear sincere, and unfortunately, he seemed to have become more handsome in her absence. She folded her arms to her chest and searched her heart for an answer. She had missed him desperately in the beginning. But now those feelings had faded—it was Kolton's presence in her life. He had left a permanent impact on her heart, and she couldn't deny it. She knew she couldn't settle for someone like Adam anymore.

"Adam, your visit has caught me off guard," she said. "I don't think I still have the same feelings for you. We've been apart for weeks, and in the time away from you I've changed my opinion of you. I'm not the same trusting woman I was. I see you in a different light now."

He nodded. "I realize that I hurt you, Carly. I am sorry. I was hoping we could start over."

Unwilling to commit, she moved away from him to lean on the counter.

He smiled warmly and cocked his head to the side. Her countenance softened slightly at seeing the familiar gesture, and he jumped at the opportunity. "I would like to take you out to dinner, Carly. Could I come back this evening?"

Carly looked at the floor. Her body was tense, and she instinctively felt like declining. To gain time she changed the subject. "Were you planning on staying all day?" she asked.

"Actually, I'm spending the night. I'm staying at the bed-and-breakfast."

Carly nodded. The "bed-and-breakfast" was a private residence that a local widow ran to make extra money. There were only two or three rooms, but the service was good, and it was the only place in town to get a room for the night.

"Adam," Carly confessed, "I've had a bad day, and I don't think it would be a good idea to go out—"

Adam stepped close to her and interrupted her softly, "It's okay, Carly. I'm sorry I dropped in unannounced, but I came to spend time with you. If today is bad, then I will come by tomorrow. What time do you go to church?"

"Our meetings start at nine, and we're out at noon. Perhaps we can talk after church."

He considered the idea for a moment and then smiled contentedly, "Good. I'll see you tomorrow."

"Okay, I'll see you tomorrow," Carly said. She walked him to the door and closed it as soon as he had walked outside. Relieved that he was gone, she leaned back on the closed door and shut her eyes. Her day was gradually getting worse. First, Kolton had tried to get her out of his life, and now Adam was trying to persuade her back into his.

Both men were attractive in their own ways, but they were extremely different. She knew that she had the strength to sever a relationship with Adam. She had done it before, and she would do it again. Kolton was a different story. Her heart ached to think that he didn't want her in his life, and Adam's attentions did little to compensate for that loss. She made up her mind to tell Adam tomorrow that there was no chance for reconciliation.

Carly stayed home that evening, avoiding her parents. She didn't want to discuss Adam's arrival. In the morning she awoke early to get ready for church. She realized she was still grumpy from her confrontation with Adam, and wanted to be fully awake before she saw her parents. She dressed in a light summer dress and sandals, brushing her hair straight. After finishing her makeup, she was completely ready to go when she entered the kitchen for breakfast.

Her father sat at the table, reading the newspaper. "Good morning, honey. Did you sleep well?"

"Yeah," she mumbled. "The nights are getting warmer."

Her mother stood at the stove, cooking eggs and frying bacon. "The days are getting warmer too. Today is supposed to be over eighty." She flipped an egg and turned to Carly. "Are you hungry?"

"Not really," she said as she opened the refrigerator and pulled out some orange juice. "Thanks." She grabbed a glass from the cupboard and sat across from her father at the table.

"Your father has already eaten. I have plenty left."

Carly hesitated for a moment and then accepted, "Oh, okay. I'll have an egg and a couple slices of bacon."

Raymond folded up his paper and tucked it under his arm. "That's a woman for you," he teased. "You can never make up your mind."

Carly bantered, "No, we're just not quick to make rash decisions."

"Even when it comes to the heart?" he smiled at his daughter.

Carly gave him a direct look. "What's that supposed to mean?" she demanded, realizing that her extra alone time hadn't done much to calm her mood.

"Raymond," Emma warned, "mind your own business."

Ignoring his wife, he commented, "That was a very handsome beau you had come calling yesterday."

"Dad, Adam is not a beau. He is a friend."

Her tone had been firm, giving him the impression that the issue was not to be discussed. Both her parents looked at her, surprised by her aggressive attitude, but no one said anything else.

Carly remained silent while her mother delivered her plate to the table and sat it in front of her. Raymond stood up and carried his plate and glass to the sink. Giving his wife a playful pinch, he teased, "I wasn't a rash decision, was I?"

Emma smirked at her husband. "You'll have more than a rash if you pinch me like that again."

Raymond laughed as he walked out. "I'm going to get dressed. We'll leave in twenty minutes."

Emma started washing dishes, calling out, "We'll be ready."

Carly ate in silence, hoping to avoid any more conversation. She had tossed and turned all night, thinking about Adam and Kolton. She truly hoped that Adam would investigate the Church, and hoped that it would be a new beginning in his life, but her feelings for him had dissipated. She hadn't realized it until she had seen him, but it was true. It was amazing how differently she looked at him now.

"Carly," her mother interrupted her thoughts. "Will Adam be coming over today? You're welcome to have him for dinner if you want."

"No thanks, Mom. He might stop by after church, but that will be all. I doubt he'll be staying for dinner."

"Well he certainly is a nice-looking young man, and very charming. He said—"

Carly knew how easy it was to be swayed by Adam's charms. She cut her mother off. "Don't forget why I left him."

"I know, honey. But he did show an interest in the Church," her mother reminded her.

"He did—and I really hope that he's sincere." She looked at her mother's encouraging expression. "Mom," she explained, "I don't regret leaving Adam. For a while I had doubts, and I was really sad when I first came home. But I don't think he's changed at all. I don't trust that his newfound interest in the Church isn't just a ploy to win me over."

Emma joined her daughter at the table and looked at her earnestly. "Well, then, I think you're wise to follow your instincts. Your father and I enjoyed meeting him, but he was trying very hard to win our affections." She paused, and then said slyly, "If you're no longer interested in Adam, then I'll assume that you *are* interested in Kolton."

Carly kept her eyes locked on her plate and fought to control her emotions. Her voice trembled as she confided in her mother. "He doesn't want to see me anymore."

"No!" Emma exclaimed. "Why not?"

Carly shook her head. She really didn't want to get upset before church. "I don't really know. I guess it's too hard with the families not getting along."

"Did Kolton say that?"

"He said I deserved better than being caught up in the problems he has with his past."

Emma tried to console her daughter, "He may see things differently over time. You're still friends, right?"

"I guess so," Carly whispered.

"It's not like you were already dating seriously, Carly. Kolton could have a change of heart. But I can see how frustrated you must be. Even if the argument between Stacey's family and Kolton isn't the reason why he doesn't want to see you, I hope the Powers family decides to let go of this grudge. Kolton needs to let go of it too. Nobody progresses spiritually when they refuse to forgive. Stacey certainly wouldn't have wanted this hatred between her loved ones."

Carly nodded in agreement. She believed her mother was right, but she didn't know how to remedy the situation. Emma glanced at her watch and jumped up. "I have to finish getting ready." She leaned down and wrapped her arms around her daughter. "Trust in your faith. I'm sure you will make the right decisions, and things will work for good."

Carly sighed heavily. After her mother left the room, she said a silent, heartfelt prayer that everything would work out for the best.

As her mother had predicted, the day was warm and bright as they drove to church. A swift glance around the parking lot confirmed that Kolton's truck was there. They entered the chapel for sacrament meeting, and Carly caught Kolton's eye. He immediately looked away when he saw her. Her heart sank as she followed her parents and sat down a few pews in front of Kolton and Kyle.

She didn't want to believe that their relationship was truly over. The prelude music was ending, and Carly felt a light tap on her shoulder. She looked up to see Adam standing above her with a wide grin.

Shocked, she questioned in a loud whisper, "What are you doing?"

"Do you mind if I sit down?"

Carly reluctantly scooted closer to her parents, who each smiled a greeting at Adam. He sat close to Carly and rested his arm behind her shoulders. "Adam, what are you doing here?" she repeated.

He smoothed his silk tie. "I'm coming to church, Carly. I told you that I'm interested in your religion."

Carly glanced at his well-tailored, charcoal-colored suit, red silk tie, and Italian leather shoes. A few members of the congregation smiled knowingly at Carly. *This is not good,* she thought angrily. She didn't want anyone to assume that Adam was her steady boyfriend. A man like Adam was going to be the center of gossip for the entire day.

Knowing that they were in Kolton's direct line of vision, she tried to inch away from Adam to make it clear that she was not willingly sitting so close, but there was no room left in the pew. Adam leaned down to her and whispered in her ear, "Tell me about this meeting."

Before Carly could speak, the bishop rose to the podium and began the meeting. Throughout the rest of the meeting, Adam whispered thoughtful questions, but Carly only gave short concise answers. And his arm never left the back of the pew behind her. His forward approach was gnawing at her nerves.

When the meeting concluded, Adam asked, "Where do we go now?"

"We are going outside to talk," she said firmly.

Without a word to anyone else, she led Adam out to the foyer and through the glass doors. She stood with her back against the doors, Adam facing her one step away. Folding her arms, she blurted indignantly, "What are you doing? Why do you keep showing up unexpectedly?"

He put his hands on his hips. "Carly, I told you that I'm willing to investigate your church. Why can't you believe that? That meeting just now was great."

Carly had to admit that the speakers had been very good, and she had felt the Spirit in the room—despite her growing irritation with Adam. "Adam," she began, "I don't know what you want from me."

Adam reached out to stroke her cheek, but she pulled away. "Carly," his voice grew firm, "I want to try again with you. I think we made a mistake."

Carly held her ground. "No, Adam. I think we made the right choice." She looked into his eyes and saw the familiar signs of his temper rising. "I'll be blunt with you, Adam. I don't feel the same way about you that I did before." Adam pursed his lips. He looked upset and slightly confused. She took a deep breath and spoke more softly. "Adam, I think you're making a wise choice to investigate the Church, but I don't want anything more than friendship from you."

"There's someone else," Adam guessed.

Carly avoided his eyes and looked at the sidewalk. She wasn't about to explain that there was someone else, but that he wasn't interested in her.

"Is it that hayseed standing over there?" Adam asked directly.

Carly turned around, and over her shoulder she could see Kolton watching them from the foyer. He looked away when Carly turned, but she got the distinct impression that he was keeping a watchful eye on her and Adam. She faced Adam and explained, "He's a good friend. I've known him all my life."

Adam sighed and shook his head in disbelief. He showed no emotion other than irritation, and Carly wasn't surprised. Adam had never been overly sentimental with her. She didn't feel that he loved her as much as he liked the idea of being in love. His friends had liked Carly, and she was beginning to think that maybe he was here because he missed having her around for their approval.

"Adam," Carly said gently, "I want us to be friends. I don't want to argue about it with you anymore."

"I thought we had something special," he said.

"We did," she confirmed, "but it ended."

Adam's expression was sour, and he kept glancing over her shoulder to where she knew Kolton was standing. Carly reached out and rested her hand on his arm. "I did love you. I wanted to be with you, but we obviously have different ideas of what a good relationship should be like. I'm still getting over you, and I still care about you. I just see things differently now. Everything went smoothly between us until a time when you didn't get what you wanted. It was then that I realized that we're too different in our values and morals to have a relationship."

Adam nodded reluctantly. "What can I say?" he shrugged.

"I hope we can remain friends," Carly said.

He paused, and then agreed. "I guess you're right. When you left I was upset, but I thought everything would work out. I figured that I would move on and find someone else. But then I realized how much I missed you. I even missed your stubborn convictions. There are so many women willing to do anything to be with someone, and you're different. I couldn't quite see it then, but I see it now."

The sincerity in his voice tugged at Carly's heart. "I'm sorry, Adam. For what it's worth, leaving you really broke my heart. I wish things were different, but I feel like this is the right choice for me now," she explained.

Adam pulled his sunglasses out of his coat pocket and put them on. "Well, I will admit that I enjoyed your meeting. I didn't think I really would, but I did."

"You will always be welcome in the Church at any time," she said sincerely.

"Thanks, Carly. If you ever need anything, you know where you can reach me." He reached out to give her a hug and a gentle kiss on the cheek.

As he turned to leave, she offered, "Adam, you don't have to go. We can still go to church together—as friends."

He turned back to face her and confessed, "I thought I could come down to Bridger and sweep you off your feet, but the minute I saw you I could tell you weren't thrilled to have me here. I'm sorry that I interrupted your life. Whatever you have going," he glanced in Kolton's direction, "I hope that it works out for you. Thanks for the invite, but I think you have someone waiting for you."

Carly smiled kindly at him, and without another word, he walked away. She watched him walk around the building toward the parking lot. She felt relieved and grateful to have things cleared up with Adam.

Their confrontation had given her the closure in her life that she had needed. Now she just had to work out her feelings for Kolton.

By the time she returned to the foyer, most of the members had moved on to their next meeting. Kolton had left, but it pleased her to know that he'd been watching. Assured that Kolton still cared, she smiled inwardly. In time, she hoped to win his affection and discover what he was hiding about his past.

Several friends asked her about Adam before she left church, and she told everyone the truth—he was an old boyfriend and a new friend. There was nothing left to discuss, and she didn't offer any more information than that. She didn't see Kolton the rest of the morning. She didn't know if he had been avoiding her or if their paths just hadn't crossed.

When the church services were over, Jennifer caught up with her in the parking lot, smiling broadly, "You sure know how to stir up the gossip around here!"

"Really? What did you hear?"

Jennifer laughed. "Like you don't know! Tell me that was Adam and not an entirely new boyfriend."

Carly nodded. "It was him. We had a good talk, and I think we're going to be okay just being friends."

"How do you feel about that? He's very cute." Jennifer added hastily, "I don't mean that a relationship can be based on appearances only, but he is far more handsome than I had even imagined."

"He is handsome," Carly agreed, "but you're right. Appearances aren't everything, and when I saw him again I just knew that he wasn't right for me. I mean, I already knew that, but seeing him again confirmed it."

Jennifer smiled and leaned toward her friend. "Well, I think you have other admirers to keep you busy."

"I wish. Kolton won't have anything to do with me."

Jennifer rolled her eyes in the direction of the parking lot. "He seems to take notice of you from a distance."

Carly glanced at the spot Jennifer had indicated with her eyes and saw Kolton standing in a group of men, talking. He had been looking in her direction, but immediately glanced away when she looked over.

After church, she stayed home with her family for dinner. Chad and Leann came over, and there was a peaceful feeling between everyone. Carly had decided to make a friend of Leann and dismiss the earlier incident with Kolton. She grieved for the loss of Leann's baby, but there was more to Carly's forgiving attitude than just compassion. She didn't want to be a part of the kind of intolerance that had eaten at the Powers family and Kolton for so many years.

Carly decided to ignore the differences of opinion that she and Leann had, and move on with their relationship. Chad appeared to notice that they seemed to be getting along better, and after dinner he asked Carly to join him out on the porch swing while Leann and their folks watched television.

Chad sat down first and motioned for Carly to join him. "Have a seat, sis."

Carly sat down and gazed out at the horizon. The sunset was beautiful. Waves of red and orange hues and streaks of lavender filled the horizon. She leaned back and softly rocked the seat. For a few moments neither one spoke.

"You know, Carly," Chad began, "I appreciate all your support lately."

"I can't imagine how you two feel," Carly said sympathetically. "I don't think I could handle losing a baby."

Carly noticed that Chad looked confused at her statement. "What? Did I say something to upset you?"

"No, no," he insisted. "It's not that."

Carly looked at her brother more closely. Tears were forming in his eyes, and he looked away from her.

"Chad," she said softly, "whatever it is, you can tell me."

He laughed softly and smiled. "You know, I never thought about us growing up and being adults. I always looked at you as just my pesky little sister. Now we're all grown up and having adult conversations."

Carly didn't know what to say, so she waited for her brother to compose himself. "Leann and I have been having some problems," he began. "Actually we've had this same problem in our marriage for a while. I can't handle her attitude toward Kolton. Her whole family hates him." He paused. "Well, I guess I wanted to talk to you about the whole Kolton incident."

Carly interrupted him before he could continue, shaking her head. "No, I don't want to talk about it. I don't want to cause problems with you and Leann, and I don't want to argue with her. I'm really starting to like her," she confessed.

"I've noticed. She feels like she's found a friend in you too. I wanted you to know she feels bad about the incident with Kolton. She would take it all back if she could."

"I know. And I think that her physical and emotional state played a part in her actions."

Chad nodded his agreement.

"I'm not going to judge her, Chad. Whatever her reasons were, they're hers. I have a different opinion of Kolton, and we'll just have to agree to disagree."

Chad smiled. "Your attitude about this has left a big impact on Leann."

"Really? How?"

"Well, the Powers family have all been so wrapped up in their own personal views that they don't really remember what happened eight years ago."

Carly remained quiet, listening with interest as he continued, "It's just my opinion, but I think now they're starting to see things differently—at least Leann is. For so long she only heard from her family how terrible Kolton was. There was always a family member around who was willing to lay some blame on him—whether he was deserving of blame or not. I became tired of all the backbiting and harsh words they said about Kolton when we were dating, and it only seemed to get worse after we were married."

"How has it changed?"

Chad smiled ruefully, "It seems that Leann's family is confused at how someone could love Kolton. After all, for years they've all agreed that he's some kind of monster. This is the first time Kolton has had a close woman friend since his wife's death."

"They think I care for Kolton?"

Chad threw her a sidewise glance and raised his eyebrows. "Well, you two might be the last to admit it, but you obviously feel something intense for each other."

Carly blushed faintly. She wouldn't admit to anything, but she didn't deny to herself that she liked him and could love him, if given the chance.

"Anyway," Chad's voice turned more serious, "the whole family and even the community respects you. They know the kind of person you are, and I think they can feel in their hearts how good you are."

Carly smiled warmly at her brother. They had never before talked so frankly with each other. She kept swinging contentedly and continued to give Chad her full attention.

"What I started out to tell you is that all this contention between Leann's family and Kolton is tiring. It's caused a strain on our marriage and on all our family relationships." Chad swallowed hard and continued, "But now I can see that Leann is starting to soften toward Kolton. She doesn't want her mom to know, but she has started to agree with me about letting things go. She may only be making baby steps, but she's definitely progressing toward forgiveness."

"I don't know the whole story," Carly admitted, "and Kolton isn't willing to discuss it—as a matter of fact, he isn't very willing to discuss anything with me right now—but I've prayed about my relationship with Kolton, and I have a sense of peace. I know that Heavenly Father will guide me in the direction I need to follow. So, if I keep trying to stay worthy, I know that I'll be happy, whether I'm with Kolton someday or someone else."

"You wouldn't be happy with Adam," Chad stated.

"You didn't even meet him," she protested. "You only saw him at church today."

"I have loser radar," Chad teased. "He looked a bit pompous, and he stuck out like a sore thumb. He's definitely not your type."

"What is my type?" Carly was amused.

Chad had a serious glint in his eye. "Homegrown and down to earth."

Carly assumed he was referring to Kolton, and she silently agreed.

"Trust me, Carly. You would not be happy with Adam."

"No, I don't think I would. I had a hard time getting over him, but I think I'm now fully recovered from our breakup."

"Well, I hope that you can somehow make a difference in Kolton's life. I hope he sees how special you are and how beneficial you could be to Kyle and his relationship with Stacey's family. I'm hoping that this whole mess will be resolved soon. I can't go on with this anger and tension in my life. I don't take an active role in it, but it's definitely putting a strain on Leann and me."

Carly was touched by Chad's kindness to her. "I wonder why they all choose to hate instead of forgive," she mused aloud.

"I don't know." Chad seemed to be trying to remember something. "All I know is that the family speaks of Stacey as being some wonderful little angel. They thought she was marrying beneath herself when she married Kolton."

"I wonder why."

Chad looked a bit perplexed. "You know, I really don't understand it. But anyway, apparently she loved Kolton and insisted on being married. She was a bit younger than he was—I think she had just graduated from high school and moved out here with her family."

Carly absorbed every word. "Go on," she encouraged.

"Well, I remember someone once saying that Stacey had a full scholarship to college. She was very smart, and a gifted pianist. Her mother wanted her to go to a fancy music college in New York City."

"Really?" Carly was impressed. "She must have been very good if she was even considering a career in music."

"She was. The whole family thought she gave up her life to marry Kolton. But I remember things a little differently than the family remembers."

"How so?"

"According to the family, she never seemed very happy after they got married. But I saw her with Kolton when they thought they were alone, and she appeared to be very happy. To me it was when she was around her family that she never seemed happy. I think she felt torn between her family and Kolton. When Kolton realized the family didn't think he was good enough for Stacey, he was really offended. He made it clear he wasn't fond of her family either."

"So the family didn't like him from the start?"

"No, they never did get along. The family blamed Kolton for Stacey being so unhappy. They feel that Kolton dampened her passion for piano and kept her from furthering her education. I've never heard Kolton's side of the story, although I suppose he has one."

Good luck getting him to tell it, Carly thought.

"The real victim in all of this is Kyle," Chad surmised. "He has a whole family of relatives that he doesn't know."

"I've noticed how Leann and her family watch Kyle, but never interact with him."

"They don't dare. Kolton told the family at Stacey's funeral to back off and stay away from Kyle forever."

"Really?" Carly thought that sounded a bit drastic, but she considered what Kolton's feelings might have been like at the time. "Perhaps he was grief-stricken and not thinking straight. Besides, the family was apparently pointing fingers at him for causing Stacey's death. I'm sure he wasn't exactly rational at the time," she offered.

"See?" Chad confirmed. "You have a way of shedding a different light on Kolton's actions. He doesn't sound like a monster when you speak of him. Maybe in time, through you and Leann, her family and Kolton will forgive and finally forget.

"Whatever happens, I hope that Kyle can someday meet the rest of his family. He could benefit from their love." She thought on how she had assumed his naughty behavior at school was a cry for attention. She could see now why he might lack attention despite a loving father and paternal grandparents. The other half of his family was missing.

Leann called out from the house and Chad stood up. "I better go see what she wants." He gave his sister a sincere smile. "Thank you. It was good talking to you. Thanks for your influence on Leann."

"You're welcome." Carly waited for her brother to enter the house, then she slowed the swing as she thought about what her brother had said. She hadn't been aware that she was making a difference in Leann's attitude. Then she focused on Chad's concern for Kyle. Perhaps Kyle's welfare was the one thing that could make Kolton have a change of heart toward the Powers family. As the last bit of light left the sky, she vowed to herself that she wouldn't give up on Kolton, and that she would do whatever she could to bridge the gap between him and his in-laws. Maybe if he could learn to forgive and be forgiven, he could allow himself to love her.

Chapter Nine

Carly had decided to let some time pass before she made another attempt to visit Kolton. He had made it clear to her that he didn't want a relationship, so she was positive he wouldn't try to see her. And she had been right. A full month had passed since he had talked to her at Sister Gayle's house, and they had both kept their distance.

At church he would occasionally glance her way, but if their eyes met he would immediately look away. Carly hoped for the best. She was assuming that he was still interested—even if he was admiring her from a distance. She was called to serve as a teacher in the Relief Society and was grateful for the distraction from her personal life while she prepared her Relief Society lessons and kept herself busy with work and church service.

Gossip spread fast in Bridger, and it was becoming common knowledge that she and Kolton were not dating. Friends and co-workers tried to set her up with other men, but Carly politely refused every offer, although she did go out with some of her work colleagues to dinner and a movie a couple of times. It had been casual group dating, and Carly had enjoyed herself. Most of her spare time was spent at work catching up on projects, with her family, or with Jennifer and her family.

Every day she prayed for the Lord's guidance and direction concerning her relationship with Kolton. Something within her heart told her she still had an opportunity to grow closer to Kolton, and she hoped she could somehow be a part of his life—if not in a romantic capacity, at least as a close friend, and she didn't want to do even the slightest thing that might damage the chances of that. All she could do was to go about her life and have faith that everything would work out for the best. Her office work at the elementary school was becoming routine. She finally felt as though she had mastered the office computer programs, and she was building solid work relationships with her co-workers. The children could be challenging at times, but she was enjoying her job.

Every chance she got to see Kyle at school, she would try to talk to him, but he kept his distance just like his father. One day she caught Kyle staring at her over the office counter, but when she smiled at him and asked him what he needed, he became shy and quickly ran away.

The next day before school started, he brought her a picture he had drawn. "This is for you, Carly," he said as he handed her the picture.

There were three people standing in a row, and they were all holding BB guns. "Kyle, this is nice. Thank you."

He smiled proudly. "It's a picture of my dad, and you, and me."

"I love it. I'm going to hang it next to my desk where everyone can see it."

His smile grew broader. "Maybe someday we could go shooting again."

"I would like that, Kyle," she said sincerely. He nervously shuffled his feet, and then waved good-bye before he ran off.

"See you later," she called.

As she taped the picture to the wall next to her desk, she smiled to know that Kyle wasn't scared to show her that he liked her. *Well*, she thought, *he's smarter than his dad.*

One Saturday morning she awoke to the ringing of the telephone. Surprised that no one else in the house had picked it up, she glanced at her nightstand clock. It was after eight o'clock. She suddenly remembered that her parents had planned on leaving early that morning to go shopping. Reaching over her clock to the phone, she sat up in bed as she answered it.

"Hello." Her voice cracked, and she quickly cleared her throat.

"Carly?"

She recognized the voice immediately. "Sister Gayle?"

"Yes, dear. How are you? I hope I didn't wake you."

"It's okay. I need to get up." Carly sat up and shifted her night-gown. "How are you?"

"I'm good. I wanted to invite you to lunch today, if you don't have any plans."

A bit surprised, Carly stated, "I thought I was your visiting teacher. I'm supposed to plan visits with you."

Sister Gayle laughed. "Yes, well, I thought I would take the initia-tive. You can still count it as your visiting teaching appointment."

"Well, it sounds like fun. What did you have in mind?"

"Let's go to Lucky's Diner." It was the only restaurant in town besides the drive-in where most of the teenagers hung out.

Carly immediately responded, "I would love to."

"Good, Carly. I'll meet you there at noon."

"Thank you, Sister Gayle."

"Good-bye."

Carly hung up the phone and threw off the covers. She secretly hoped that Kolton would mysteriously show up, but after Sister Gayle's last attempt to have her and Kolton meet unexpectedly, she doubted that he would.

She was sincerely looking forward to her visit with Sister Gayle. Carly hadn't made the time to visit her elderly friend recently, and she always enjoyed her old teacher's wit and wisdom.

She got out of bed and took a shower. The days were becoming warmer, so she chose lightweight capri pants and a T-shirt. Carly left her hair down and only applied lip gloss. She noticed that her face was beginning to tan and her hair was lightening more in the sun, and she liked the summer look.

She spent the morning hours catching up on laundry and tidying her room. By the time she arrived at Lucky's, she felt as though she had accomplished some real work at home. Sister Gayle's car was already in the parking lot, so she entered through the front door and glanced around.

Carly hadn't been to the diner for years, but not much had changed. The diner had a country theme. There were wooden tables with red-and-white plaid tablecloths. The floor was made of wooden planks covered in sawdust. Large barrels of peanuts were placed sporadically around the restaurant, and guests were encouraged to partake, and then throw their shells on the floor. Huge ceiling fans were circulating the air, and Carly appreciated how comfortable it was inside.

She looked around and admired her surroundings. The walls were painted a deep cream and covered in old black-and-white photographs, homemade quilts, and antique mining equipment. Everything appeared to be hung on the walls haphazardly, but the overall effect was coordinated and welcoming.

Carly spotted Sister Gayle sitting at a back booth, and she joined her. "Hello, Sister Gayle, how are you?"

"Good, Carly. Thank you for coming." Sister Gayle was dressed neatly, and her white hair had been curled.

Carly scooted along the bench and placed her purse on the seat beside her. Before they could say another word, a young waitress approached and asked if they would like something to drink. Both women ordered sodas, and the waitress left them with menus.

Sister Gayle laid her menu on the table and smiled at Carly. "I always get the patty melt. I know I should try something different, but I always stick with the sure thing."

"That does sound good," Carly agreed. "I think I'll join you." Carly set her menu on top of Sister Gayle's and asked, "Do you come here often?"

"Oh, there are a few old sisters that I meet once a week for lunch. We have to get out and visit, and there aren't many places to go."

"Yeah. I miss the advantages of a city, but I love the country too," Carly responded thoughtfully. "It's the people that really matter. I think I could be just as happy living here in Bridger as anywhere."

For a bit they talked about Carly's life in Langdon, then they ordered their meals. Carly couldn't help but notice that Sister Gayle seemed a bit nervous. She fidgeted with her napkin, and her hands were trembling slightly all through the meal. When they were both done, Sister Gayle saved a piece of meat and rolled it in her napkin.

"It's for Pumpkin," she explained to Carly. "She knows when I go to lunch, and she expects her treat."

Carly smiled, and Sister Gayle continued. "I suppose I treat her like a family member, but she keeps me company so I don't mind spoiling her a bit." The older woman suddenly opened her heart to

Carly. "When my Paul died, I really thought I would curl up and wither away. I couldn't imagine living without him. He had always been my rock. I know it sounds silly, but my dog does distract me from focusing on the loss."

Carly remembered Brother Gayle as being a tall, lean man with graying hair and a wide smile. He had always seemed quiet in social groups, but Carly remembered him being very kind and gentle. She also recollected that he and Sister Gayle had been inseparable, doing many projects and going on outings together. It had been several years since she had seen him, although only a few years since he had passed away.

"I can't imagine how you must miss him," Carly offered.

"Well, luckily I have the gospel. We were sealed in the temple before we had our children, so I know that we will all be together someday. My faith has never wavered, nor has my love for Paul." Carly remained silent, listening with interest, and Sister Gayle continued, "There is nothing more important to me than my family and the gospel. That is why I really wanted to meet with you today."

Carly was confused. "What do you mean?"

"Well," Sister Gayle began, "I don't know why I feel inspired to share this with you, but I need to tell you something."

Carly's interest was piqued, and she listed intently.

"Many years ago, when Paul and I were first married, we had a lot of financial problems. There was always work to be found, but the pay was low and there were always so many bills. Our children are all grown now and have moved away, but they were very close in age. We had four children in six years, and it was a big responsibility trying to keep them all clothed and fed the first few years."

Sister Gayle fidgeted with the rings on her fingers and kept her gaze on the tabletop. Her words were slow and deliberate. "Well, the point is that I did something I shouldn't have done. Paul was working two jobs to make ends meet, but it seemed as though we were only getting deeper in debt. Our oldest girl had become ill and the doctor bills were horrendous. The old car we owned was more of a liability than an asset—it broke down nearly every month, and Paul wasn't a very good mechanic. He had a head for business, but he just wasn't knowledgeable in car mechanics," she explained.

The more Sister Gayle talked, the more she seemed to relax. "We didn't have the means to pay our bills, so against Paul's wishes I went to work. It was a part-time job in a small bookstore, and the pay wasn't very good—but at least I felt like I was contributing. My mother helped with tending the kids and for a short while it seemed as though things were getting better.

"We lived in a small town in California where we had both been raised. We knew just about everyone in our community, and I suppose we were well known also." Carly sat motionless, intrigued as Sister Gayle's story unraveled.

"Well, to make a long story short, just when I thought we were getting a grasp on our finances, Paul lost his job. It took him weeks to find a new one, and we were slipping into debt again." Sister Gayle sadly recalled, "I can't remember all the details of what happened then, but we were accumulating a lot of bills. Everything around us seemed in need of repair. I just didn't think I could stand it anymore. I came home one night, and there was only half a loaf of bread, some butter, one apple, and two cans of soup left in the pantry.

"My mother tried to help us financially, but she was struggling also, so I made a choice." She paused for a moment, and Carly resisted the impulse to urge her on before she was ready. Sister Gayle shook her head in disbelief. "When I think back, I just don't know what I was thinking." She looked Carly in the eye. "I began stealing money from my employer."

Carly's mouth opened wide. She quickly closed it, but she knew that it was too late to hide her reaction. Sister Gayle knowingly nodded her head. "Oh, Carly, I know what you're thinking—and you are right. It was a terrible thing to do—no matter what my circumstances were at the time."

"No," Carly began, "you obviously had circumstances that—"

"No," Sister Gayle repeated firmly. "There was no excuse for my actions then, and there is none now. I was wrong."

Carly began to feel uncomfortable. She didn't want to see Sister Gayle in this light, nor did she understand why Sister Gayle was sharing these intimate details of her life with her. "I don't know why you're telling me these things, but I—"

Again, her words were cut short. "Please listen so you can understand the whole story, Carly."

Obediently, Carly leaned back in her bench seat and politely listened, despite her discomfort.

"I only took a little bit at first, and no one seemed to notice. But it became easier and easier the more I got away with it. It seemed like magic. I was able to help pay the bills, Paul and I didn't have so much tension between us, and my kids were fed and clothed. Paul did find a job, but I still kept taking a little extra money from the till every week."

The older woman sighed heavily. "Paul was so busy working that he didn't notice the extra cash I had. But eventually my conscience caught up with me.

"I can still remember clearly the day I told Paul. Our only son wanted to play an instrument in the band at school, and I wanted him to participate. Paul and I went in our room and talked about it because it was going to cost us about twenty dollars to rent the instrument and buy him a uniform. That doesn't sound like much now, but—believe me—it was a lot back then. Paul didn't want him to do it. He said we couldn't afford it. I kept insisting that we could and that I would make a way for it to happen. For some reason Paul began questioning me about money, and I just couldn't lie to him. So I told him that I had been taking a little from the bookstore."

Fascinated, Carly asked, "What did he say? He must have been so surprised."

"At first he sat down on our bed and put his head in his hands. I didn't know what to do. I had been feeling so guilty, but I also didn't want to stop. I thought the money was making my life easier, but I realized later that it wasn't. I was cheating my employer, my family, and myself." Sister Gayle paused for several seconds. When she continued, her expression was one that Carly could only describe as pride. "Paul finally rose up off that bed, took my hands in his, and told me that together we would make it right. He told me that he loved me, and he would stand by me and we would pay back the money—and we did."

"How did you do that?" Carly asked.

"First, I talked to our ward bishop and confessed what I had done. He counseled me on repentance. Then Paul and I went down to the bookstore together, and I confessed to the owner. He was a nice man, but not completely forgiving. We worked out a deal to pay back all the cash. I had a pretty good idea how much I had taken, although I didn't know the exact amount. Of course he fired me on the spot, but I had expected that. What I didn't expect was for him to broadcast my sins all around town. I guess he thought he needed revenge of some sort."

"How terrible," Carly remarked. "If you were willing to pay back the money, then he should have forgiven you."

"Well, that would have been ideal for me, but he didn't see things quite that way. We don't always get to choose the consequences of our sins. After word spread about what I had done, I didn't even try to find a job. You see, gossip is a vicious monster. By the time word had circulated through our community, the story had been changed and distorted. Some of my close friends confided in me the things that were being said about me, and it hurt terribly. But there wasn't a thing I could do about it."

"I don't know how people can be so ruthless," Carly said sympathetically. "Why would people find comfort in ruining your reputation? I could never do what that store owner did to you."

"Well, I think some people are just plain mean, others are miserable with their own lives and want to spread the misery, and others are maybe self-righteous and take it upon themselves to be judges. It was a terrible time for our family. But we got through it. And do you know how?"

"Patience and endurance?" Carly guessed.

"Yes, but it was mainly our love for one another. I knew I had hurt Paul and even humiliated him, but he stood by me, kept his head high, and we managed to overcome those trials together. Eventually the gossip died down. We had a few friends who forgave me and continued our relationships, and life went on. No matter what life brings and no matter what choices we make, we can be forgiven and move on in life.

"Carly, there must be a reason I felt like I needed to share this confidence with you. I sense that you're going through a trial of sorts lately, and though I don't know what it is, I do know that sometimes we don't have a way to fix our trials or get rid of them. We must only endure them and grow by learning from them and making wiser decisions. I couldn't take away the slander and gossip that followed me. I couldn't take away the pain that I caused Paul. But I repented, tried to right my wrong, and I did progress in my life despite the adversity."

Carly thought of Kolton and immediately she understood Sister Gayle's message. "Thank you for sharing this with me," she said. "I promise I'll keep it in confidence."

"It's not such an embarrassment for me anymore, but I do appreciate your discretion. I have made some bad choices, but I've also tried to make good choices, and I'm not that person anymore."

"I guess that we all have to make our own choices and deal with the consequences," Carly observed. She inwardly hoped that she would have the strength to accept whatever life had in store for her, and that regardless of what that was, she would make good choices. She decided to confide in the older woman. "I think I know what I want from life, but I'm not sure it's obtainable. I have one man interested in me who I don't want, and the man that I want to be with doesn't want me."

"Oh, Carly, if you're talking about who I think you are, don't give up on this special young man. I think that, like I did, he is facing a trial that has clouded his good judgment. It's not easy to go through life's struggles alone—I had Paul to stand by me and help me. It's a lot easier when you have someone who loves and supports you."

Carly's eyes moistened. *I want to help Kolton. I just don't know how.* "He doesn't want me to help him."

"Oh, I think he does, Carly. I really think he does."

Carly sighed. "He has made it clear to me that I'm not going to be an important part of his life."

"Carly, what does your heart tell you? Have you ever had someone lie to you, when you knew that they were lying?"

"Of course," Carly admitted, laughing. "The kids at the elementary school are terrible liars."

"Most adults aren't good liars either—especially when they're lying to themselves and not following their hearts. Kolton has some ill-conceived notion that he needs to avoid people for their own good. I've seen how Kolton looks at you. Follow your heart, Carly. Pray about Kolton and let your heart and mind guide your behavior."

"But he said—"

Sister Gayle's voice was firm, "Carly, you're not listening to me. Forget what he said to you. Sometimes we need to swallow our pride and move forward—whether we have a green light or not. I know Kolton as if he were my own son. That boy just needs a good woman in his life. And I think he has his eye on you."

Carly agreed with Sister Gayle's advice, but she thought for a moment. "I guess I just don't know what steps to take. I don't know how to interfere in Kolton's life in a positive way."

"Well, I hope something changes soon. Kolton isn't happy, and neither is Kyle. Kyle has a whole family that loves him from a distance, and he doesn't even know them. He knows that they are relatives of some sort, but he doesn't really know them like he should." Sister Gayle shook her head in disapproval. "It's so sad to see a family divided for so long. Kyle's baptism is coming up soon, and it should be a joyous event. It should be a time for a family gathering, but none of Stacey's family will be there."

Carly thought of Chad's feeling that Leann was beginning to change her opinion of Kolton. If it were true, then Carly assumed that she would probably want to be at the baptism. Leann's family would surely want to attend if they felt welcome. It was a shame that Kyle was missing out on so much attention from his extended family.

Sister Gayle suddenly noticed the time and excused herself so she could prepare for company later that evening. The two women hugged before they parted ways and promised to get together soon. The visit had been uplifting for Carly, and as she drove home she pondered Sister Gayle's experiences. She was grateful for Sister Gayle's friendship and wise advice, and felt confident that she would be able to find the answers she needed.

* * *

Kyle sat on the couch, listlessly clicking the television remote. It was Saturday morning, and there were cartoons on every channel. He flashed through the same channels over and over, but nothing caught his interest. Scooting to the edge of the couch, he leaned over the coffee table and reached out to take a bite of cereal. It was soggy.

Disappointed, he dropped the spoon back into the bowl and slouched back into the cushions.

His father was next door at the feed store. Kyle usually had to go to work with his dad on Saturday or go visit his grandparents, but today he had begged his dad to let him stay home and watch cartoons. He wasn't in the mood to play at Grandma's house or work at the feed store. He wasn't really sure what he was in the mood for.

Before his dad left, Kyle had asked Kolton to do something fun with him. Kolton had been in the kitchen, making toast, and Kyle had been on his heels at every turn. "Dad, can we go see a movie today?"

"No, I told you, I have to work."

"Can we ride Grandma's horses?"

"No, Kyle. We've been over this." His father's voice was beginning to show his exasperation.

"Can we go shooting?"

This time his father didn't even respond, and Kyle knew that he was pushing him too far. "But there's nothing to do," Kyle complained.

"Kyle," Kolton had said firmly, "I have to go to work, and you can come with me. There's plenty to do at the feed store."

"I don't wanna work. Can I please stay home? Just for a while? I promise I'll be good," he'd pleaded.

"Okay, Kyle. You can stay here if you watch television, but you have to leave the front door open so we can hear each other if we have to. I'll be at the feed store if you need me. And when I have to run deliveries later, you'll have to come with me."

"Okay," Kyle had answered, finally somewhat cheerful.

Kolton had paused at the door, thinking of something that would interest his son. "Perhaps this afternoon we can go shoot a few rounds. You can shoot my old BB gun."

"Great," Kyle exclaimed. He had always admired his dad's gun. It was bigger than his own and had an eagle engraved on it.

"But not until after the deliveries are taken care of," he reminded his son.

After his father left, Kyle had poured a bowl of cereal and sat at the coffee table in front of the television. Being alone in the house had sounded great until his father actually left. He had thought it would be fun, but instead he just felt lonely.

He didn't feel like playing video games or watching any more cartoons. He switched off the television and thought for a moment. He could call a friend, but his dad usually didn't allow friends over when he was working. His father's old BB gun came to mind. He got up and ran his cereal bowl to the sink. It had been many weeks since he and his father had been shooting.

Racing through the house, he entered his father's room cautiously. He wasn't allowed in Kolton's room unless he had permission. Kolton had explained to Kyle many times that his personal gun collection was dangerous and that Kyle should never touch any of his father's things. There was a large, steel gun case in his closet, and Kyle was never permitted to touch it. But he really wanted to see the gun.

He walked through his father's bedroom and peered into his closet. He looked behind him before he stepped into the large closet and looked around. The shelves were filled with old clothes, car and gun magazines, and home movies of Kyle.

He carefully searched the closet but couldn't find the BB gun. He tried the lock on the gun cabinet, but, as he expected, it was locked. Feeling guilty, he turned to leave. As he turned, he noticed a piece of bright floral fabric sticking out from behind a box at the back of the closet. Curious, he reached back and pulled out a large, flat, rectangular package wrapped in a flowery blanket. He had never noticed it before.

Quickly, he carried it to the bed and unwrapped the package. He studied the contents for a few moments before he realized what he was looking at. He reached out and softly touched it, surprised that the texture was rougher than it appeared. A lump formed in his throat.

Realizing that his father could come back into the house at any moment, he quickly wrapped up the package and put it back where he had found it. Glancing around to make sure that nothing was out of place, he left his father's room and went back to the living room where he switched on the television and resumed watching cartoons. He didn't want to get into trouble for being in Kolton's closet, so he decided not to ask his father about what he'd seen.

Chapter Ten

The following Monday morning was unusually stressful. The copier had broken, three teachers had called in sick, and Carly had misplaced an important file. There was only one more week of school before summer break, and at this point she felt like she was more excited than the students for the school year to end.

Carly hadn't yet planned out how she was going to spend her summer, but she definitely felt as though she needed some time off. Her contract was good through the next school year, and she was grateful for the opportunity to return to her job. She had no regrets regarding her work, and she was confident that the next school season would be easier. There were a few things in the office that she wanted to change, and she would implement those ideas when she came back in the fall.

Lunch break had just begun, and she felt as though she could spare a few minutes to eat her lunch at her desk. Laura was in the cafeteria, buying her own lunch, and the principal was in his office with the door shut. Carly pulled out a sandwich, soda, and a bag of chips from her bag. She was grateful for a few moments of peace and quiet. As she took the first bite, she glanced up to see Kyle staring at her from across the front counter.

He didn't say a word but gave her a hopeful look. Swallowing, she greeted him. "Kyle, how are you?"

"Good." His expression didn't change.

"Did you need something?" she asked.

He nodded his head.

She laid her sandwich on her desk and rose. As she moved toward the front desk, Kyle shifted his weight and appeared nervous. Concerned, Carly inquired, "What is it Kyle? Are you okay?"

Again he nodded.

She leaned over the counter and softened her voice. "Is there something that you want to tell me?"

"Yeah."

He still seemed nervous, so Carly lowered her voice more still, "I can't help you unless you tell me what you need."

He pushed a note over the counter. Carly unfolded it, and as she read it her face showed her disappointment.

"Kyle," she asked, "do you know what the note says?"

He nodded that he did, but remained silent.

"Your teacher is asking for you to sit in the office during your lunch recess because you put a cricket in Amber Smith's desk. Have you eaten your lunch?"

"Yes."

"Well, I guess you'll have to come around the counter and sit in the chair next to the principal's office door."

Kyle obediently did as he was told. As soon as he sat down, Carly sat back at her desk and resumed eating her lunch.

"I'm getting baptized on Saturday," he blurted.

"Oh, that's great. Did you have your birthday already?" she asked.

"It's Saturday too. My dad said I could get baptized on my birthday."

"That's great, Kyle." Carly's excitement was genuine. "I remember when I was baptized, and it was a great experience."

Kyle nodded in agreement.

"Have a happy birthday. Turning eight is an important birthday."

Nodding again, he mentioned, "My dad is going to have a party for me after the baptism. We're going to have cake and ice cream in the yard."

"That sounds like fun."

"And a piñata—I hope," he added.

Carly couldn't help but smile at Kyle's excitement.

"Do you want to come?" he asked.

"I don't know, Kyle. I'd like to, but I don't know if I'm invited."

"You are. It's my baptism. I can invite anyone I want."

"I don't know if your dad would like it if I came to your party," she stated plainly.

Sadness washed over Kyle's face. "My grandparents will be there, and my Primary teacher. But I don't know how many friends will come."

Not wanting to hurt his feelings, Carly suggested, "I'll check my calendar, and I'll try to make it, okay?"

Before Kyle could respond, Mr. Stout came out of his office. "Well, Kyle Raywood, how are you today?"

"Good, sir."

"Are you waiting to see me?"

Kyle looked at Carly, and she handed the principal the note from Kyle's teacher. Mr. Stout quickly read the note, and then shook his head. "Kyle, we've talked about teasing other kids before, haven't we?"

Kyle nodded.

Mr. Stout sighed heavily, and then stated, "I will agree with your teacher's punishment this time, but if anything like this happens again you will have to come see me in my office. Perhaps we will have to invite your father to attend our meeting, and together we'll work out a form of punishment."

Kyle swallowed nervously. "Yes, sir."

Mr. Stout turned to Carly, "The recess bell is going to ring soon. I'll be in the halls checking on things."

"Okay," she acknowledged and cleared off her lunch from her desk. Kyle remained quiet as she returned to work.

A few minutes later, the recess bell rang, and Kyle looked at Carly for permission to leave. "You can go, Kyle. Remember to be nice to the girls."

He turned to leave, but then remembered something. "My baptism is at four o'clock. And then be at my house afterward for cake. Oh, and I like sports stuff and baseball cards."

He quickly ran off, and Carly felt a wave of sadness. She knew she wouldn't be welcome, but she did want to attend for Kyle's sake. She wondered what Kolton would think if she crashed his son's baptism and birthday party. The thought made her smile. It would be fun to see him a little uncomfortable. After all, she still owed him for the Stan episode.

Mr. Stout soon returned to the office and commented to Carly, "I just don't know what to do with that Raywood kid."

"What do you mean?" she asked.

"Well, it seems to me that he gets himself in trouble on purpose," he confided to Carly. "He never breaks any major rules, he gets top grades, and yet he seems to enjoy being disruptive. I've talked to the father multiple times, and I feel the boy comes from a good home. I suppose he just needs a little extra attention."

Carly nodded that she agreed. "He can be a very good kid," Carly said in Kyle's defense.

"Oh, I know. But lately, it seems like he's in a bit of trouble daily. This morning on the playground he told a bunch of kids he seen a spacecraft land behind the school. The duty teacher said she had a couple of kids crying because they thought aliens had landed." Mr. Stout shook his head, "I think he's a good kid, but like I said, he seems to be reaching out for attention." Changing the subject, he requested that Carly hold his calls for a while since he'd be working on a report.

Thinking of Kyle's need for attention, Carly wished she could attend his baptism. She sat back at her desk, entertaining herself with creative ideas for getting revenge toward Kolton. She could crash the baptism wearing her old prom dress and make a huge fuss over Kolton. Better yet, she could show up in a wedding dress and sit in the back row, pouting. That would definitely embarrass him in front of his family. Actually, Carly thought, the sad part would be that there wouldn't be anyone there to witness her stunt. All of Kolton's siblings lived out of state, and none of Stacey's family would be there.

She dismissed the urge to seek revenge, since she suddenly had an idea that could help change Kyle's situation. Immediately, she made a phone call to execute her plan.

* * *

Carly woke up early Saturday morning feeling daring, yet apprehensive. The previous day had been exhausting as she'd tried to tie up all the loose ends at work. The children had all been dismissed from school early Wednesday afternoon for summer break. She had spent the rest of the week taking care of unfinished school business. Friday had been a late afternoon, but she felt relaxed now that her job was near completion for the school year. She still needed to take care of a few odds and ends at the beginning of the next week, but then her vacation would officially begin.

She crawled out of bed and wrapped a robe around herself. As she entered the kitchen to fix some breakfast, her parents both wished her a good morning from the kitchen table.

"Good morning," she countered cheerfully.

Her father noticed her demeanor and piped up, "Who's the lucky guy?"

"What do you mean?" she asked as she poured some cereal.

"Well," he explained, "you seem unusually cheery this morning. There must be someone special on your mind."

"Kind of," she admitted.

"Speaking of men, did you get the message on the counter?" her mother questioned.

"No, what does it say?"

Emma got up from the table and ruffled through some papers on the counter. "It's a message from Adam. I took it yesterday. He wanted to talk to you about work. He said that he would hire you for the summer if you were looking for work. I wrote his number here somewhere."

Dismissing the offer with a wave of her hand, Carly sat down at the table. "I wouldn't work for Adam if he paid me triple. He'll find someone else."

Emma returned to the table. "Well, maybe he's trying to change—"

Carly interrupted her mother as she poured herself some orange juice. "Adam is not for me. Besides, I think he's using the gospel as an excuse to get closer to me."

"Carly," Emma said, "you could be a big example in his life and help him investigate the Church."

"Mom," Carly countered impatiently, "I really think he was trying to manipulate me by using the gospel to get me to see him again. If he really is interested in the Church, he'll be able to investigate it without my help. He might be rich and handsome, but I definitely don't need him. Don't worry—I won't be an old maid. And I don't need the job he's offering. The school district spreads out my paychecks so I get paid through the summer. I'll be fine. Maybe you should take the job with Adam, Mom," Carly teased.

Raymond stifled a laugh, disguising it with a cough. "Raymond." Emma pointed a finger at her husband. "You keep laughing, honey, and I might just take that job."

"I think our daughter has good judgment," he answered, looking directly at his wife.

"You know I agree. I just wanted to see how Carly would react to the offer. He was a hottie, but I do think Carly has made the right decisions."

"Mom," Carly drawled. "A 'hottie'?"

Her father bluntly announced, "Well, I think you would be better off with Kolton Raywood. If I were you, I'd get back in his good graces."

Carly swallowed a bite of cereal and rolled her eyes. "Since when is my love life the topic at breakfast?"

"I will admit there is something about Kolton that I like," her mother offered. "He is a special young man."

"And I see the way he looks at you," added her father.

"Really?" Carly asked hopefully and looked at her dad.

He gave her wicked smile and admitted, "No, but I wanted to see if you were still interested in him."

Her parents both chuckled. "Go ahead," Carly encouraged. "Laugh all you want. I know who is good for me and who isn't. Adam will find someone else. And I'll deal with Kolton."

"Is there something we don't know?" her mother asked.

Carly couldn't help but grin. "Yes, but you'll have to wait to find out."

"Hmm. Sounds intriguing."

"It's a secret," Carly said.

Disappointed, her mother asked, "You're not even going to tell me?"

Carly shook her head as she took a drink of juice. "You'll find out."

Losing interest in the conversation, her father noted, "It's getting hot already. I'd better get busy out in the garden."

"Yes, me too," her mother agreed. Her parents cleaned up their plates while Carly finished her breakfast. She sat alone at the table after her parents went outside, pondering the possible outcomes of her day. Her plan could be a huge success, or it could be an embarrassing failure. Either way, she had nothing to lose. She knew that she had no hope of either success or failure if she didn't try something. Like Sister Gayle had said, she was going to push ahead even if she didn't have a green light from Kolton.

* * *

Kolton was rattled as he entered the church bathroom to change out of his wet clothes. Kyle was trying to peel off his own wet clothes with little success. As he helped his son undress and change into his dry church clothing, Kyle bubbled, "Isn't it great? There's at least forty people here!"

Kolton was amazed at the attendance at his son's baptism. He had expected his folks and a few close friends from their ward, but he had been shocked to see the entire Powers family show up. His emotions were mixed, and he couldn't quite pinpoint how he felt. Initially, he had been offended that they would come uninvited, and he expected to feel angry. But as the meeting progressed and he baptized his son, he felt the Spirit testify of the love in the room—and he knew that the love was centered on his son. Kolton's heart softened at the excitement on his son's face.

"Dad," Kyle gushed, "I hope that they all come to my party. Do you think they will?"

Kolton actually hoped that they wouldn't, but he changed the subject and helped Kyle with his tie. "Go comb your hair and I'll get dressed. We still need to finish the meeting."

Kyle moved quickly as his father had instructed, and they both returned to their chairs. As Kolton sat down, he glanced at the back of the room and saw Carly looking straight at him. He looked away, but then did a double take. She looked guilty. What was she hiding?

At the conclusion of the meeting, everyone helped stack the chairs and congratulated Kyle on his choice to be baptized. Kolton noticed how his son glowed from all the attention and affection bestowed on him. The Powers family seemed grateful to be a part of this important day, but Kolton kept his distance. He watched as Kyle shook hands with Chad, and as Leann gave his son a hug. Thoroughly confused, he went along with the apparently temporary truce for the sake of his son, but he still kept a watchful eye on Kyle and those surrounding him.

Carly stayed near the back of the room, and as she slipped out of the meeting she bumped into Kolton's mom. "Hello, Sister Raywood. How are you?"

"Good, Carly, how are you?"

"Fine." Carly remembered her mother's message from Sister Raywood several weeks ago about choir practice. "How did everything go on Thursday night?" she inquired.

Sister Raywood seemed surprised by her question and answered, "Well, I got all the invitations done that night and delivered the next day." She noticed Carly's confused expression, and then it dawned on her what Carly had been talking about. "Oh, choir practice. I'm sorry, Carly. I was thinking of something else. Actually, we haven't had practice for a few weeks. Brother Spriggs has been sick, and we haven't had anyone to play the piano. But do come this next week. I believe we will be practicing then."

"I'll try," Carly promised. "Now that I'm off work for the summer, I should have more time."

Sister Raywood looked at her watch, "I don't mean to rush off, but I'd better get going to Kolton's house. I'll see you later." They exchanged good-byes and they both left.

Everyone seemed to leave rather quickly, and Kolton and Kyle headed for home. Kyle talked nonstop about the baptism and all of the people who had come to see him. "Do you think that my Primary teacher will come to my party?"

"No, son, I don't think so. I didn't invite her. We're just having a family party with a few of your friends from Primary."

Disappointed, but still hopeful, Kyle questioned, "What about Leann? Isn't she family?"

"Oh, I don't think she'll be there." Kolton always felt uncomfortable talking about Stacey's relatives.

"But she said that she would see me later," Kyle insisted.

"I don't think she's coming over, Kyle," Kolton said.

Kyle sighed and informed his father, "I knew Carly would come. She said she didn't know, but I knew that she would."

Surprised, Kolton asked, "What do mean? Did you invite her?"

"Yeah. I told her at school that I was getting baptized and that I was having a party with a piñata."

"Really." Kolton began piecing clues together. "Did you tell her when it was?"

Kyle nodded. "She's nice, Dad. She always smiles at me at school."

Kolton's temper began to simmer. He suspected that she had something to do with Stacey's family attending the baptism. He would need to have a talk with Carly tomorrow. Kyle was so happy, though, that Kolton decided he wouldn't do anything about it today. But as he pulled the truck into their driveway, Kolton realized that he would have a chance to discuss things with Carly sooner than he had expected.

Men from the ward were setting up tables borrowed from the church. Church members, along with Stacey's family, were helping set up a potluck dinner right on his front porch. Looking back, he noticed more vehicles coming down his street.

"Look, Dad," Kyle exclaimed. "The party! Thanks, Dad!"

Kyle ran off, and Kolton was left standing speechless in his own driveway. The faces were all familiar. Everyone who had attended the baptism was now surfacing in his yard. He could feel his blood pressure rising, and he gritted his teeth. He was definitely in a difficult predicament. If he was rude and angry, it would spoil Kyle's birthday. On the other hand, he didn't know if he could manage to be civil and courteous. He decided to try his best to find Carly. She was his top suspect in the planning of this surprise event, and she needed to be aware of how he felt about her meddling.

He forced himself to advance into the crowd, and he was welcomed and thanked by family and friends for his hospitality. He played along and smiled as courteously as he could manage. His mother approached and pulled on his sleeve.

He leaned down so she could whisper in his ear. "How are you, Kolton? You don't look very happy."

Nodding toward the food piled up on the tables, he concluded, "There seems to be party going on. At least there seems to be plenty of food to go around."

"Are you okay with all of this?"

"I don't know, Mom," he growled lightly. "This is a complete surprise. I sure wasn't expecting Stacey's family to come to the baptism."

"Really?" His mother seemed pleased. "Well, everyone seems to be behaving." She warned, "Don't you spoil this for Kyle. Everyone is having a great time so far."

Kolton had to admit that the party was progressing smoothly. The adults were beginning to eat, and the children were playing in the grass and climbing the trees. He heard a car pull into the driveway and recognized it as Carly's. He excused himself from his mother and proceeded toward her.

Leann waylaid him and asked, "Kolton, may I speak with you a minute?"

Her approach had distracted him from Carly, and he looked at her cautiously. "Uh, yeah. I suppose so."

Leann was wringing her hands, and her voice was shaky. "I want you to know that I really think it was great of you to make this first step." Kolton was unsure what Leann was referring to, but he kept silent and allowed her to continue. "I think it's time to let bygones be bygones. I'm sorry about our past and how I've treated you." Her eyes were moist, and she appeared to be having difficulty forming her words clearly, "I want you to know I think Kyle is great, and I hope that Chad and I can get to know him better."

Kolton swallowed hard. He was used to handling harsh exchanges with Leann—but seeing Leann humble and emotional was a new experience. "Leann, I'm sorry too. I guess both of us could have handled things differently."

Relieved, she smiled broadly. "My aunt was so touched that you invited her. It was really sweet of you."

Kolton knew that Leann must be referring to Stacey's mother, Annette. Although she wasn't here, he had seen her at the baptism. *Invited her,* he thought. *I didn't invite her—I don't even know her address.* He had heard that Stacey's father had died a few years back and Annette had been living in Wyoming with her oldest son, but that was all he knew. Annette hadn't seen Kyle since he was an infant. Kolton had mailed her some pictures in Kyle's first months, but he had stopped when the feud between him and Stacey's family escalated.

He breathed in deeply and excused himself from Leann. *Carly,* he thought. *Where is she?* He caught a glimpse of her across the lawn and began to make his way in that direction. She caught his gaze, but averted her eyes immediately. On his way over to her he was stopped twice. By the time he got to where she had been standing, she was gone. His temper was rising, but he forced himself to conceal it.

Before he could hunt Carly down, the children had thrown a rope over a tree limb and were getting ready to hit the piñata. He joined the crowd watching, but then noticed that Carly was standing back near the house talking with Sister Gayle. After Kyle had swung the bat a few times at the piñata, Kolton quietly stepped back and turned for the house. When he got there, Sister Gayle was alone cleaning off some of the tables. He was beginning to feel that Carly was purposely evading him.

"Sister Gayle," he greeted.

"Oh, Kolton," she said. "This is marvelous. The baptism was wonderful, and Kyle seems so happy."

They both looked over and saw the joy on Kyle's face. He was surrounded by friends and family, and he seemed to be basking in the attention.

"Yeah," Kolton agreed somewhat dully. "This was a great idea."

He wondered if Sister Gayle knew how all these people had been invited to the baptism and his house. He looked closely at her face, but she revealed nothing

"I think after the piñata, you should have Kyle open his presents. I'll clean this table off, and we can put out some cake," Sister Gayle instructed.

"I don't think we'll have enough cake for everyone," Kolton admitted.

"Oh, didn't you see the cake?"

"No. My mom said that she would make one, but I haven't seen it yet."

Sister Gayle motioned for Kolton to follow her into the house. On the kitchen table was a large cake box from a professional bakery. Kolton opened the lid and found a sheet cake with "Happy Birthday, Kyle" written on it in frosting script.

Sister Gayle declared, "It's a beautiful cake. I love the little race cars and hills. Look, there is even a tiny stop sign."

Kolton looked at the side of the box and noticed Carly's name written on a sticker with the pick-up time. Forcing himself to control his voice, he spoke slowly and smoothly. "Have you seen Carly around?"

"She left just a few moments ago. She said that she had to get home."

Kolton nodded his head grimly. He'd track her down eventually. For now, he would pretend to be a good host. The party continued, and everyone kept expressing their gratitude and complimenting Kolton. He wasn't sure how to act around Stacey's family, but he tried to be as polite as possible.

Sister Powers and her husband were a bit distant, but they had willingly attended, and Kolton could see that their affection for Kyle was sincere. Leann's younger sister and brother were friendly, but they had been in grade school when Stacey had died. Kolton didn't even know if they knew any of the details of his supposed involvement in their older cousin's death.

All of the guests pitched in to help clean up as the party came to an end. As they prepared to leave, Chad and Leann approached Kolton. Chad extended his hand in a friendly gesture while Leann offered a sincere smile. Kolton gave her a half smile back. He was still a bit apprehensive about his former in-laws.

It was after seven o'clock before the last car pulled out of his driveway. After everyone had left, Kyle gave his father a big hug. "Thanks, Dad."

"Kyle," Kolton admitted, "to tell you the truth, I didn't—"

Kyle interrupted his father with awe in his voice, "Did you know that I have another grandma? She was at the baptism, and she gave me a remote-control truck."

Kolton didn't know how to answer his son. The truck was impressive. It was a miniature monster truck and moved quickly around the yard. Kolton had always deflected Kyle's questions about his mother, and now his back was up against the wall. *Thanks to Carly,* he thought darkly.

"Kyle," Kolton ordered, "go and collect a few of your toys and get in the truck."

"Where are we going?"

"You're going to Grandma Raywood's house for a while. I have to take care of some business."

Kolton wasn't sure what he was going to say, but he knew that he had to get what he was feeling off his chest. He dropped Kyle off at his parents' house and sped toward the Westons' with a huge cloud of dust trailing behind his truck.

He jumped out of the truck and leapt onto the porch. But before he could knock on the door, Emma Weston walked around the corner of the house. "Hello, Kolton. How are you?"

Forcing a smile, he answered, "Fine. I'm looking for Carly."

"She's here somewhere. I think she might still be in the garden."

Not wanting to engage in small talk, Kolton brushed past her and muttered, "Thank you."

Carly was kneeling in the garden pulling weeds when she saw a figure coming across the yard. Initially she had assumed it was her father, but she realized the figure was moving too rapidly, and straight for her.

She stood up and raised a hand to her brow to wipe some sweat. "Kolton," she whispered to herself. He was still wearing his church clothes, but he had removed his tie, and his white, short-sleeved shirt was unbuttoned at the top. His tightly knitted brows and the grim line of his lips didn't bode well.

He stomped into the garden and stood facing her eye to eye, ready for battle. Carly squared her shoulders and smiled sweetly.

Once he stood across from her and looked into her eyes, he didn't know where to start. He blurted, "Why, Carly? Why did you go to such great lengths to make me miserable?"

"Kolton," she answered calmly, "I'm not sure what you are talking about."

"Carly," his voice was deep yet controlled, "I know it was you," he accused.

Carly looked down and picked the mud off her fingers. When she looked up into his eyes again, she was surprised to see the anger etched on his face. "Kolton, let me explain. I honestly wouldn't have come to the baptism if I had known how upset you would be."

"No," he pointed a finger at her, "let me explain something to you. You had no right to intrude in my business and cause my son to believe that he has a family that he really doesn't. Inviting everyone to a baptism and birthday party does not mend eight years of contention—especially when you go behind my back without letting me know what's going on."

Carly stood still, staring at Kolton with her eyes wide. His face grew red with emotion as he spoke. "I don't know how you did it, and I don't know why. But you went too far. I don't appreciate you sticking your nose where it doesn't belong."

Carly's eyes began to fill with tears. Kolton noticed, but it only added to his irritation. "Furthermore, you have put me in a situation with my son and the entire Powers family that I'm not sure how to handle. You don't go around messing in other people's personal affairs like that. Are we clear, Carly?"

"Kolton, it was just a cake," she said softly.

Exasperated, his hands flew up. "Just a cake? No, Carly. You've created a lot of problems for me."

A tear rolled down her cheek and she folded her arms tightly around her chest. "I'm sorry."

Kolton's voice was heavy with disappointment. "I never thought that you would do something like this to me, or Kyle. I hope you realize how big a mistake you've made."

Carly bit her bottom lip and wiped the tears off her cheek with the back of her hand. Kolton's anger was beginning to turn toward himself, and his heart slowly softened toward Carly. He hadn't meant to hurt her. He had just wanted her to understand how uncomfortable she had made him. He stepped back and looked out at the sunset. He could hear Carly's soft breaths and knew that she was suppressing a sob.

Carly blinked her eyes quickly to stop her tears, but held her tongue. It wouldn't matter what she said to defend herself—he obviously had his mind made up.

"Carly, it was so unexpected," he addressed her in a softer tone.

She kept her eyes downward and remained silent. Kolton felt like a heel. *Why can't I control my emotions?* he wondered in frustration.

At a loss for words, he turned to Carly and tried to look into her eyes. She kept her gaze downward and didn't respond. "Carly," he began again, "I don't want to fight with you. I just wanted you to know how I felt about what you did today."

A silent moment passed, and then she looked up into his eyes and said, "I'm sorry you're upset." The sincerity of her voice was reflected in her eyes. "I don't know what else to say."

She walked past him, and he stood speechless as she swiftly escaped into the house. He didn't blame her for walking away. He'd had no right to come to her house and chastise her like he had. Instead of feeling vindicated, he actually felt worse. Regretful, he walked back to his truck and returned to his parents' house to pick up Kyle.

It was dark when he opened the door to his parents' house and hollered, "I'm home."

"I'm in the kitchen," his mother yelled back.

"Hey," she said as he flopped into a chair at the kitchen table. "Are you okay? You look exhausted."

Kolton leaned his elbows on the table and rested his face in his hands. "No," he mumbled. "I've had such a bad day."

Sarah Raywood sat across from her son. "Are you upset about all the surprise guests at the baptism today?"

He looked up and said, "Yes, and the fact that the whole ward showed up for Kyle's birthday party. Not to mention all of Stacey's family."

His mother toyed with a cloth napkin and said, "Kyle was so happy today. He had so many friends and family around him."

"Yeah," Kolton conceded, "he did enjoy himself. Where is he?"

"He's in the family room watching a movie with your dad. I haven't checked on them for a while, but they're probably both asleep."

Kolton rubbed his eyes. It had been a tiring day. It had been a day of happiness and a day of frustration and lack of control. He had looked forward to exercising his priesthood and baptizing his son. It gave him great pleasure to know that his son had chosen to be baptized into the Church. The rest of the day was rapidly becoming a blur in his memory—except for the look on Carly's face when he was yelling at her. Her quivering chin and tear-filled eyes would be etched on his memory for a long time. His own heart ached. He wished that his relationship with her could be different.

When he had approached her in the garden, his mind had been set on one thing. But once he saw how vulnerable she was, his heart had softened. He couldn't deny his feelings for her any longer. Avoiding her had become routine, but it apparently hadn't changed how much he cared for her. But she would probably never talk to him again after his performance in the garden.

"You know," Sarah observed, "I really think that you made progress today with Stacey's family. They seemed warm and open-minded—at least they were friendlier today than they've been in the past."

"Do you think so?" he asked absentmindedly. He was suddenly more worried about Carly than his relationship with Stacey's family.

"I think that Kyle needs to know his mother's family. He needs to have a relationship with them. Even Stacey's mom came from out of town for the baptism—we haven't seen her since the funeral."

"Yeah, Mom, but it wasn't right," he insisted. He clasped his hands together and voiced his feelings. "It's not fair for me or Kyle to be forced into a situation like we were today. I had no idea that all those people were coming, and no way to prepare—and I still don't know how she convinced everyone to attend."

"Who?"

"Carly Weston. She was the one behind all of this. I don't know why she did it, but for some reason she took it upon herself to invite everyone out to Kyle's baptism and party. That's where I was just now. I went over to her house and confronted her about it."

Sarah's hands flew to her mouth. Kolton noticed his mother's reaction and added, "I know. It was such a surprise. I still can't believe that she would do such a thing."

"Oh, Kolton," his mother almost whispered. She took her hands off her mouth, and her face fell with regret. "It wasn't Carly. It was me," she confessed. Her voice was barely audible. "I invited everyone. I didn't tell you because I knew that you wouldn't agree. I sent out the invitations last week."

Kolton sat motionless and felt the color drain out of his face.

"Kolton, please don't get angry. I did this for Kyle—and for you."

Kolton was afraid to speak. He didn't want to lose his temper with his mother too. She got up from the table and went to her purse on the kitchen counter, coming back with a blue piece of paper that she offered to Kolton. It was an invitation to Kyle's baptism and birthday party.

He read the invitation. It was signed "from the Raywood family." He laid it on the table and asked tersely, "Why didn't you tell me?"

"I knew that you would never agree. Your father and I want to help you, but you resist us every time we offer help. You won't even talk about Stacey."

Kolton's voice rose slightly, "You know what happened. You know why they accuse me of Stacey's death."

"I also know that they came to see Kyle." Sarah gave her son a determined look. "This isn't just about you and your disagreement with the Powers family. It's about Kyle. He has a family within miles of his own house, and he doesn't even know them. I think that you have carried this grudge long enough. Whether you realize it or not, there was progress made today."

"Not with Carly," he interjected dryly.

"I'm sorry, Kolton. I really am." Sarah gave her son a longing look. "I want the best for you and Kyle. I'm really sorry if you're mad at me, but I really think that everyone involved needs to put the past behind them." Sarah took a deep breath and chastised her son. "Your father and I are tired of the contention between the families. It doesn't just affect you and Kyle—it affects all of us. Too much time has been lost, and it's time for you to do something about it. You need to forgive and forget so that you and Kyle can move on with your lives."

Kolton knew that his mother was right, but that didn't stop him from being angry. He rubbed his face with his hands and stood up. As he walked into the family room, he saw that his mother's guess had been correct; his father was asleep in the recliner, and Kyle was asleep on the floor. Kolton picked up his son and walked back into the kitchen.

"I'll talk to you later, Mom. I need to get home."

Sarah nodded that she understood. "I'm sorry, Kolton."

"It's okay, Mom." His tone was strained, but his anger was subsiding. "I'll talk to you tomorrow."

Sarah folded her arms and followed her son outside to his truck. He laid Kyle down on the seat and got in on the driver's side. He gave a brief wave to his mother before he left. He could see the sorrow on her face. He didn't doubt that her actions had been driven by love.

As Kolton drove home, he thought of Carly and how he had accused her of intentionally interfering in his life. He realized that she had probably delivered the cake, but that had been the extent of her participation. He was sure that Carly had been hurt by his harsh words earlier, and he wondered how he could set things straight with her. He sighed heavily. There were so many issues in his life; he couldn't possibly figure them all out tonight.

As soon as they arrived home, he carried his sleeping son into his room and tucked him into bed. The ride home hadn't disturbed him at all. The fact that Kyle had just had the most exciting birthday of his life had most likely exhausted him.

Kolton softly shut his son's door and retreated into his own room. His mind was reeling with conflicting emotions. He wanted to forgive Stacey's family, and he also knew that he needed to seek their forgiveness too. He also had to apologize Carly. Before he went to bed he knelt in heartfelt prayer and begged for help to overcome his weaknesses.

Chapter Eleven

Carly threw herself on her bed. In the distance she'd heard Kolton's truck going down her street. Perhaps she had been overly optimistic. She had known there was a chance that he wouldn't appreciate her gesture. She had ordered the cake and planned on dropping it off herself as a gift after the baptism. In their small community, baptisms were usually a ward event, and she probably would have gone whether she had an invitation or not. Besides, Kyle had personally invited her.

When she had arrived at the baptism, she had been shocked to see so many people in attendance. She sat down next to her brother, and he explained to her that he and Leann had been invited to the baptism and a birthday party afterwards. Without a written invitation she was nervous to crash the party, but she did have the excuse of dropping off the cake. No one questioned her when she arrived, so she stayed for a while and enjoyed herself.

But she had felt negative vibes emanating from Kolton, and now she knew why. Someone had extended the invitations without telling him. He had seemed to want to confront her during the party, so she'd snuck away early to avoid him. When he arrived at her house, she had hoped that he was coming to see her as a friendly gesture to thank her for the cake. But as soon as she saw the animosity in his expression, she knew that there was something wrong. And when he approached her in the garden, she made some connections with what he was saying and realized that his mother must have sent out the invitations.

There was no use in talking to him now. He had obviously assumed it was her, and in due time he would realize his mistake. Carly wouldn't stay mad at him. If he had been surprised by the attendance at the baptism and party, then he had every right to be upset. It was simply unfortunate that he hadn't waited to collect all of the facts before he confronted her.

She knew it didn't matter what he had said to her in the garden—he would try to make it right once he realized his mistake. She had forgiven him already, before he even had the chance to do so. It had been weeks since she had been near Kolton, and she had thoroughly enjoyed being around his home and family today, no matter what the consequences had been. Carly's feelings for Kolton had gone beyond attraction or admiration. She couldn't explain it, but she didn't need to analyze it. She just wanted to be with him, and she wanted to show him how she really felt about him. She curled up under her covers and relaxed. She decided to be patient. She said a prayer and drifted off to sleep.

* * *

The next day Carly didn't get a chance to talk with Kolton at church. She looked for him, but he seemed to be preoccupied with his own thoughts. Carly was disappointed that he didn't make an attempt to talk to her. She had hoped that they would clear up this misunderstanding soon.

Chad and Leann came over after Sunday dinner, and Leann asked Carly if they could talk privately. Emma was serving ice cream in the kitchen, so the two young women each grabbed a bowl and went into the family room where they could be alone.

"There's something that I want to tell you, Carly." Leann's voice was quiet.

"What is it?" she asked, mixing her ice cream with her spoon.

"It's about Kolton."

"Really?" Carly tried to appear disinterested.

Leann set her ice-cream bowl down on the couch next to her and began, "I owe you an apology. I said a lot of things about Kolton that weren't fair."

"Well, all I know is that there's a big feud in your family. Kolton has never told me the details," Carly admitted.

"I think that Kolton is trying," Leann said.

"Trying to do what?" Carly asked.

Leann clasped her hands in her lap and thoughtfully answered, "He's trying to mend fences with us. My parents aren't very trusting of him yet, but they can see a change in him. After all, he invited us to Kyle's baptism and birthday party. He's never done anything like that before."

Carly decided not to reveal what she knew about that. She continued to listen to Leann.

"Anyway, I want you to know that I am sorry for all that I said about Kolton and the way I acted. I can't help but feel that I'm somewhat responsible for your breakup with him."

"No, Leann," Carly reassured her, "it's not your fault." Deciding to confide in Leann she stated, "Kolton ended our relationship. For whatever reason, it was his choice, and no matter what you've done, he is ultimately accountable for his own actions."

Leann smiled and thanked her. "I feel better having gotten this off my chest. Thank you, Carly. I truly hope that you and Kolton can work things out. I think that my family has been too judgmental of him. Even in the beginning, when he and Stacey got married, my family automatically didn't like him. Stacey was so smart and talented, and everyone hoped that she would be something great someday. I guess they took out their disappointment on Kolton. I actually liked him. We would talk and visit, and Stacey was happy that we got along so well. But I guess when she died I took up my family's point of view. And now I see how much I've been a part of the problem."

Carly said, "I hope that someday you can all work out these problems."

"I think we are beginning to make some progress. Chad has helped me see things differently also. I now understand that she was successful in life—she was a wife and a mother."

Carly nodded and added, "I agree."

"Kolton has asked to meet with my family," Leann said. "He called after church today. He wants to discuss things with us."

Carly was a little surprised at that news, but she was happy for Leann and her family. "I think that would be great if you all could settle this—especially for Kyle's sake. He really enjoyed being around your family."

Leann sighed contentedly. "Even my Aunt Annette, Stacey's mom, is planning on being here. She was so excited to see Kyle at the baptism that she was afraid to go to the birthday party—she worried that she would fall in love with Kyle and then not be allowed to see him again after that day."

Carly hoped that Kolton truly wanted to make amends, and that the Powers family would find it in their hearts to forgive and forget all that had transpired in eight years. After Chad and Leann left that night, Carly lay in her bed, unable to sleep for over an hour. Thoughts of Kolton and Kyle swarmed in her head. A slight tap on her window startled her, and she glanced at the clock on her nightstand. It read 9:45 P.M.

She waited for a moment and didn't hear anything. She nestled back into her bed, but heard another distinct tap on her window. Slightly frightened, she got up and grabbed her robe. Wrapping it around herself, she cautiously peered out through the drapes. A large figure stood in front of her window.

"Carly, it's me—Kolton." His hushed voice could be heard through the window. Relieved, Carly quickly grabbed her slippers and said, "I'll meet you on the back patio."

Careful not to disturb her parents, she quietly exited the house by the back door and met up with Kolton on the darkened patio.

"I'm sorry to wake you." He stood before her with his thumbs in his jean pockets. His white T-shirt almost glowed in the moonlight. She thought his hair looked a bit mussed in the darkness, and he sounded tired.

"I wasn't sleeping," she offered.

"Good. I hope I didn't wake your parents."

"No," Carly looked back at the house and saw that no lights had been turned on. "I think they're still sleeping."

Kolton took a deep breath and drew up his courage. "I need to talk to you, Carly."

"Come sit with me on the porch swing," Carly offered.

Carly sat down and scooted over to make room for Kolton. He leaned back and rested his hands on his lap. Crickets chirped nearby, and the night air was slightly cool. For a moment they rocked softly in the swing in silence.

Carly noticed that his anger from their last confrontation was gone. "I can only imagine what you think of me and how I've acted," Kolton began. "I owe you an apology. I am so sorry for coming over here yesterday and accusing you of meddling in my life. I know now that you didn't invite all those people to the baptism behind my back."

"I did bring a cake, though," Carly confessed, with a bit of humor.

"And I thank you. It was really nice of you."

"Well, I shouldn't have brought it. You made it clear to me that we weren't even friends, and I still found an excuse to come over."

Kolton pondered her words, and his voice trembled. "And I am so glad that you did. Honestly, Carly, I will understand if you want nothing to do with me ever again. But I want you to know that I am very sorry for the way that I've treated you." Carly could feel the sincere emotion behind his words, and her heart swelled. "I had my reasons for not wanting you in my life, but now I'm trying to change those things."

"Kolton, I understand—"

He cut her off and insisted, "Please hear me out. I couldn't sleep last night because I felt like I need to share some things with you."

Carly gave him her full attention as he continued. "When Leann lost her baby, I felt as though it was my fault. If my presence hadn't caused her to flare up like she did, then her miscarriage wouldn't have happened. So I figured it would be better for everyone if we didn't see each other. I didn't want to drag you into this mess."

"Kolton, it wasn't your fault she miscarried," Carly argued. "Leann was already having problems when she came over here that night. She came over to talk to my mom about it. I think that her miscarriage was already in motion. She was in an emotional state, but nothing that you did caused her to lose the baby."

Kolton felt a wave of relief wash over him. "I didn't know that. I just jumped to conclusions, as usual."

"You never gave me a chance to tell you."

"Carly, there is so much more that I want to tell you. I need to clear the air between us."

"Okay, go ahead."

"You said something to me at my house that Sunday that Kyle was sick. You said that my private business might be mine, but it affects all the people who care about me. Well, my mom has been saying that for a while, but I guess I wasn't listening. But now, I feel like I've been stagnating for eight years. I need to move on with my life—especially for Kyle."

Carly nodded in agreement. "I just wanted you to be happy, Kolton. I thought I was helping."

"I know. And I'm not upset. I guess it's just taken me a while to learn this lesson." He hesitated and then said, "I want you to know what happened with Stacey and her family." Kolton paused to try to remember all the details before continuing. "I met Stacey at church when she was pretty young. She had recently graduated from high school and had just moved here. We began to date, but Stacey's family was disappointed. Her parents didn't want her to become serious with anyone at such a young age. They had high hopes for her because she had a great musical talent and exceptional grades in school. She had been offered scholarships, and prestigious schools even showed an interest in her piano capabilities.

"We dated for a short while before we both agreed that we should be married. I know in my heart that it was the right thing for me to do at the time, and I believe that she felt the same way, but her family was really upset. Her father came to me privately and asked me to have a long engagement—he wanted his daughter to have time to go to school and consider her future. I rejected his request, and I never told Stacey about the conversation.

"They also thought that I should give up the family business and take Stacey away to school, but I told them no. I had just drawn up all the paperwork to buy the business from my folks. It was my dream, and I didn't want to move anywhere else. I made it very clear that I wanted to stay here and start a family. Well, they didn't like it one bit. Stacey knew what I wanted, and she understood. I talked with her about it, and she said that she wanted to stay here with me."

Kolton stopped rocking in the swing and searched his memory for the right words to explain his past. "She knew that she had disappointed her family. They didn't hate me, but they thought I was selfish and demanding of Stacey. They blamed me for taking away her dreams—but I really thought they were just their dreams. Stacey never once told me she desired to go to college. Perhaps she just didn't want me to know—I don't know. When I look back on it all, I suppose it was very difficult for her to please both me and her family. I know she felt torn, and I think that she may have sacrificed her education to marry me.

"Anyway, I took things too personally and avoided her family as much as possible." Kolton began to relax and the words came out more easily. "I guess that made things worse for Stacey, even though I didn't realize it at the time. Not long after we were married, she became depressed. It seemed as though she rarely smiled. We began to argue a lot, and I think it was mostly because of me not getting along with her family. I thought she was having second thoughts about marriage, but I was ready to start a family. I was pressuring her to have a baby, while her folks were pressuring her to go to college—even if it was through correspondence study.

"It wasn't long before she was expecting Kyle. I was so happy—I couldn't wait to have a child of my own. During her pregnancy I put in a lot of time at the feed store, trying to make extra money to prepare for the baby. I knew that I had been neglecting time with Stacey, but I felt like I really needed to provide well for her and the baby. She spent the time I was working with Leann—so the family knew how often I was gone."

Kolton stared out into the darkness as he recalled the details of his past. "When she was in her last trimester, she began to go out in the evenings, and it wasn't to Leann's. I would come home late and find her gone. When she arrived home I would ask her where she had been, and she always insisted that she was with friends. Something inside of me didn't believe her, so I began to ask around. Pretty soon I found out that she had been lying to me."

Carly kept her attention on Kolton. She was glad he felt able to confide in her.

"I was pretty insecure," he confessed. "I was always worried that Stacey would get tired of living here in the country and run off to school somewhere. I guess a small part of me believed just like her parents did—that I had married above myself. She was so smart and talented. We could all see the potential in Stacey, and it scared me. I was scared that someday she would realize that she had made a mistake marrying me, and regret not pursuing an education."

"If she told you that she wanted to be married, then that was her dream. That was her first priority or she wouldn't have done it."

"I know that now," Kolton admitted. "But I didn't know that for sure then. Anyway, she continued to go out in the evenings, and I couldn't get her to tell me where she was going. She asked me to trust her, but I kept badgering her. We began to argue even more."

Kolton paused, and then forced himself to continue recounting the events. "One night we had a bad argument. I was tired from working late, and when I arrived home after eight o'clock she was gone. She came home around nine o'clock. I know it was wrong, but I lashed out at her and demanded that she stop going out. I really lost my temper."

Finding it hard to resist, Carly asked good-naturedly, "You? Lash out at someone? I can't imagine."

Kolton grinned. "Yeah, I know it's hard for you to believe." Turning more serious, he continued, "Well, I said some stupid things. I kept demanding answers about what she was doing, and she just kept asking me to trust her. She said she had a surprise for me, but I just couldn't let it go. It turned into a week-long fight."

Trying to help him feel better, Carly sided with his actions. "She was keeping secrets, Kolton. That does make a person seem guilty."

"I know, Carly, but I should have had more faith in her. I should have trusted her." He shook his head in disbelief, "I look back at how I acted, and it was unforgivable. I began to confide in Leann," he explained. "I told Leann what was going on, and pretty soon the whole family knew our business. But—for once—her family was on my side. They too began to question Stacey, and it only made her angrier. She was angry at me for betraying her and sharing our problems with her family, and she was mad at her family for prying into her business. I think that she probably would have told me her secret if I hadn't made her so angry. I never should have gone to Leann and confided our personal business."

"Everyone was worried about her," Carly said, feeling bad for Kolton. "She was young, pregnant, and acting suspicious. Surely she understood why everyone was questioning her."

"Well, she was real upset at me and her family. One night we exchanged some especially harsh words. She hadn't gotten home until after nine o'clock, and I was sick of wondering where she had been. She and Leann had had an argument earlier in the day—Leann wanted her to confide her whereabouts, but Stacey wouldn't budge. She just kept telling everyone to stay out of her business. So she was already upset about her argument with Leann before I started yelling at her that night."

Kolton choked up, and it took him a few moments to gather his thoughts. "Stacey left our house about ten that night. She told me she was going to her cousins'. Sister Powers was trying to calm her down when her water broke. They said that she was really emotional when she arrived, and her water broke when she began to relate our argument." He thought for a second, calculating in his head. "She was two weeks away from her due date. They called me and said they were going to take her to the hospital because the contractions were so close. I grabbed the bag she had prepared and jumped into my truck. By the time I met them out on the highway she was bleeding real bad. So I parked my truck and got into her aunt's car. By the time we got to the hospital, she was as pale as a ghost.

"It didn't take them long to rush her into the emergency room. I waited for what seemed like an eternity, but I think it was less than thirty minutes. The doctors had saved Kyle through a C-section, but Stacey had slipped away."

Carly's eyes grew misty. She reached out and took Kolton's hand. He gave it a squeeze, and she squeezed back.

It was difficult for Kolton to talk so candidly about his past, but he wanted Carly to understand. "At first I just couldn't believe it. The whole family showed up that night at the hospital. The days were a blur. All I really remember is my mom being by me every minute, and that I just wanted to hold Kyle and never put him down. He was my only tie to Stacey.

"At the time of the funeral, Kyle was four days old. My parents were a big help with the baby—I didn't know how to take care of him. I couldn't sleep, and I couldn't stop crying. Before the funeral services began, I took him for a walk outside of the church building to get some fresh air. I walked around the building and overheard some of Stacey's family talking. Her mom, dad, her aunt, siblings, and cousins were all there. At first they didn't see me, but I overheard one of them say that Stacey would still be alive if I hadn't married her and forced her to have a baby. Her father said I should have let her go on to school and waited for her to grow up. Someone else said that she wouldn't have gone into early labor if I hadn't upset her so much with my constant badgering. And then Leann saw me and accused me of killing Stacey. She was sobbing, and she said that it was entirely my fault because I had upset her so much.

"I knew that they were hurting as much as I was, but I just couldn't handle it. I was so angry that I told them all to stay away from me and Kyle. I wasn't going to let them touch our baby. I must have been screaming because they all just stared at me."

"Everyone says things that they regret when they are upset," Carly said, trying to understand how horrible it must have been for the Powers family.

"I know. But they seemed so hypocritical. Stacey had told me that marriage and a family came before her career. She assured me that I was the one she wanted to marry. I wasn't a perfect husband, but her family never took responsibility for the stress they caused her. They were constantly asking her about her education, and they had the same suspicions about Stacey's whereabouts that I did.

"They were as worried and confused as I was. I confronted my wife, and they did too. I remember how Stacey felt—as though her family and I had banded together against her. I'm sure that the whole situation was very stressful for her—especially when you consider the fact that she was emotional from the pregnancy, as well as nauseated all the time.

"But as soon as Stacey died, they alienated me as if I were the only one who had upset her. They acted as though they had no part of it. But I remember the truth—Stacey was upset with me *and* her family.

"So I told Stacey's family to stay away from me and Kyle, and I never talked to them again. It wasn't long before her parents moved away from Bridger. They were partially right about me, though. I think we all killed Stacey, including me. If we hadn't been badgering her all the time, maybe she wouldn't have been so upset. Maybe she wouldn't have gone into labor."

"No, Kolton, you can't know that," Carly insisted and continued to hold his hand. "Just like with Leann, you don't know if there was a previous condition. I'm not a doctor, but I know that there are complications in pregnancy all the time. Even if the argument threw her into labor, who's to say that the outcome wouldn't have been the same if she had gone into labor on her due date? If there was a problem, it would have been there no matter when she went into labor."

"I don't know though. And it's hard to live with myself when I don't know the truth."

"Kolton, you have to get over this. Forgive yourself and Stacey's family too. It's too much for you to carry this burden all your life."

He looked her in the eye. "There's more."

"What?" she asked anxiously.

"I found out where she was going at night."

"Where?"

"A couple of weeks after she died, a man came to the door with a package. It was a portrait that he had been painting of her."

"Oh," Carly groaned, sorrow for Kolton washing through her. "She was posing for an artist."

Kolton nodded. "She met the art teacher from the high school and asked him to paint a portrait of her. She wanted to surprise me with it for my birthday in July. It's really nice. I keep it in my closet and look at it every now and then. Stacey is standing in a white, flowing gown with her hands resting on her stomach. It's really beautiful. The artist did a great job. He had heard that Stacey died, so he quickly finished it and dropped it off at the house. He thought Kyle would like it when he was older. He was really nice—he wouldn't even let me pay for it."

It was clear why Kolton acted the way he did. He was holding onto a lot of guilt and shame for his actions.

"Carly," he added, "I don't know why, but I never told Stacey's family about the portrait. I was so angry with them that I didn't want them to know the truth. I didn't think they needed any more ammunition against me. And as ugly as it sounds, I wanted them to have a little doubt about Stacey, just so they wouldn't judge me so harshly."

"Oh, Kolton, you need to tell them. You need to be honest so you can begin to forgive yourself and them."

Tenderly, he said, "Thank you for being so understanding. I didn't know how you would react when I told you what really happened."

"I have faith in you," she told him simply, "and I think that you'll make the right choices."

"I know that I need to fix this mess. I finally see that I'm missing out on life by living in the past, and I'm hurting my son and Stacey's family. I'm going to talk to Stacey's family and show them the painting. I've made arrangements to go over tomorrow night and explain everything."

"I'm glad that you are." Remembering her conversation with Leann earlier in the evening, Carly said, "I know that they'll be welcoming to you, Kolton. I think that enough time has passed that everyone wants to forgive and forget—especially for Kyle's sake," she added.

"I'm anxious," Kolton admitted, "but I know I need to do this. I need to swallow my pride and settle this matter."

"You won't regret it," she assured him.

"I know. And I'm so tired of regretting things. Including the way I've been treating you. I don't expect anything from you, Carly, but I'm truly sorry for the way I've behaved toward you. You've proven to be so loving and patient. I always thought you were special—even when we were kids I admired you."

"You're already forgiven, Kolton."

"I'm sorry for lashing out at you, and—"

"Really, Kolton, you are already forgiven."

"But I need to tell you that I—"

Carly leaned into him and hushed his lips with a kiss. Kolton was taken aback, but quickly recovered. She pulled back and softly raised her finger to his lips.

"Don't tell me how sorry you are, Kolton. Show me."

Kolton gratefully gathered her in his arms, and at that moment they both knew they were making a choice to love.

Chapter Twelve

Kolton was dreading Monday evening, yet a part of him did anticipate the meeting between him and Stacey's family. He decided to leave Kyle with his mother so he wouldn't be distracted.

When he dropped Kyle off, his mother gave him a big hug. "I am so proud of you, Kolton. I have a good feeling about this."

Kolton thought about his mother's words as he drove to meet Stacey's family. Although he was a bit nervous, he too had a good feeling that he was making the right choice.

As he pulled into the drive of their large home, he noticed there were several cars parked in front of the house, including one with out-of-state plates, which he figured was Stacey's mother's car. Chad and Leann's truck was parked next to Carly's compact car. He was a bit surprised that Carly was there, but he was grateful for her support. He immediately felt more relaxed.

He parked his truck at the side of the house and pulled out the large painting, still wrapped in the floral blanket. He didn't intend to part with it forever, but he was willing to share it.

He knocked on the front door and Stacey's mother immediately swung it wide open. She had obviously been waiting at the door for his arrival. She smiled at Kolton and awkwardly moved forward to give him a hug. He graciously hugged her back and stepped into the hallway.

"Hello, Annette," he said softly, trying to hide his surprise at such a warm reception.

"Hello Kolton. Before we go into the living room, there's something I must tell you."

She had barely begun to speak, and tears were already forming in her eyes. "I know that it has been a long time since we've talked—since we moved away right after Stacey's death. No matter what is said this evening, and no matter how you feel about us, I do hope for some resolution. I've lost my husband as well as my only daughter. I don't want to be estranged from my grandson any longer. I do feel that I've been wrong in many aspects. But when I saw Kyle at the baptism . . ." She began to cry and was unable to continue.

Kolton put an arm around her and gave her a squeeze. "It's okay," he told her. That's why I'm here. Hopefully, we can all come to an understanding."

Annette tried to compose herself and pulled away from his embrace. "I just want you to know that I really want to spend some time with my grandson. When I saw him, I realized that I need to put the past behind me. Of course I will respect your wishes, but if it's at all possible, I would like to visit with him often."

Kolton's own eyes filled with tears of varied emotions—regret, remorse, and forgiveness. "Of course," he promised. "That's why I'm here. That's why we are all here—for Kyle."

She nodded that she understood. "Thank you, Kolton. Should we join the others?"

"Of course."

He followed her into the large living room and was surprised again at how welcome the Powers family made him feel. Brother Powers, Leann and Chad, and a few other family members were in attendance. He saw Carly sitting next to Chad, and he gave her a wink. She responded with a loving smile.

He noticed that Sister Powers was not in attendance, but he didn't ask about her whereabouts. He figured that some of the family might still be too angry at him to attend. They would have to come around in their own time. Perhaps Sister Powers would be able to find strength in her family members who did want to work out a resolution.

The visit lasted two hours as Kolton explained how the past had affected him, and why he had made so many of the decisions he now regretted. He listened respectfully as many family members apologized and expressed their feelings. It turned out to be truly edifying, since everyone was willing to listen and reach an understanding.

As he unwrapped the picture of Stacey, the room fell silent. Stacey's mom had tears streaming down her face, and she made no effort to wipe them away. She simply stared at the beautiful picture of her daughter.

Kolton felt impressed to hand her the painting. "I would like this to be a keepsake for Kyle. But I think it would do well to hang in your home for a while." She nodded in appreciation, and her gratitude showed in her eyes.

After Kolton finished discussing the things he wanted to share, the main topic turned out to be Kyle. Everyone wanted to spend time with him and get to know him better. Kolton was agreeable but insisted that visits and gatherings be done gradually. He wanted his son to adjust to Stacey's family without being overwhelmed.

After all was said, Kolton excused himself to leave. Not all of the family was as eager as Stacey's mother to find a quick resolution, but the remaining family was at least cordial. Leann's father and her siblings kept silent during the meeting, but shook Kolton's hand before he left. There was still a feeling of awkwardness with them, but Kolton hoped that it would slowly dissipate as they all worked together to get along. He knew that it would take time for everyone to come to terms with him. And he realized that he would have to make changes in his own attitude in order for the outcome of this visit to be successful. He said his good-byes, and Carly rose to leave also. As they walked out of the house, Carly reached out to hold his hand.

As soon as they were outside and alone, she said, "It was a beautiful thing for you to give Annette the picture of Stacey."

Kolton's eyes were soft and sincere. "It was killing me to see her crying. I guess I was prompted to share what I have left."

"I think that this visit went well, Kolton. I really feel like it's going to be a turning point."

"I do too," he agreed.

Kolton stepped closer to her, putting a finger under her chin to lift her face to his. "Thank you for being here. I really appreciate your support."

"Anytime," she answered softly.

He gathered her in his arms, and they both felt that they had passed a turning point for them too—in the right direction.

* * *

At church the next Sunday, Kolton and Carly sat together during the services. After sacrament meeting closed, he asked her to go for a drive after lunch. She was so excited to begin a meaningful relationship with him that she only picked at her lunch in anticipation of his arrival. Her father teased her about her wide smile and bright eyes, but she only smiled wider.

They had spent the previous week apart except for brief phone conversations. Kolton had been trying to spend time with Stacey's family to allow them enough time with Kyle. When Carly finally heard his truck pull up into the driveway, she quickly said good-bye to her parents and rushed out the door. Like her, Kolton had changed out of his church clothes and was wearing jeans and a T-shirt. He got out of his truck to open the passenger door for her, and she realized that Kyle wasn't with him.

Once he was seated and they were on their way, she asked, "Where's Kyle?"

"I dropped him off at my parents' house."

"You didn't have to do that. I love having Kyle around."

"Are you kidding? I know he'd get all your attention if I brought him."

Knowing he was only teasing, Carly insisted, "Really, Kolton. I don't mind having him with us."

"I know, Carly. I can tell how much you like him. And I really want the two of you to spend time together. But I think we should spend some time alone, too." He reached over and held her hand, giving it a gentle squeeze.

The day was warm and bright—a perfect day to be outdoors. "So where are we going?" she asked.

Kolton paused for a moment and then said, "I'd like to go for a walk."

"Okay." She didn't care what they did as long as they were spending time together.

Carly sat quietly as they arrived at Bridger Cemetery. Kolton parked and turned off the ignition, but he made no move to get out of the truck. "I feel like I need to make some changes, Carly. And I want to thank you for our conversation last Sunday, and for being at my meeting with the Powers family on Monday. So far, I feel like I've made progress with them. Kyle has received a couple of phone calls and an invitation to lunch with Chad and Leann. He is definitely enjoying all the attention."

"Good. I'm sure they're thrilled to come to an understanding with you, too."

"There is something I want to do today. I feel like I need to say good-bye to Stacey somehow. I need to tell her how sorry I am and somehow make amends with her. Do you think I'm crazy?"

"No, not at all. I think that you've been carrying around a huge burden of guilt. I didn't know Stacey, but I think she would want you and Kyle to be happy."

He nodded in agreement. They both got out of the truck and walked hand in hand across the parking lot and through the cemetery. They stopped in front of Stacey's headstone. It was a simple stone, with remnants of once-beautiful, cut flowers lying beside it. Carly wanted to give Kolton some time alone.

She looked around and noticed the perfect place to sit. "I'm going to walk over to that gazebo over there," she said. "Take as much time as you need."

Kolton gave her a weak smile as Carly squeezed his hand and walked off. He watched her walk away and sit down on a bench under the gazebo. Then he kneeled down and silently opened his heart to Stacey, hoping it would help to relieve the pains he still held in.

Carly sat on the bench for twenty minutes, trying not to watch Kolton. She closed her eyes and wondered what he was thinking and feeling. She casually glanced toward him, but he was still kneeling. Closing her eyes again, she breathed in the warm air and felt a soft breeze play in her hair.

When she opened her eyes she was startled to see Kolton standing right in front of her. She jumped slightly and he grinned. His eyes were moist, yet he looked at peace.

"Sorry. I didn't mean to scare you," he apologized.

"It's okay, but you should never sneak up on someone in a cemetery."

He smiled and looked out into the distance. "Do you want to go for a walk? We could follow the path around the cemetery."

She nodded in agreement and they began their walk, hand in hand. For the first few minutes they remained silent.

Kolton broke the silence, posing the question, "What do you want out of life, Carly?"

His tone was serious. Instinctively, she knew that her answer would have a direct bearing on the future of their relationship. With all honesty she expressed her most important dreams and hopes.

"I want to be happy. I want a family. Most of all I want children. Not a lot, but three or four. I don't need a big house, but I need a home. I've always wanted a husband like my father—a husband who wants to be there for me and the kids. I've always felt a strong feeling of love in my home, and I want the same for my kids."

Kolton nodded. "Anything else?"

"No, I think that would be enough to make me happy."

He paused for a moment and then stopped. He turned toward her and held both her hands in his. "I know how important the gospel is to you, Carly. It's very important to me also. I think it's a good foundation for us to start a relationship."

"You're right." She smiled. "I think we could probably help each other through anything."

Kolton nodded. "Your strength and insight have already helped me a lot. This day was important for me, Carly. I never came back to visit Stacey after she died. My mom would bring Kyle to put flowers on her grave, but I just couldn't face her. I worried she would be disappointed in me. But I don't feel that way anymore. I have a warm feeling of closure that I can't explain."

He continued, "What I do know, Carly, is that I have very strong feelings for you. And I haven't had feelings this strong for anyone since I met Stacey. I need to know if you feel the same way."

Carly nodded. "I do. I like the way I feel about myself when I'm with you. You make me feel special, and I love to spend time with you."

Her words were exactly what he wanted to hear, but he wanted to explain himself further. "I also want the same things that you want, Carly. But I realized that in order to achieve those things I need to work on making some personal changes. I don't want to be prideful and unforgiving anymore. I don't want to be as short-tempered and judgmental as I've been in the past. I'm working on these things,

Carly, and I want to know if you're willing to give us a try. I'd like to date you exclusively and see if we have a chance."

"I'd like that."

Kolton smiled in relief, but there was one more issue. "You know how I feel about my son . . ."

Carly stated, "I know that you're package deal, Kolton. I would never do anything to hurt Kyle. I want to date you, and therefore, I want to date Kyle and get to know him better too."

Kolton knew that Carly had been a huge influence in improving his life, and he knew that together they would be able to face any obstacle. He put his arms around her and gave her a tight squeeze.

As they embraced, Carly's heart told her that they had a very good chance. They finished their walk holding hands, yet somehow joined heart to heart.

Epilogue

"Where are you taking me?" Carly demanded playfully. "I have to get back to work." Kolton and Kyle smiled at each other knowingly. Carly had been at the school getting the office ready for the new school year. She only had two days left to get everything in order before the students would be starting their first day back. Kolton and Kyle had dropped in during her lunch break, promised her a surprise, and whisked her off in their truck, blindfolded. The ride only lasted ten minutes, but she was anxious to see what the surprise was.

Kyle opened up the passenger-side door and helped her out. "It's so cool, Carly. You won't believe it." The excitement in his voice was contagious.

Kolton got out of the truck and took her by the hand. "Follow us, we're almost there."

The threesome had spent the entire summer together—swimming, going to movies, or just hanging out. With Carly not working, she had the extra time she needed to devote energy to Kyle and become better acquainted with him and Kolton. At first, Kyle was apprehensive about being her friend without his dad joining them, but he soon grew very fond of Carly. When he wasn't spending time with his mother's family or Kolton's parents, he was Carly's little shadow. He had helped her in her mother's garden, they had gone on bike rides, and Carly had taught him how to do the backstroke in the local pond. Carly's affection for him had grown into a lasting love. Sometimes she wondered which one she loved the most—Kolton or Kyle.

She stumbled, and Kyle laughed. "Be careful, Carly."

"I can't see!" she exclaimed.

Kolton guided her. "We're almost there. You should be able to figure out where we are."

As they continued to walk, she smelled the unmistakable scent of fresh manure. "Are we in a meadow?"

"Close," Kyle answered.

She felt the air around her become cooler, and she imagined they could be entering a building. "Okay," she insisted, "where are we?"

Kolton pulled off her blindfold and watched her face. They were inside a barn. She wasn't sure whose barn, though.

Kyle smiled and jumped up and down excitedly. "Did we surprise you?"

"Yes," she answered, a bit confused.

"Look over there," Kolton motioned to her right. Carly couldn't believe her eyes. In a soft bed of hay there was a red plaid blanket. On the blanket there was a three-piece setting of dinnerware and glasses. A beautiful spray of red roses served as a centerpiece.

Kyle couldn't contain his excitement any longer. "It's a picnic! We got chicken and salad and rolls and soda."

Carly smiled and gave Kolton a kiss. "Thank you. This is great."

She moved to have a closer look, but Kolton pulled her tightly to him. "First things first." He gave her a passionate kiss that made her weak in the knees.

Kyle groaned. "Yuck." As much as he was beginning to love Carly, he couldn't understand why his father always wanted to kiss her.

"Okay, Kyle," Kolton instructed, "remember what we practiced?"

Kyle nodded and came toward his father. Kolton pulled away from Carly and bent down on one knee. Kyle followed his father's example.

In anticipation, Carly put her hands over her mouth. Her eyes instantly filled with tears.

"Can I go first, Dad?" Kyle asked as he pushed his hand into his pocket.

"Go ahead."

Carly watched as Kyle pulled out a toy engagement ring. He reached up to take her hand and gently pushed it on her finger. Earnestly he asked, "Carly, will you please be my stepmom?"

Unable to speak, she nodded and gathered him up in a bear hug. He wiggled out, but smiled from ear to ear.

"It's my turn," said Kolton as he slipped a beautiful diamond ring on her finger next to Kyle's ring.

Carly looked deep into his eyes, and she could see that he too was blinking back tears. Kolton began, "Thank you, Carly, for showing me that it's never too late to love and forgive. Will you give me the honor of being my wife?"

Carly knelt down next to him and gratefully accepted. "Oh yes, Kolton."

They hugged tightly, knowing that they were making the best choice. Carly had never been happier in her life.

Kolton helped her to her feet. "There is one more thing."

"What's that?" she asked.

"I get to decide where we have the honeymoon."

Carly was so happy she was willing to agree to anything. "Where?"

"Here," he demanded.

"Here in Bridger?" she questioned.

"No. Here in this barn. Remember how you told Adam that you would rather have a honeymoon in a hay barn than be married to him?" With a sheepish grin he added, "I'm just making all your dreams come true."

Carly laughed and gave her fiancé a kiss. Her dreams had come true.

About the Author

Nancy Cratty was born in Las Vegas, Nevada. She has lived in Pahrump, Nevada, for twenty-six years. Nancy and her husband Joe have been married for fourteen years and have ten-year-old twin boys, Logan and Trevor, and a six-year-old daughter named Kayla.

Nancy spends most of her time with her family and also enjoys reading, writing, gardening, practicing the piano, and her Church callings with the youth. *Never Too Late* is her first published work.

PROLOGUE

Winning a case was not an everyday occurrence for the county's contract defense attorney. Meredith Marchant handled the cases the courts ordered her to take and did the best she could to ensure her clients a fair day in court. She enjoyed her work, and she felt like she was good at it. But winning with a clear finding of "not guilty" by a judge or jury—or even by persuading the prosecutor that his case was weak and he should move the court for a dismissal—just wasn't her fate very often. Most of her *victories* weren't victories at all, just plea bargains.

So why did she feel so empty now as she walked back into the courtroom to join her client? After all, she was about to win. The county attorney had just thrown in the towel on this one. And unlike most of her cases, the man sitting at the defense table waiting for her return was not a typical client. He'd contacted her at her office, dropped two thousand dollars on her desk in hundred dollar bills, and said smugly, "The cops ain't got a case, and it's your job to prove it for me."

She had agreed to defend him, but certainly not because he was a nice man, nor because she was convinced he had been framed by Detectives Osborne and Fauler. The money had been the deciding factor. Any case she took in addition to her court-appointed ones helped her save for the future.

"Well, is he going to drop it?" her client asked with a sneer.

"Of course," she said as brightly as she could muster.

Her client sat back with a satisfied grin on his face, not a word of thanks for her efforts. She glanced at him as she waited for the judge to enter the courtroom. Except for his eyes, her client looked the part of a successful businessman. She supposed he was, but she was almost certain that his business was anything but honest.

The client's eyes caught hers, and once again she was vaguely aware of the impression that there was an evil person within the facade of honesty and integrity he was trying to put on. But those eyes made her skin crawl, and they caused a slight panic in her heart. She silently prayed that after the next few minutes, she would never see this man again in her life.

Desmond R. Devaney was the name his Alabama driver's license gave him. But if Meredith had to guess, she'd say that New England was more likely the area of the country where he'd come from.

The judge entered the courtroom. Meredith and her client stood, as did everyone else. After being seated, the county attorney rose and said, "Your Honor, due to new information that has just come to my attention, I am, in the interest of justice, moving the court to dismiss the state's case of aggravated assault against Mr. Desmond Devaney."

"Is that so?" the judge said as he leaned forward and peered menacingly at the prosecutor. "Twenty minutes ago you talked like you were ready to set the matter for trial. What sort of new information are you basing your motion on?"

"Ms. Marchant, counsel for the defendant, just revealed to me that she has located several witnesses who are prepared to testify that the defendant was at a social gathering in Roosevelt at the time the assault occurred in Duchesne."

"I see," the judge said. His stern gaze turned on Meredith. "How many witnesses?" he asked.

"Six, Your Honor," she said as she rose to her feet.

The judge continued to stare at her for several seconds as if that figure were suspect, then looked in the direction of the prosecutor. "Your motion is granted; the charges are dismissed, and we are adjourned," he said with a shake of his head and rap of his gavel.

There was a groan from behind her, and Meredith turned in her seat. Luke Osborne and the new detective, Enos Fauler, were shaking their heads in dismay. Her client rose to his feet and pushed his chair back. Two men on the second row of seats were looking right at him as he turned toward them. One, a good-looking fellow of maybe twenty-one or twenty-two, grinned at him and gave a thumbs-up. The second, older, sober, and with a surly face, simply nodded. Then they both left the courtroom. Meredith's client turned to her and said, "Maybe those two detectives learned a lesson today," before quickly moving away.

Meredith gathered up her papers and then followed him into the lobby. She spotted the rich, auburn hair of her young daughter and smiled in her direction. Deedee's face was flushed and her hair windblown. *She must have ridden her bike up here from town,* Meredith thought to herself. She froze as her client approached Deedee and she heard him say, "Hey, babe, you're very pretty. Need a lift to town?"

Meredith stepped forward quickly and shouted as she neared them, "Get away from her, Desmond!"

He turned around, apparently surprised at her protest, but didn't say a word until she walked up and put a protective arm around Deedee. His attempt at an innocent smile was marred by the slight leer, and he said, "Just being friendly to the girl, Counselor. Know her, do you?"

"She's my daughter," Meredith fumed, "and she doesn't need a ride with you."

Desmond's face grew dark, and he turned to Deedee. "Would you like a lift?" he asked again defiantly.

Meredith was suddenly so angry that she clenched her fists, ready to claw his eyes out if he so much as touched Deedee. Then a tall presence appeared beside her, and Enos Fauler said, "Why don't you just leave, mister? Is this any way to thank the lady who just saved your guilty hide?"

Desmond bristled and looked up at the tall detective. "It won't be any too soon. Not exactly my kind of town." He moved toward the door, but as he pushed it open, he made one last parting shot, looking straight at Meredith's thirteen-year-old daughter. "I'll see you again, beautiful."

For a big man, Enos Fauler moved awfully fast. He had to, or Meredith Marchant would have lit into her former client. Enos deftly stepped in front of her, effectively blocking the way as Desmond smugly left the courthouse.

Everyone in the lobby had been watching the tense drama unfold, and Meredith was suddenly embarrassed. "Thanks," she said to Detective Fauler, whose gaze suddenly dropped to the floor.

"He's not a nice man," the detective said without looking up.

Deedee moved to her mother and clutched her arm. Her eyes were wide. "Who was that horrible man?" she asked with a trembling voice.

Meredith tried to appear calm. "No one you ever want to know. He was a client of mine."

"He scares me," Deedee said.

"He scares me too, sweetheart," Meredith replied even as she was trying to stop her shaking hands.

"I don't dare ride my bike home now," the girl added.

At that moment, Detective Luke Osborne arrived. "Enos and I will see that your bike gets back to your house. You go on home with your mother."

"Thanks, Luke," Meredith said, then added, "I've defended some creepy people over the past few years, but that guy takes the cake."

"You got him off," Luke reminded her with a lopsided grin.

"Well, I did have six signed affidavits from people who are willing to testify that he was in Roosevelt the night your victim got himself beaten up. And you've got to admit that your victim is not exactly a nice guy himself."

Luke nodded in agreement, then turned to Deedee, who was still clinging to her mother. "He'll be out of town in no time. You don't need to worry about him. He knows that if he ever shows up here again, Detective Fauler and I will be on him like glue."

At the mention of the new detective's name, Meredith glanced at Detective Fauler. She met his eyes, and he immediately dropped his gaze. Luke smiled and said, "We'll be seeing you around. We'll get that bike back down to your place in a few minutes."

Just then the sheriff's secretary came in. "Luke," she said breathlessly, "a detective from Los Angeles says he sent you an e-mail you might want to look at. It's about the case you have today. He says it's very important."

Meredith felt a sinking in her stomach as Luke replied, "The case is over, but I'll come have a look anyway. Maybe you'd like to join us, Meredith."

As they walked the few yards to the sheriff's office, Luke couldn't help but notice the way Enos glanced at Meredith. *Maybe I ought to try to line those two up,* he thought. He also thought about Deedee, her young daughter. She was already as pretty as her mother, and even though she was only thirteen, she looked every bit of sixteen. *The boys will be after her long before her mother's ready for it,* he concluded.

Meredith interrupted his thoughts as they entered the lobby of the sheriff's office. "Did you notice those men who were seated two rows behind me in the courtroom, Luke?"

"I did notice, actually. The young one is Stuart something-or-other. I've never seen the older one before. Why?"

"Oh, nothing, I just wondered what they were doing in the court-room."

"I wondered too," Luke said.

Deedee visited with the sheriff's secretary while Luke, Enos, and Meredith checked Luke's e-mail. None of them looked more distressed than Meredith over what they learned. The man who called himself Desmond R. Devaney looked suspiciously similar to a man the detective in Los Angeles knew as Jim White, a man suspected of international slave trading—women, mostly young prostitutes, who came up missing from time to time. Yet there was no way to know if they were actually the same person.

"Probably not," Luke said when he noticed the anguished look on Meredith's face.

"He saw Deedee," Meredith said softly. "He threatened her."

CLAIR M. POULSON

CHAPTER 1

Two years later

"You don't even know Stu!" Deedee screamed in anger as she leaped to her feet from the sofa.

"I hardly know you anymore," her mother answered, willing herself to stay calm.

"It would be better for you if I hadn't ever been born."

"Maybe better for you too," Meredith said. "Don't think it's easy raising a teenager."

"Maybe I ought to just leave," Deedee shouted. "You don't want me here anyway."

"Sometimes you make me feel like that," her mother retorted. "Don't think my life wouldn't be more peaceful without you." She regretted those horrible words the second she'd spoken them. Deedee was her life, and she loved her more than anything in the world.

The fifteen-year-old glared at her mother for a moment, then her eyes filled with tears, and she spun away as she shouted, "I hate you!"

Meredith took a deep breath as the door to Deedee's bedroom slammed. She wiped at her eyes and slowly sank to the sofa, dropping her head into her hands. Deedee's stinging words cut deep.

Being a single parent was not an easy thing.

Being an only child wasn't easy for Deedee, who had also been rejected by a father she never got to know. Meredith's marriage had lasted just over a year. She'd married too young, hadn't really gotten to know her fiancé, and had seriously underestimated the strains of married life. He'd left her when Deedee was only a couple of months old. She hadn't seen him since, and the one who had paid the greatest price for his treachery was Deedee.

It was hard not to cry. Meredith loved Deedee, and she'd worked hard to provide for her, to raise her and give her the opportunities she deserved. But earning a good living meant many hours spent away from the girl, many hours that Meredith now realized should have been spent building more of a relationship, with the stability Deedee needed. Life had become a balancing act, one at which she thought she'd been doing quite well. She now admitted in her sorrow that it hadn't been quite so successful.

The years she'd spent getting through college and then law school had meant many days during which she'd interacted very little with her young daughter. But the time they did have together had always been special, and she'd always believed they'd been as close as a mother and daughter could be. Following admittance to the Utah Bar, money became less of a problem as Meredith established a successful law practice in rural northeastern Utah. But finding time to spend with Deedee became more of a problem as Meredith found herself working long, hard hours.

There had also been several men in her life, for Meredith was both attractive and fairly well off. However, she had resisted all serious advances, choosing to sacrifice romance during some of the best years of her life in deference to her daughter. While her decision may have broken some hearts along the way, the only heart she really cared about had been Deedee's.

Even though there was never enough time to do everything she would have liked to have done with or for her daughter, things seemed to be going fine. Then . . . well, Meredith was unsure just when the serious problems between her and Deedee began to develop. It was almost as if she woke up one day to discover a stranger in their house. And now, scarcely a day went by without a serious disagreement. Deedee was sluffing school occasionally, and she was balking at going to church, sometimes outrightly refusing to go. Something had to change, Meredith decided, and only she could bring about that change. She had to sacrifice whatever she must, for Deedee was her life.

Meredith stood, wiped her eyes as she entered her bedroom, and approached a mirror. She brushed her long red hair, applied some makeup to her cheeks, then brushed on a little eye shadow in an attempt to give life to her green eyes, eyes that usually were bright but were now dull with pain, worry, and regret. She hated what she'd just said to Deedee. She couldn't believe she'd done it, and she certainly hadn't meant it. She forced a smile onto her face and then looked herself over, resolving to mend things with Deedee, to treat her with more respect, more trust. And for some strange reason, she felt she had to look good for her.

Finally, feeling that she looked as cheerful and pretty as she was capable of at the moment, she turned away from the mirror and headed for Deedee's room. There would be no shouting, no recriminations, no anger. She'd offer a sincere apology and somehow demonstrate to Deedee that she loved her. She tapped softly on the door.

"Deedee, honey," she called softly.

She wasn't surprised when there was no answer. Deedee had recently perfected the art of administering the silent treatment. Meredith turned the knob and stepped into the room. "Deedee," she said as she looked around the room for her daughter, "I love you, sweetheart. I'm sorry for what I said. I didn't mean it. We need to talk. You talk, and I'll listen."

Meredith stopped. A cool breeze stirred the curtains of Deedee's open window. The closet door was also open. Dresser drawers were pulled out, their contents spilled carelessly about; clothes were strung across the floor and bed. A quick check in Deedee's bathroom revealed that her makeup kit and other essentials were gone. A hollow pit developed deep in Meredith's stomach as she looked in the large walk-in closet for Deedee's suitcase, also missing from its usual place.

Deedee had threatened to run away before, but she'd never seemed to mean it and had certainly never attempted it. Meredith approached the window as if in a trance and parted the curtains, peering into the deep blackness of the night. In despair she realized that she didn't have any idea where Deedee might go. She didn't know where to begin to search. But search she must.

And search she did after several intense and tearful minutes on her knees, pleading with her Father in Heaven for both forgiveness and help.

By morning Meredith realized that Deedee's anger and determination had run far deeper than she'd thought. None of the girl's friends had seen her or heard from her, and the sheriff concluded shortly after ten in the morning that Deedee must have caught a ride out of town. Meredith was enveloped with fear and pain that threatened to destroy her sanity.

Deedee, though only fifteen, looked three or four years older than that. At 5'5", she was still a couple of inches shorter than her mother, but she had inherited her good looks and attractive figure. Her auburn hair was long and thick, hanging halfway down her back. Her eyes, a dark brown like her father's, were expressive as well as pretty. Slim, willowy, even a little athletic, Deedee attracted boys much older than her.

It had been about one of those older men that they had argued. Meredith had reminded Deedee that dating before sixteen was simply out of the question—especially dating someone like Stu Chandler, a seemingly well-to-do twenty-four-year-old from the eastern end of the county. Meredith knew Stu had been giving Deedee some attention lately, and she had forbidden her daughter from seeing him again when Deedee mentioned that Stu had asked her out.

And now, looking back, Meredith couldn't even be sure if Deedee had been asking permission to date him or if she'd only wanted someone to talk to about the whole thing. Meredith had blown up so quickly that she hadn't even taken the time to learn what Deedee's response to Stu had been. Now, with her despair deepening, she suspected where Deedee had gone—toward the very man she had hoped to stop the girl from associating with, a man she feared might not be unlike Deedee's own unfaithful and unstable father.